Blessed Are Those Who Weep

By Kristi Belcamino

Blessed Are the Dead

Blessed Are the Meek

Blessed Are Those Who Weep

Blessed Are Those Who Weep

A Gabriella Giovanni Mystery

KRISTI BELCAMINO

WITNESS
IMPULSE
An Imprint of HarperCollins*Publishers*

EPub Edition APRIL 2015 ISBN: 9780062389404

Print Edition ISBN: 9780062389398

10 9 8 7 6 5 4 3 2

For Father Seamus Genovese

Blessed Are Those Who Weep

Chapter 1

AT FIRST I think she is a doll. Sitting there so still on the floor in her pink dress, chubby legs sticking out from her diaper, big black eyes unblinking, staring at something I can't see. A ribbon hangs loose in her hair. Something that looks like chocolate is smeared around her mouth and one cheek.

The front door is only open wide enough to frame her small body in the dim light. I can't see the rest of the room.

"Mrs. Martin?" The words echo in the silent apartment. At my voice, the baby turns her head toward me in what seems like slow motion. Even though the apartment door was ajar when I arrived, something stops me from pushing it open more. My hand hangs in the air, frozen. The rhythmic drip of a faucet is eerily loud. And something smells funny. Off. A smell I recognize but cannot place. A smell that increases my unease.

"Are you in there, Mrs. Martin? It's Gabriella Giovanni from the *Bay Herald*. We spoke yesterday."

Silence.

As if my voice has flicked a switch, the child moves and talks, babbling. "Mamamama. Maaamamama." She picks something up. Something floppy and pale and long. Something with short red fingernails. An arm.

A wave of panic rises in me as I figure out what I smell.

Blood. Urine. Feces. Death.

I nudge the door open. My hand flies to my mouth.

Blood oozes across the floor, seeping in puddles around bodies lying helter-skelter. Seemingly too many bodies to count. But I do. Clinically. Subconsciously. Five dead bodies. Because for sure they are all dead. No one could survive those gaping, slashing wounds.

I don't turn my head. Only my eyes dart around the room, taking it all in. My legs turn into mush, and I grab the doorknob to support myself, worried I'll collapse onto the floor. The sound of the dripping faucet seems magnified and is suddenly, extraordinarily loud.

The girl chants, "Mamamamama." She drops the arm, and it makes a slapping sound as it hits the scratched wooden floor. I nudge the door wider with my knee. The arm belongs to a woman in a green dress lying face down. The child tugs at the woman's shiny black hair, as if trying to wake her or get her to lift her head. A sticky pool of dried blood ripples out from the woman's torso.

Directly in front of me, another woman, older with white hair, is spread-eagle on her back, her stomach slashed open, insides strewn on the floor beside her. One arm reaches toward the door. Across from her, an elderly man is slumped on the couch. A wide gash across his neck yawns open, revealing pink and red and something white. What looks to be a teenage boy's body is propped up against the far wall, as if he were taking a break, resting, but the top of his head is matted with something awful looking. Bloody slash marks stripe the boy's arms—*defensive wounds.* The clinical term jumps into my mind. There is also a blond woman slumped in the corner, eyes staring at nothing.

Drip. Drip. Drip. The noise from the faucet sounds distorted. Everything seems to be in slow motion.

I've lost track of time. My feet remain planted in the doorway, stuck, frozen. Fear crawls up my neck. How long have I been standing here? A tiny part of me is tempted to get out my notebook and take notes, but I push it aside. *Get the baby.*

She holds up a bottle and looks at me. "Baba?"

The word releases me from the spell, making the drip of the faucet sound normal again. I carefully choose my footing, stepping over the body of the white-haired woman. Her eyes stare up at me as I pass.

Up close, what I thought was chocolate on the baby's face is dried blood. Her tiny fingers are covered in it. She holds up her bottle to me again. "Baba?"

Good God, how long has she been here? But I know it can't have been more than a day. I spoke to Mrs. Martin yesterday afternoon. At the time, I heard a baby in the background squealing with delight. Maria Martin apologized for the noise, and laughed, saying her ten-month-old was just learning how to use her vocal cords effectively.

Scooping the child up in my arms, I head to the bathroom. The shower curtain is open. Inside the tub is a large open window without a screen. Cold air hits my face from the ocean breeze streaming in.

Wetting a washcloth I find near the sink, I dab at the child's face. She shakes her curls to get away, but I scrub until her cheeks are finally pink—not black with dried blood. I work on her tiny fingers one by one. Even though she tries to pull them away, I soap them until the basin is full of pink suds swirling down the drain.

Once the water turns clear, I dry her face and hands and head back into the kitchen. Balancing the girl on my hip, I tug on the refrigerator door with a trembling hand. Vaguely, I realize I'm leaving my fingerprints all over a murder scene. I smell the milk before rinsing out her bottle and filling it.

Once it's full and the nipple is screwed back on, the girl snatches it and gulps, her head tilted back, eyes on me. At the same time, her other hand reaches up to my hair, tugging on a strand until she has it wrapped and twirled around her chubby fingers.

With her balanced on my hip, I head for the bedroom, crowded with a bed, a crib, and a dresser. The girl watches me solemnly with big black eyes as I lay her on the bed and change her diaper. She lifts her legs to make my job easier. "It's okay, baby. It's okay," I coo as I gently wipe away all the dried feces stuck to her legs. I strip off her bloody dress and maneuver her into a tiny pair of flowered footie pajamas lying near the crib.

All the while I'm blocking out what is in the living room. I'm pushing back the reporter voice in my head describing the scene. I ignore what else I should be doing. *Something important.* Once I get the baby changed, the smell reminds me.

The bodies.

But first I need to get out of here. I focus on the front door. With the child in my arms, I step across and around bodies, making my way through the carnage. Finally, after what seems like forever, I'm in the hall.

I close the door to the apartment and slump to the floor. I bury my face in her curls for a moment before reaching into my bag.

My fingers are shaking as I punch in the numbers. 9-1-1.

It is all I can manage. I don't even hold the phone up to my ear as it rings. A sign above me on the wall shows all the emergency exits in the building. I stare at it, wondering which one the killer took to escape. Beside me, a small box has the UPS logo on it. It is addressed to Maria Martin. The return address is Babies"R"Us.

The girl snuggles into my neck and chest, slurping the rest of her bottle with loud sucking noises. She holds a strand of my hair, twisting it in her fingers and pressing her body close to mine. In the distance, from what seems like a place far removed, I hear a small voice.

"Nine-one-one . . . nine-one-one? What is your emergency? This is nine-one-one . . . State your emergency, please."

Chapter 2

EVERY ONCE IN a while, I catch a Spanish word I recognize.

Baby. Police. Blood. Grandparents. Knife.

A uniformed officer holds back a crowd clustered at the end of the hall shooting alarmed looks my way. One officer comes into focus, kneeling right in front of me. He asks my name. When I answer, my voice sounds like it's coming from a distance. The child starts to cry when he attempts to take her out of my arms. I cling tighter to her as she thrusts her fists into my hair, holding on so hard my scalp stings.

I come to life, gritting my words. "Leave us alone. She doesn't want to go to you."

He gives me a look I've seen cops give drunken people, then heads toward a petite woman in a brown suit. The woman, whose hair is cut like a boy, stops her conversation, looks at me over the top of her cat-eye glasses, and presses her lips together. I look away. Instead I focus on the army of legs moving past me. Cops come and go out of the apartment. Some cast sideways glances my way, but most ignore me.

After a few minutes, the petite woman comes over to me. She crouches down to my level.

"Heard you found them inside. I know you are shaken up from what you've seen, but the EMTs need to check this little guy out."

"It's a girl."

The woman reaches out to the baby, who buries her face in my neck and shakes her head, murmuring, "No no no no no no."

"You heard her," I say.

Annoyance flashes across the woman's face, but only for a second. "Hey, I'm not in the business of traumatizing little kids, but this one needs to be checked out. Please give me the girl." The woman is persistent, staying crouched down a few inches from my face. "The EMTs are waiting outside."

I close my eyes and nod, my brown hair falling in a curtain across my face. "I'll carry her. She needs me."

As soon as the words come out of my mouth, I know they are true.

I stand, murmuring into the child's hair. "It's going to be okay. I won't let them take you. Let's get you checked out." As if she understands me, her grip on my hair loosens, but she doesn't let go.

"Baba?"

I reach down and pick up her bottle. She holds it with one hand, chewing on the nipple. Her other tiny hand is still wrapped, tangled, in my hair.

The woman in the suit nods and stands, running her palms down her slacks. "Follow me. The reporters have descended like vultures. I'll take you around the back."

A strangled laugh makes her turn and give me a questioning look. I shut my mouth. She obviously doesn't know I'm one of those "vultures." They are my people. Okay, maybe not the TV reporters.

The bright sunlight outside the building makes my eyes squint and water a little. A camera guy from one TV station spots us and scrambles closer, followed by the rest of the mob of reporters, leading with their microphones and leaping toward the yellow crime-scene tape separating us.

"Miss? Miss?"

"Can you tell us what happened?"

"What happened to your baby?"

The words stop me dead in my tracks.

Chapter 3

The petite woman in the suit continues walking, but I'm frozen.

"Hey. Isn't that Gabriella Giovanni from the *Bay Herald*?"

"Gabriella! Gabriella!"

"It's Victor from Channel 9!"

"Gabriella?"

A clump of reporters points microphones our way. Another cluster of people stands behind them, probably neighbors, whispering and darting horrified glances my way, with the exception of one man in dark glasses, who leans against a telephone pole, preternaturally still, watching. The street is quaint, with small trees lining the sidewalk, and the tall bell tower of a Spanish-style church is on the horizon.

The woman in the suit appears in front of me again and nudges me. I snap out of it. The reporter was asking about the baby in my arms.

"You're a reporter?" the woman says. I nod. Does she regret calling reporters "vultures" now? I don't bother telling her that my being a reporter doesn't mean I condone the behavior of all the other journalists in the world. We round the corner where the ambulance waits, and we're finally out of view of the news crews.

Sitting on the edge of the open back of the ambulance, I hold the girl while the EMT checks her out. She hides her face in my neck and hair but lets him do his probing. Her curls smell like baby shampoo. When he's done, the woman in the suit comes back over.

"I need to ask you a few questions."

When she says this, it sinks in—she's a *detective*. I thought she was a social worker or something, since I know most of the detectives in San Francisco.

"Are you new?" I squint, noticing the badge peeking out from her suit jacket.

"Started in May. Was with San Jose PD for fifteen years." She recites it like she's been forced to defend herself this way a lot. Given some of the cops in San Francisco, she's probably had to do just that—prove she's no new kid on the block. A soft spot for her starts to grow, but my main concern is this child. And if this woman is trying to take the baby away from me, she's no friend of mine right now.

"Why don't you let me give the girl to Officer Jackie," the woman says, pointing at a ponytailed uniformed officer who looks about twenty-five. "She's got four kids of her own. She'll take care of her."

Officer Jackie reaches down and gently wraps her hands around the girl's waist, trying to pull her away from me. The baby shrieks and cries and clings tighter, burying her face in my neck. "No no no no no!" the girl screams.

"I can talk to you and hold her at the same time," I say.

The woman in the suit shoots a glance toward Officer Jackie, who backs off and walks away.

"Okay. We'll do it your way, little one," the woman says to the girl and turns to me. "I'm Detective Khoury."

She doesn't offer her hand but meets my eyes. Behind the cat-eye glasses, her eyes are soft, concerned. "I'm lead on this case. So far, you're my only witness, you need to tell me everything you know, and you'll need to come into the station later and go over it again."

As long as she lets me hold the baby, I'll talk. Sitting in the back of the ambulance, I spill everything—which isn't much. Mrs. Martin called me at the newspaper yesterday and told me she had a big story—possibly the biggest one of my career.

I usually blow people like that off, but for some reason, Mrs. Martin seemed different, sincere. Not like the usual nut jobs that call me with wacky story ideas. She'd read something I'd written that made her decide to trust me with her story, but she was afraid to tell me over the phone. I agreed to meet her at her apartment at 2:00 p.m. the next day. Today when I showed up, the apartment door was ajar and a horror show awaited me.

"So, you don't know this child?" Khoury asks.

I swallow and look away. A few faces peer out of windows at an apartment building across the street. I scoot over until I can't see them anymore.

"Ms. Giovanni? Do you know this child or have any connection to her besides finding her?"

I bite my lip and shake my head. The woman looks around as if someone can help her with me. She unclicks a small radio from her belt. "Swenson, call CPS for me, would you?"

Without waiting for a response, she puts the radio back down and turns to me.

"You realize she needs to go into Child Protective Services while we find her parents."

A long white van pulls around the corner. Another identical van arrives. The coroner's office is here. I've never seen two vans arrive at a crime scene before, but I've never covered a story with this many bodies.

"Her mom is dead. I saw her body." I realize I don't know for sure the woman in the green dress *was* her mom, but I don't take it back.

"CPS will find her family or find a foster home." Detective Khoury says it matter-of-factly and I know she's right, but handing this child over to strangers seems horribly wrong.

"Can she stay with me?" I'm begging.

Khoury shakes her head.

"She's obviously bonded with me. Why put her in a stranger's hands? Do you want to traumatize her more? You saw how she acted when someone tried to take her away from me."

Her eyebrows lift, and I know what she is thinking. *Crazy lady.*

"Ella?" We both turn at the deep voice. Donovan. Relief floods my body. I leap up and throw myself into his arms, hugging him with the baby in between. His five o'clock shadow scratches my cheek.

"You okay?" He pulls back and holds my chin, meeting my eyes. His dark eyes under heavy brows look worried.

I shake my head. *No, I'm not okay. I just saw an entire family that had been slaughtered.*

"Heard you were here," Donovan continues. "What's going on?"

"Detective Sean Donovan. What are you doing slumming in

my city?" the detective interrupts. Her voice sounds too familiar for my liking. It's the same thing everywhere Donovan goes.

It doesn't help that this year he was on the cover of the Sexiest Bay Area Cops calendar. He only did the calendar because sales go to fight kid's cancer. Every other cop in the calendar went shirtless, but Donovan refused and still made the cover wearing his tight black tee.

"Hey, Khoury. I see you met my fiancée, Gabriella Giovanni."

"You still keeping the streets clean in Rosarito?" she asks him.

"Yes, ma'am." He smiles at her, and she smiles back.

Even after two years of dating, the low rumble of his voice never fails to make me weak in the knees, so I suppose I can't blame other women for turning to mush. He rakes one hand through his perpetually messy hair, making it stick up more than usual. I don't like that he does this sort of anxious, nervous gesture around another woman, but I brush away the flicker of jealousy.

The thudding of a small, dark helicopter above us drowns out Khoury's response to Donovan. She looks up, scowling.

"What the hell is that?" Khoury shouts. Her hair blows in the wind from the chopper. She turns toward Officer Jackie. "Get them the hell out of here. Nobody has clearance to fly over my crime scene. And most definitely not this low."

Donovan squints up into the sky. I tuck the baby's head into my neck as bits of trash start whirling on the ground around us.

Khoury shades her eyes from the sun with one hand and glares at the helicopter. Almost imperceptibly, the helicopter rises. Pretty soon it is a small dot heading toward the ocean. Almost as an afterthought, Khoury turns back to Officer Jackie. "Find out who that belongs to. If that's a TV news station, I'll have their ass for this."

Khoury gives me an appraising look and turns to Donovan. "Sean, can I talk to you privately?"

He turns toward the detective, but I touch his arm, feeling the hard muscle underneath, and he stops. He leans in to hear my voice. My mouth brushes his ear as I speak.

"Donovan, they want me to turn this baby over to CPS. I can't do that." I hate the pleading in my voice. "Can you please talk to them? Tell them she should stay with me. I'll keep her until they find the rest of her family. I'll take care of her."

Donovan doesn't answer; he only nods grimly before walking over to where the detective is waiting a few feet away.

The baby's eyes are closing, so I rock her, watching Donovan and the detective speak in hushed voices. I can make out some of the words. Bloodbath. Baby. Shell shock.

Every once in a while, Donovan looks my way and gives me a small, tight-lipped smile, as if he wants to be supportive and encouraging but is more worried than anything. His mouth is set in a grim line as he makes his way back to me. It's not good.

"You have to turn the kid over to CPS," he says. "No way around it. It's the law."

Screw the law. I hold the baby even tighter and don't answer.

He hesitates a moment. "You know, maybe you feel this way because—"

"No," I interrupt. "It is not because of that. It's not." Deep down inside, I worry he's right. But I tell myself I would act this way about a helpless child no matter what.

"You don't have a choice. Amanda says she's okay with you taking the child to the police department. CPS is meeting us there."

Amanda?

"Donovan, she needs me. Look." I lean my head so he can see how the girl's chubby little fingers are wrapped in my hair. The girl has fallen asleep in my arms, her head nestled into me, her mouth open, her warm breath against the hollow of my neck. "I'll take her to the station, but I'm not handing her over to anyone."

"I'll meet you there." Donovan turns to leave.

"Can't we go together?"

He points toward a waiting squad car. "They want to drive you."

The police officer, a kid of about twenty, holds the back door of the squad car open for me. "Sorry, miss, we don't have a car seat right now, but the station is only about eight blocks away . . ." He trails off.

I pull the seat belt around the baby and me and click it into place. The backseat of the squad car smells like piss and vomit and sweat, all thinly masked with a pine air freshener. The officer meets my eyes in the rearview mirror as he starts the engine. Across the parking lot, Donovan is on the phone, pacing, as if he is agitated. I can tell he thinks I'm being difficult, unreasonable. I don't care right now. This baby needs me. Her entire family was slaughtered in front of her. For whatever reason, she is clinging to me, and I'm keeping her with me as long as I can.

Another baby-faced cop holds up the crime-scene tape and our car slides under it. I make the mistake of looking out the window right in time for the photog at our competition—the *San Francisco Tribune*—to snap a picture. The camera is so close to the window that I'm surprised his toes aren't run over from our tires. The flash momentarily blinds me, and when I can focus again, we are past the mob of reporters that had been running alongside our car. I close my eyes and dip my head into the girl's curls.

Chapter 4

My cat, Dusty, is kneading the pillow near my head and meowing loudly with hunger when I wake the next morning.

The sun is streaming through the windows of my studio apartment. Donovan is long gone.

During the several hours I spent at the police station last night, I repeated my account of finding the bodies once again, got fingerprinted to rule my prints off anything in the apartment, and handed the baby girl over to a woman from Child Protective Services.

"It looks like most of her relatives were in that apartment, but luckily, the police have located her father. We'll take good care of her until he can come get her," the woman said and handed me her card. Mrs. Kirkland. No first name. Like a kindergarten teacher.

The last image I have of the girl is her reaching over the woman's shoulder, arms outstretched toward me, her face bright red from howling.

I know she'll be with her father soon, but I can't help feel I let her down.

The clock shows it's past nine. I'm late to work.

Thinking of work sends me sitting straight up in bed. I never returned the messages on my cell phone last night. I meant to call my editor, Matt Kellogg, and tell him everything as soon as the police released me, but when I saw it was past midnight—past our deadline—I went home and fell into bed.

A knot forms in my stomach when I think about the newspaper, but I couldn't exactly excuse myself from being questioned as a witness in a mass murder by telling the cops I was on deadline.

Guilt is replaced by a pang of longing. Even though I never saw her before yesterday afternoon, my arms yearn to hold that baby, as if they'd spent the last year cradling that girl and now there's a phantom feeling of something missing. It doesn't make sense. I don't even know her name.

In the kitchen, Dusty winds himself around my bare legs as I dump some cat food in his bowl and cut up some small pieces of cheese to make up for his late breakfast.

Next, I head straight to the bathroom and stick the thermometer in my mouth before logging the numbers on the chart I have taped to the wall. When I'm done and see today's temperature next to the number from yesterday, my heart pounds so hard that I feel it in my throat. I'm ovulating.

I dial Donovan. His voice mail picks up.

"Are you in the city? I just took my temperature, and I need you to come home if you're still around. Otherwise, let's meet back here tonight. Love you."

I hang up, and a tiny tendril of hope unfurls. We can try again tonight. *Please make it work this time.*

After starting the moka pot on the stove, I heat some milk and set out my big coffee bowl. Donovan has left out the sourdough bread for me on the kitchen table and scribbled a note:

"Wanted to let you sleep in. Call me if you need to talk or grab lunch or something. See you tonight." He signed it "D" with a big heart around it.

Once the coffee percolates, I pour the liquid gold into my big mug and top it with the warm milk. Hopefully the caffeine will give me the kick start I need. I slept fitfully, glancing at my red clock numbers every half hour until about 4:00 a.m., when I must've fallen into such a deep sleep that I slept through Donovan getting ready for work.

Besides the note and bread, other signs he was there remain . . . an empty press pot of coffee, bread crumbs from his toast on the table, a knife smeared with Bonne Maman wild blueberry preserves in the sink. The stack of newspapers he usually leaves for me is missing, though. The coffee table in front of my beat-up red velvet couch is also bare. I peek out onto my balcony, where we sometimes have coffee on sunny mornings, but the papers aren't there, either.

I need to know what the *Bay Herald* had on the murders. That way I'll know how deep shit I'm in when I get to work.

As the hot water beats down on my head in the shower, a memory rushes back, as it sometimes does when I'm especially tired, like this morning.

I'm staring at the monitor off to the side of the exam table. Anxiety surges through me. The cold, flat metal slides around the slimy jelly on my abdomen. The flickering gray-and-white image on the monitor shows a tiny, shrimplike object curled into a comma. Not moving.

Please, God. Please let there be a heartbeat.

Wetness slips down my cheek into my ear. It takes me a few seconds to realize the doctor has removed the cold metal from my belly and gently pulled down my exam gown. She takes my hand in hers. Before she says a word, I see her eyes as she leans down. Before her lips move, I already know what she'll say.

Chapter 5

THE SIDEWALKS OF North Beach are teeming with people, jostling on their way to work. Some of the older Italian men have already staked out spots at sidewalk tables, where they're sipping espresso and smoking cigarettes. The salty ocean breeze mingles with the aroma of fresh coffee and baked goods.

The strip clubs are still buttoned up, but the restaurants and cafés are bustling. People are lined up in front of one small Columbus Avenue restaurant famous for its breakfast.

Café Tucca is on my way to where I parked my car last night. I'm so sleepy I'll need more than my regular bowl of coffee today. Plus the coffee shop will have all the morning newspapers. I get a few admiring glances as I head for the café in my high-heeled sandals, and I'm glad I'm fooling people.

My Italian mother has drummed into me *la bella figura*—looking your best—but I fail at achieving it ninety-nine percent of the time. I interpret the philosophy my own way—by dressing up on the days I feel the worst, sort of a bait-and-switch maneuver. Since today is an especially shitty morning, I spent extra time on my hair and makeup. I also threw on my nicest formfitting black wool pants, a silky navy blouse with white polka dots, and black patent-leather slingbacks, which are totally inappropriate for covering the crime beat.

Inside the café, I flip through the stack of discarded newspapers someone left on a table while I wait for my cappuccino.

The *Bay Herald* has a tiny front-page story by May, the night cops reporter. It has the bare basics of what happened: Five dead. Police investigating. It doesn't even identify the victims or say how they were killed. At least we have something, even if it's not much.

The *San Francisco Tribune* is on another table. I'm nervous to see what they wrote, but even so, I'm not prepared for the giant photo.

It's a picture of me. Above the fold. Under a huge headline. "Massacre in the Mission: Five Dead. Family Slain by Samurai Sword," with a subhead: "Reporter found with baby at scene of gruesome slayings."

In the photo, I'm looking out the backseat of the squad car with the baby's head tucked under my chin.

My index finger traces the contours of the baby's face in the black-and-white photo before my eyes move up to the image the photographer caught of me.

I don't recognize the look in my eyes. I don't recognize myself at all. My hair is ratty from the girl twirling it in her fingers. My lipstick is rubbed off. My mascara is smeared. The look in my eyes is what floors me. I look . . . unstable. Frantic. Deranged.

I read the headline again. Samurai sword. Yes, I suppose that would have caused the carnage I saw, but who carries around a samurai sword? And how did Andy Black at the *Tribune* get info on the murder weapon so early? Usually the cops won't release that until the coroner's report is complete. The *Tribune* kicked our ass on this story. And I was there as a witness. The realization makes my mouth dry.

Grabbing my coffee, I rush out, taking the paper with me. Did Donovan hide the papers from me? I scan the story as I walk to my car. It contains no hint that the cops have a suspect or that an arrest is pending. It says that Maria Martin's husband is in Iraq. It will take at least a week for him to get back to the U.S. because of national security issues. Along with his wife, the dead include his parents, his sister, and his nephew. The story says the child apparently has no other living relatives besides her father. My heart breaks for him. He's lost his entire family and is thousands of miles away. That little girl will grow up without knowing her mother or her grandparents or aunts and uncles or cousins.

I can't imagine life without a big family.

As soon as I get to my car, I call Kellogg.

He answers on the first ring.

"Giovanni, what the hell is going on? How do you think it looks that the *Tribune* has more details on this massacre, when you were *there*? Arnold is going off the rails about this. One of his reporters is in the middle of the biggest crime story in San Francisco since Harvey Milk was shot, and you're on the front page of the fucking competition. Jesus Christ."

Guilt swarms over me, making my face flush with heat. I crank up the air conditioner in my car even though it's cool outside.

"They kept me past midnight, questioning me. I wanted to call, but I couldn't."

His long sigh is a bit reassuring, but I'm still braced for an ass chewing.

"That's what I told Arnold. I know things have been tough for you lately, but I'm worried you're losing your reporter instinct."

I pull over to the side of the road and press my forehead against the cool glass of the window, staring, unseeing, at a man waiting for a bus. What *is* wrong with me?

The images of the slain bodies come back full force. I only have time to throw open my car door before I vomit onto the pavement and convulse until I'm dry heaving. From my phone on the passenger seat, Kellogg's tiny voice asks if I'm okay and repeatedly calls my name.

When I'm finally done, I wipe my face on my sleeve. It was a delayed reaction, but I feel better. I've been operating on autopilot since yesterday.

"I'm sorry," I say in a hoarse voice. "I don't know what happened. This has really fucked me up."

"Head on in when you feel up to it. I'll see what I can do to try to salvage your job."

Chapter 6

I CAN'T SHAKE the memory of that girl stretching out her arms toward me or the look on her face—like I'd thrown her to the wolves. Thinking of her as I drive across the Bay Bridge through thick, low-hanging fog makes my heart ache and fills me with anger at the same time. *She's not yours.* But I can't help the way my body felt when it held her. As if she were my own child. Something about being the person to find her in that horrific scene has bound me to her. It doesn't make sense, but it feels more real than anything I've felt in my life.

Driving to work, the landscape is brown and gray today, leached of all color. Usually, emerging from the Caldecott Tunnel into the East Bay means a welcome change in climate from coastal fog to sunny skies. Today, coming out of the tunnel, I'm greeted with more cloud cover that stretches for miles, obscuring the summit of Mt. Diablo in the distance.

Everything seems ugly, as if my rose-colored glasses have broken. Even other drivers on the freeway are scowling and flipping the bird and cutting people off.

In the newsroom, a few people look at me askance, but most ignore the fact that I was on the front page of the competition today. At least nobody says anything. At this point, they probably expect this kind of thing from me.

Last year, I was in the paper, too. All the Bay Area papers. For killing a man. Oh yeah, and I was in the paper the year before that, as well. Same thing. Killing someone. Both were bad men. Horrible men. One was a serial killer who preyed on children. The other was a crooked, murdering cop. Even though every single second of my life I regret killing someone, both acts were in self-defense. If I hadn't killed them, they would have killed me or someone else.

Even so, I've been in heavy-duty therapy about it. The guilt will haunt me to the grave. Even my priest, Father Liam—after hearing me confess the killings nearly every week for six months—has banned me from confessing it ever again. I've considered doing confession at another church without telling him.

And it has earned me a bit of a reputation in the newsroom. Terrible jokes abound, like the sign in the copy editor area that says, "Don't fuck with Giovanni's copy or she'll send you swimming with the fishes."

The sexy cops calendar didn't help any, either. Someone hung it up in the newsroom, and there is endless teasing about it. And it's not only jealous women who give me a hard time. The men are just as bad. For instance, Jon, the investigative reporter, will make a big scene, saying, "Gee, I wonder what day it is today? Let me go consult with Giovanni's hunky boy toy and find out."

Finally Kellogg made them all back off. But I'm sure they still talk about me behind my back.

Today it doesn't help that all the TVs in the newsroom are showing recaps of the massacre footage, including me driving away in the squad car with the baby. A brief glance reminds me I look like a crazy, homeless lady. Not my finest TV moment. Not in line with *la bella figura*. At all.

KXYZ is on the big screen, and even from across the newsroom I can read the words under the footage of me holding the baby—"Gabriella Giovanni, reporter with the *Bay Herald*."

It explains the stack of missed message slips waiting for me on my desk. The news clerk adds two more to the pile as I slide into my chair.

"Thank God you're here," she says. "People have lost their fucking minds this morning calling for you." She rolls her eyes and stalks off as only a five-foot-tall, eighty-pound woman can.

"Not my fault," I say to her back. Flipping through the stack of messages, I roll my eyes, too.

One message is blunt: *What's your alibi? Pretty convenient you were the one to find them.*

Another is kinder: . . . *is a psychic. Wants to meet with you to tell you who the Mission Massacre killer is.*

Sometime since last night, the hive mentality dubbed the slayings "the Mission Massacre"—probably based on the *Tribune*'s headline.

After the third message—*Baby is possessed and killed family telepathically*—I stop reading.

But my phone doesn't stop ringing. Unfortunately, the publisher insists we answer calls to our desk, even if they are wack jobs. He says you never know. Every once in a while, he's right, too.

In between answering calls, I wade through the voice mails waiting for me and nibble on a packet of cracker-and-cheese sandwiches from the vending machine. One call is from a radio announcer. He actually sounds pretty nice. And normal.

"Dave Schrader here. Darkness Radio. I heard about your . . . experience . . . with the Mission Massacre. I was wondering, with all that you've seen and done in your job, if you'd be my guest on *True Crime Tuesdays*. If so, can you please give me a call?"

Chris Lopez, my good friend and favorite photographer at our newspaper, is always trying to get me to listen to Darkness Radio, says I'd dig it. I hit save and go to the next message. I delete most without listening to them in their entirety, but one makes me pause. I listen to it twice, taking notes the second time.

The woman doesn't leave her name, but she has a lot to say:

"Isn't that poor woman's husband military? Good luck with him getting any support on dealing with that tragedy. The military is trying to hide it, but my sister's husband is stationed in Kentucky, and there's at least one soldier she knows who killed himself after he found out his wife had been in a car accident. She was in a coma and died before he even got leave to come back home to see her and say good-bye. And I know at least one other soldier who killed himself and his wife in front of their two kids only a week after he got back from Iraq. They are seeing some horrific things over there, and our military is doing nothing to help."

I start jotting down notes on what she is saying, sensing a story in here somewhere. It has been nearly a year since the invasion of Iraq and somehow none of this has been reported yet. Or if it has been, it's only been on a small-scale level.

"And there's more," she continues. "Not just suicides. There have been at least three soldiers who come home from Iraq and beat the living daylights out of their wives. They are seeing things over there that we don't know about and that they can't handle once they get back here. The worst part is the military isn't doing anything about it. My sister said that her husband suffers from depression and he's afraid to go to the doctor on base because he's worried they will pooh-pooh his disease and might not even cover the cost of his meds."

I wish this woman had left her phone number. It sounds like a good story. I'm sure Maria Martin's husband will need a lot of support after what happened to his family, and if this woman is right, it doesn't sound like the military will be the one to give it to him. I wonder if he'll talk to me about it. Not now, but maybe later, after some time has passed?

What an injustice. They risk their lives and get worse than nothing in return? As I'm getting angry about it, my phone rings again.

The next caller points out that it is "disgusting" that I was holding a baby while my face was covered in blood. I take a peek at the photo in the *Tribune*. There is no blood. The caller is either blind or crazy.

"Thank you for calling," I say and hang up without bothering to argue. The phone immediately rings again as I'm tossing most of the disgusting cheese-and-cracker things into the trash.

I snatch up the phone and say in an irritated voice, "Newsroom."

"Gabriella Giovanni?" The woman has a thick accent.

"This is she." I'm tapping my pencil on the desk, waiting for another crazy stream of nonsense.

"I am Maria Martin's mother."

My pencil freezes. Didn't the *Trib* say all of the baby's relatives had died in the massacre except her father? Is this a crank call?

"Yes. What can I help you with?" I scramble to find a notebook in the mess of papers on my desk.

"I want my Lucy. They say that she has to go to her father. That *pendejo*." She sort of sputters out the last word.

The black-eyed baby's name is Lucy. And I don't know much Spanish, but I do know this woman didn't call the father a prince.

"Ma'am, what is your name?"

"Teresa Castillo."

I scribble it down.

"Mrs. Castillo, have you talked to the San Francisco Police Department?" She could still be a kook, but if she called the police, she's probably legitimate.

"Yes. Detective Khoury says the father gets Lucy. Nothing I can do about it. They will not give her to me."

She knows Khoury. It is the girl's grandmother.

"Why are you calling me?"

"TV. I saw the look on your face. You care about her, not just getting a story in the paper."

She's right.

"Miss Giovanni, you have to believe me when I say this: That man, that *devil*, cannot get my granddaughter. I will die before I let that happen."

The way she says it makes me believe her. I don't understand.

"What do you mean? He's her father."

"Come see me in person. I will tell you."

Just like her daughter. She wants to talk in person. She rattles off her address. She lives in San Juan Bautista, at least a two-hour drive. I scribble the address down obediently, but she hangs up before I can tell her I probably can't drive that far to talk to her in person.

I can't help but worry about what she has said. She'd rather die than let the father have the baby? I wonder if this is some weird "no man is good enough for my daughter" deal. But she called him "the devil." There was something in her voice that indicated she doesn't use that word lightly.

The grandmother's desperation is so real that for a few brief seconds, I consider making a road trip to San Juan Bautista, until Kellogg swaggers over to my desk, butting his big belly up against my cubicle by accident. For a minute, the books I have balanced on a shelf wobble precariously.

"You okay?" he asks. Without waiting for an answer, he tells me that Nicole, my best friend and the courts reporter for the paper, will cover the massacre.

I nod.

"You're too close to this one," he says in a voice that leaves no room for argument. "There's a way you can make up for today's snafu. Arnold says if you write a first-person account of what you saw inside that apartment, we'll save face a little."

What you saw inside that apartment. I swallow and nod.

"Can you handle that?" Kellogg's brows knit in concern. "I could tell him no, but he's so pissed off at you right now, I think you should do whatever he wants to appease him."

Kellogg clears his throat and continues. "You didn't hear this from me, but there's been some talk of layoffs. The classified ads from Silicon Valley are shrinking, and the big guys at Knight Ridder are starting to panic."

That sounds like blackmail. "If I write what the publisher wants, I can keep my job?" My words drip fury. How dare the publisher tell a reporter what to write?

"It's not like that," Kellogg says, not meeting my eyes and picking at a piece of loose plastic on my cubicle wall. "You know I'd quit before I let that happen. This is just an account of what you saw. Taking advantage of being there first. No sweat. I think you need to do this for several reasons: probably good therapy for you to get it out of your head, it is something only our paper will have that might help make up for the *Trib*'s scoop, and it wouldn't hurt to have Arnold on your good side."

"What if it hurts the investigation if I put those details in the paper?"

Kellogg straightens up, tilts his head, and looks at me sideways.

"What?" I narrow my eyes at him, wary of what he'll say next.

"You know I've never said squat about you dating a cop. You've done a good job staying professional and not letting it affect your newspaper instincts. But right now you need to remember what side you're on. You're a goddamn good reporter, but you're walking a thin line here. I know you've had a lot of personal shit go on the past two years, and I've given you a ton of slack. Because you're damn good. Someone else—well, I would've let them go a long time ago. What you just said, about hurting the investigation? Don't forget what your job is here, or there'll be some big problems.

"You're not a cop. You're a reporter. Don't forget it. Now, write the story. If you don't want to do it for the publisher, do it for me."

He lumbers back to his desk and squeezes into his cubicle, causing a minor earthquake around him. He could have taken over the big corner office when he was promoted to executive editor, but he wants to stay in the trenches with his reporters. He's the smartest and best editor I've ever had, and I'd do anything for him, so his words sting. I'm not only shocked by his accusation; I'm also ashamed that I've given him reason to doubt my loyalty.

At that moment, the big-screen TV on the opposite wall

shows the apartment building where the slayings occurred and once again cuts to a shot of me in the back of the police car with that same dazed look in my eyes. Aren't people sick of seeing that footage?

I stare at the screen, seeing the baby girl's head nuzzled in my neck. It's a big story. A huge, giant, behemoth story. Kellogg is right. Of course I should write a first-person account about it. It's something no other newspaper or TV station could possibly have.

At the same time, I can't jeopardize any case the cops might have. Whoever deprived that baby girl of her family needs to be behind bars. And I'm not going to do anything to prevent that from happening. I'll write the story. For Kellogg. Not the publisher. But I'm not putting anything in my story that may hurt the case.

As I open a new document on my computer, determined not to hurt the investigation with my story, a nagging voice in the back of my mind remembers how my first instinct at that apartment was to help the baby, not compose a story about what I was seeing. Deep down inside, I wonder if Kellogg is right. Have I forgotten whose side I'm on?

Chapter 7

I've crossed a line. Broken the rules of Journalism 101—never show a source a story before it runs—because after I finish my first-person account of what I saw in that apartment, I e-mail it to Detective Khoury with a note: *My editors are on me to write about this. Will this hurt your case?*

And I don't even particularly *like* Khoury, either.

The story is about six inches long. Incredibly short by newspaper standards. More a "brief" than a story. But it's all I'm willing to give.

In my story, I talk about having an appointment with Mrs. Martin. I leave out that she called me and wanted to tell me "the story of a lifetime."

I describe walking up to find the door of the apartment slightly ajar, then give a brief account of what I saw when I nudged it open: *"Bodies lay strewn across the apartment, pooled in blood. A baby girl sat in the middle of them all, untouched."*

These two sentences are the lead of my story, going into the article through the back door, so to speak. Later, I go into how

I scooped up the girl, changed her diaper, and gave her a bottle. Putting it on paper makes me realize how stunned I was. Why did I do all that *before* calling 911? I was acting on pure instinct. Although I was taking notes in the back of my mind, my urge to care for that child overcame anything else I knew I should do.

Drumming my fingers on my desk, I wait for an e-mail back from Detective Khoury. Every once in a while I cast a guilty glance over at Kellogg, as if he can read my mind and knows I showed a source a story.

Khoury's response comes in less than three minutes. I click it open in a hurry.

"I'd prefer you didn't write anything," the e-mail says. "But what you have seems to be fine. Won't hurt the case."

I file the story in the editor's queue and check my other e-mails.

But I can't quash the guilt in the pit of my stomach for running the story by the detective. I know it was the right thing to do ethically as a person, but not the right thing to do as a journalist. And that's the crux—they should technically be the exact same thing, right?

We never, ever read or show stories to sources before they run. But I needed to. The last thing I wanted to do was harm a case that would put a mass murderer behind bars.

When my phone rings, I snatch it up, thinking it's Khoury changing her mind about my article, but it's Nicole.

"Hey, how's it going?" Her words are soft, guarded.

"I'm okay."

"That was . . . awful . . . you know . . . that you had to see all that . . ." She starts and stops, clearing her throat. "Kellogg has me covering it. Did he tell you?"

"Yes." Handing off the biggest story our newspaper has probably ever seen to another reporter—even my best friend—stings.

"Any arrest?" I ask, even though I just exchanged e-mails with Khoury.

"No. Off the record, my D.A. source told me the investigators are stumped. Nobody saw a thing."

"Yeah. I'm their only witness, and I didn't see anything." I let out a strangled laugh.

Nicole is quiet for a minute. "I'm sorry this got punted to me. It feels weird."

It is odd to have Nicole covering the story. It's my story. It's my beat. The Mission Massacre is one of the biggest stories to hit the Bay Area in my lifetime, and I'm benched, sitting on the sidelines. Like a chump.

I wait a second to answer. "No, it's better you than anyone else. I know you'll knock it out of the park."

"Kellogg says he's running your first-person account as a sidebar."

There's another long pause. "I'll send you over my story. Tell me what you think," she says.

"Thanks," I say. And mean it. It's not her fault.

Her voice brightens. "When are you and Donovan coming over for dinner? Ted has a new grill and wants to feed you two."

"Sounds good," I say. "I'll find out when Donovan has his next Saturday off."

I say the words, but the truth is I'm not asking Donovan anything. Although I love Nicole like a sister, I've been avoiding invitations to her house for months. I'm not sure I can handle seeing her baby boy cooing in his bouncy chair. I've only met him once—I went to the hospital when he was born. But that was before.

That's the thing I don't understand. It's been excruciating lately to be around babies, yet all that disappeared when I held Lucy. All I want to do is hold her again.

"Maybe you and I can meet after work this week for a drink?" I say.

"Let me check with Ted." Now she sounds apologetic. "It's been a little bit of a challenge to get to day-care pickup before they start charging us an arm and a leg for being late. I'll figure out a night Ted can take off from work early so I can meet up with you."

Again, the line is silent. Both of us contemplating just how much our worlds have changed in the past year. She has to check with her husband before she meets me for a drink?

I want my old friend back.

But it is more than that. I want my old life back. I want it like it was last year before every day was filled with longing and heartache.

Chapter 8

WHEN I WALK in, Donovan is sitting on my couch, scratching Dusty behind the ears and nursing a beer. The kitchen is dark. It's Friday night, and we're both home early. A year ago, he would've had something yummy to eat on the table. We're like an old married couple now. We no longer try to impress each other. It makes me sad and wistful.

All that disappears as he stands and wraps me in his arms.

"You okay?" he whispers in my ear. His warm breath sends a shudder of desire through me. Dusty wraps himself around my legs, trying to be part of our embrace.

I push back an image of that apartment filled with bodies. It is instantly replaced with the memory of holding Lucy in my arms. I can almost feel her tiny fingers wrapped around my hair. I can't stop thinking about how she reached for me when CPS took her away.

When I don't answer, Donovan draws back. Holding onto my shoulders, he searches my eyes. "It's going to be okay."

Pressing my lips together tightly, I nod before disengaging myself from his arms and checking my side table for today's mail.

Unearthing a postcard from Tomas in Russia, I lean over my chessboard and make the move he has sent me: Queen e2. I can see immediately that he's aiming for a smothered mate. If I move knight to df6 to defend, he will move bishop to b4 mate. I study the board, biting my lip for a few seconds until I move my own piece. Knight to d6. That should give him something to think about. Grabbing a stack of postcards that have been preaddressed and stamped, I scribble my move and sign it with my signature, G.G. Can't wait to see what Tomas has planned to defend against *that.* I set the postcard on the small table by my door so I won't forget to mail it in the morning.

Donovan is watching me with a sexy half smile. "Why *do* you like chess so much? As opposed to, say, poker or something. Have you thought about it?"

He already knows that after my sister was murdered, learning to play chess helped me cope with the trauma and begin speaking again after six months of silence. But that's not what he means.

"I've thought about it a lot, actually. What I've also thought about is why you won't give it a try. I think you'd like it. It would be something fun we could do together." I watch him down the rest of his beer. "Are you sure you don't want to learn how to play?"

"Nah," he says, winking.

Donovan walks over and undoes the top few buttons of my silky blouse.

"Tell me more about why you enjoy chess," he says in a low voice that sends a shiver through me. He runs his hands down my back and even lower.

"There are certain truths you can find in chess." I catch my breath as his fingers roam.

Donovan's face is now only inches away from mine. His eyes are lowered, staring at my mouth as I speak.

"Go on," he says with a sexy growl, his hands roaming down my sides, lifting my blouse to find bare skin.

"You can't find a universal truth in life, but you can find it in chess," I say, nearly losing my train of thought as I watch his mouth come even closer to mine. He smells so good, a musky man scent with the faint hint of cologne. "In chess you can achieve the seemingly impossible, such as the ability to confront a superior force and overcome it."

With a flick of his wrist, my silk blouse is on the floor.

"But for you," he says, his mouth coming closer, "chess is also a way for you to escape, isn't it?"

He knows me like nobody else does. I feel like he's always known me. I don't answer, only stare at his mouth until finally it crushes mine. I melt into his embrace, closing my eyes for a second before an image of the massacre leaps into my mind and I pull back in dismay.

"What's wrong?" He searches my eyes, concerned.

I shake my head back and forth. "When I close my eyes . . ."

"Shhh," he says, kissing my forehead. "It's going to take some time. Is there anything I can do?"

I answer by grabbing his head and pulling his mouth down to mine. He responds eagerly, pulling me close until it feels like every inch of our bodies is touching. When I finally pull back, it's only to move my mouth over to his jaw, down his neck, my hands under his shirt and behind his back, holding him to me.

He pulls my hips even tighter against him, and I moan. He has picked me up and is moving toward the bed, when his phone rings.

Putting me down on the bed, he glances at the number on his cell. When he starts to reach for it, I know it is his work calling. I put my arm on his to try to stop him from picking up the phone.

"It's Finn." His partner. Which means a ninety percent chance he's calling about a dead body. A homicide case means Donovan gone for at least the next twelve hours, if not longer.

He's listening to Finn and nodding. I'm lying on my back on the bed, half dressed, wild with desire, and knowing in the pit of my stomach that I'll be spending the night alone.

"I'll be there in twenty." He disconnects and runs a hand through his hair, making it stick straight up. "Goddamn it."

At first I think he says it because he has to leave me.

"Gang shooting. This time it was one of my C.I.'s." Confidential informants.

I flop over onto my belly and put my chin on my folded hands. I don't look at him as I ask, "Can't Finn handle it for the first hour? Can't you stay just for a little while?"

He leans down, lifts my hair, and kisses the back of my neck. "I'm sorry. Hell, I don't want to leave right now, either, but I have to. Be back as soon as I can."

I don't answer. My entire body is limp with desire, and he's going to leave me.

When the door shuts behind him, anger surges through me. He knew I was ovulating today, and he still walked out. I thought he wanted a baby as much as I do. The window for getting pregnant each month is small—maybe twenty-four hours, possibly as long as forty-eight. I try to push back my frustration. It's not his fault. But it lies there, simmering under the surface, even as I try to distract myself.

I'm not hungry for dinner. I don't want to read. I don't want to watch TV.

My computer is on a small desk across the room. I'll check my work e-mail and see if there's anything new on the Mission Massacre. Maybe an arrest? I scan the return addresses, looking for something from Kellogg or Nicole. Nothing.

My heart leaps into my throat when I see this return address: FA2858.

It's him. Frank Anderson. The man who kidnapped and killed my sister. Even though I have no proof, I know deep down inside my sister's killer is e-mailing me. He's taunting me. But I haven't told Donovan about the previous e-mails from Anderson. When I first got pregnant, he asked if maybe we could take a small break from hunting Anderson (aka me obsessing about finding my sister's killer) while we concentrated on starting a family.

He pulled some strings and got a new detective assigned to Caterina's cold case.

"I know it's hard, but give it a try," he said. "Let's turn it over to the investigators and let them do their job. I'm worried about you. This guy knows how to get under your skin. I don't want that monster in your head. He's done enough damage. If you can, just let go for a little while and enjoy being pregnant." His eyes were so shiny with happiness and excitement that I agreed to let go. Temporarily.

I promised to send the new detective any leads that came my way. But I soon found out that's much easier said than done.

The first e-mail came right after my miscarriage.

The subject line said, *Sins of the Father.* The body of the e-mail said this: *Exodus 20:5 You shall not bow down to them or serve them, for I the Lord your God am a jealous God, visiting the iniquity of the fathers on the children to the third and the fourth generation of those who hate me.*

I immediately knew it was Anderson. And while I didn't have proof, I believed he knew about my miscarriage and was telling me that it was my punishment for being a killer—that my unborn child was punished for my sins. He knows. I don't know how, but he knows. I forwarded the e-mail to the detective.

Tonight's e-mail has a subject line that says, *Thou Shalt Not Kill.*

My hand hovers above the keyboard, trembling slightly. I want to click it open so badly, but instead, without reading it, I forward it to the detective. I know I'm doing the right thing for my relationship with Donovan—and probably my mental health—but I can't help feeling as if I am once again turning my back on my sister.

Chapter 9

THE STACK OF police scanners is crackling with radio traffic when I settle in at my desk the next day. The normally monotone voices have something about them this morning that makes me lean over and turn up the volume, catching details in snippets.

"Motorcycle vs. center median."

"Highway 10."

So far nothing newsworthy. Then I hear it.

"Severed foot."

And to seal the deal: "Cannot locate extremity."

I grab my bag and dial Lopez in photo.

"Yo," he answers.

"Motorcyclist. Severed foot. Highway 10. Meet you in the parking lot." I reel it off staccato.

"I'm on it," he says.

Even though it's Saturday, I came in to work because Donovan is working that homicide all day. Nicole is in our Martinez bureau, scrounging for anything new on the Mission Massacre.

On the way out of the newsroom, I holler to the copy desk. "Motorcyclist vs. median. C-Lo and I are on it. There's a severed foot involved."

Someone nearby snickers. As I head for the back door, I hear someone in sports mutter, "Only in a newsroom would someone giggle hearing about a severed foot."

As WE COME up on the highway-patrol vehicle, I can't decide whether to pull in behind it or in front of the tow truck parked in front of him. With the cars whizzing by at sixty-five miles an hour, I decide we're safest in front of the tow truck.

In my passenger seat, Lopez screws the telephoto lens on his camera and adjusts the ubiquitous earbud cord trailing down to the police scanner clipped to his belt. He is a true newspaperman from a bygone era. He's also ex–Green Beret, wiry and small and usually packing a gun or two. He pulls the earbuds out of his ears for a second and turns to me as I pull over. "Dude is on way to hospital. Can't figure out if they found his foot or not."

The tow truck is parked so close to the cables separating the freeway from the median that we can't squeeze by. Lopez doesn't hesitate and army-crawls under the cables into the weeds. Within seconds, he's upright, snapping photos of the wrecked bike being hoisted onto the back of the tow truck. I see a highway-patrol officer walking toward his vehicle.

Worried he'll leave before I get the details of the accident, I scurry under the cable, knowing I look less than graceful and worried I'll be the one to find the foot.

I stand and attempt to brush all the stickers and weeds off my dress while holding my phone, notebook, and a pen. I rush over to the officer, who is now in his vehicle. I hold out my CHP Press Pass dangling on a chain around my neck. "Gabriella Giovanni with the *Bay Herald*. Do you have a second?"

"I know who you are," he says and smirks.

My heart skips a beat. He either knows who I am and hates me, or he knows who I am and likes me. He must see the confusion on my face, because he continues.

"I was there when they yanked Sebastian Laurent out of the ditch last year."

Oh yeah. They let me in for the close-up because at first they thought it was a fatal accident, but it ended up being a homicide, the first in a string of them that led to me killing the killer. I feel heat flush across my cheeks. He knows exactly who I am and what I've done.

He's started his car, but his window is down. The cool air from his air-conditioning blows on my sweaty face as I lean down. This part of the Bay Area is having a heat wave, and I'm not sure if I hate it or like it. Sometimes the temperature where I work and where I live varies by thirty degrees.

The sound of a helicopter overhead drowns out my voice as I speak to the officer. He peers through his windshield with a creased brow. I squint and try to see any markings on the small dark helicopter, but it's too far away.

"One of yours?" I ask.

He frowns and shakes his head. A second later, he opens the door, but as soon as he gets out, the helicopter zooms off.

"What can you tell me?" I ask as soon as it is quiet.

"Don't have a whole lot. You should talk to the PIO about it."

The public information officer for the CHP is a good guy, but he's sometimes hard to get hold of before deadline.

"Can you just give me the bare basics?" I ask. "I don't even need to use your name."

I wait as he thinks about it. He sighs, and I know he'll spill it.

"About fourteen hundred hours, motorcyclist hit some gravel and swerved into the cable median. No other vehicles involved. Driver was transported via ambulance with non-life-threatening injuries."

Looking up from the scribbles in my notebook, I wipe my brow and meet his eyes. "Heard something about a severed foot . . ."

"Not allowed to talk about injuries."

"Come on!" He's leaving out the most interesting part of the crash.

"That's all I got," he says.

"I heard the whole thing on the scanner, I just need you to verify it."

"Sorry." He smiles in a maddening way. This is fun for him. It's all a big game.

Lopez is in the median, gesturing at me, for some reason. He paces and beckons.

With the cop watching me, I get down on my knees and crawl under the cables. I'm concentrating on watching the weeds in front of me, hoping that I'm not the one who finds the severed foot somewhere. Finally, I'm through and leap to my feet, brushing the grass and sticky weeds off my dress. I'm making a face as I gingerly step through the weeds in the median. When I turn to look around, I catch the cop watching from his window. He's snickering.

"Don't you dare say a word," I say.

He laughs. Right before he pulls away, he says, "Don't worry, they found the foot."

Bingo. Confirmation.

In the car on the drive back, Lopez is frowning. "What was up with that helicopter?"

I shrug. "No clue." He's chewing at his lip and looks worried.

"Why do you ask?" I say.

"Helicopters like that are what we saw in 'Nam. Black helicopters. Called 'The Quiet Ones.' Used for some covert shit. The military uses copters like that for stealth missions, inserting and extracting personnel. No reason for a chopper like that to be out here in East County."

Lopez is the best, but sometimes I worry that what he saw in Vietnam might make him a little more paranoid than the average person. Instead of answering, I look out the window and decide not to tell him I saw the same kind of helicopter at the scene of the Mission Massacre.

BACK IN THE newsroom, I ignore the night cops reporter, May, as I sit down.

She wears crisp, pressed slacks, a starched blouse, and fat pearl earrings, and she smells overpoweringly like Chanel. Doesn't she ever have to cover wildfires or crawl under freeway medians like I do?

We are only civil to each other when we absolutely have to be. I tolerate her—barely—because she's good at her job and I don't have to worry about her missing any big stories on the cop beat overnight.

She owes me for her beat. I intervened to get her off covering education. But that doesn't mean we need to be best friends. As if she is reading my mind, she proves why we can never be pals by sneering slightly at me, eyes pointedly fixating on the big grass stain on my dress.

Note to self: never, ever, ever wear a dress to work again. Even as I say it, I know I'm lying. It's too hot here in the summer to wear pants every day.

Digging through my purse, I can't find the reporter's notebook I took out to the crash. I try to remember if I threw it in my bag when I got back into the car. I was so busy talking to Lopez about how stupid it was for me to wear a dress to work that I'm not sure what I did with the notebook. Rushing out to the newspaper parking lot, I check inside my car. No dice. Damn it. It's somewhere in the center median of the highway. It isn't the ideal way to write an article, but I write my severed-foot story based on memory.

Before I pack up, I get online and search "Iraq War," "samurai swords," "black helicopters," and "soldiers with PTSD." I print out about fifty pages of information and tuck them into my bag. Some light reading for bedtime.

Donovan is working the homicide again, so I'm on my own for dinner. Back in North Beach, I eat some sourdough toast and slice a tomato, but my heart isn't into it. I grab the sheaf of papers I printed out, hop in bed, and vow to stay awake reading until Donovan gets home so I can ravish him. We should be spending every second tonight making love in case there is still a chance I can get pregnant. Instead, here I am reading about the Iraq War in bed. Alone.

Chapter 10

I WAKE IN the night, screaming. It takes me a few seconds to realize Donovan is back home and holding me in his arms, rocking me back and forth and whispering soothingly in my ear that it is just a bad dream and everything is okay. I fell asleep reading the papers I'd printed out.

I flick on the light by my bed, hoping it will dispel the memory of my dream. In it, I was in the Martin apartment again, nudging the door open. This time, the girl has her head turned away. I make a soft, cooing sound to get her attention. Her head snaps in a 360-degree arc like the girl in *The Exorcist,* and her eye sockets are black holes. Her pointy vampire teeth are still chewing on chunks of flesh she's ripped from her dead mother's breast.

I'm afraid to tell Donovan about the dream. He'll think I'm even more in need of therapy than I really am.

He holds me as I calm down, allowing my breathing to get normal again. Sweat is trickling down my brow, and my body is trembling. But Donovan's presence calms me. He breathes into my hair and rubs my back until I'm not panting for air.

After a while, I pad over to the kitchen sink and fill a large glass with water, drinking it all in several gulps. Donovan is sitting up in bed, leaning against some pillows propped on my headboard. "You okay?" His eyes are soft, squinting in the bright light. He's been asking me this a lot lately. The question itself makes me feel high-maintenance and guilty.

"How long have you been home?" I say.

"A few minutes ago. Have to be back in two hours."

I walk back over to him, and we lie down with his arms wrapped around me and my face pressed against his chest. I kiss him, lifting his shirt up as my lips make their way downward. But then I hear it. Snoring. He's asleep.

I'm tempted to wake him up. I shake him a little, but he rolls over on his side. Anger, disappointment, and frustration shoot through me as I stand. I also feel guilty for being so angry with him. He has to go back to work in two hours. And he just got home. No wonder he fell asleep. But it still feels like rejection. If he wants a baby as much as I do, wouldn't he have tried to stay awake just in case there was still a chance?

Wide awake, I grab a blanket and head out the sliding-glass door to the balcony. Pulling out a metal bistro chair, I sit, putting my bare feet up on the balcony railing. The smell of jasmine and basil from the pots in one corner combines with a whiff of ocean carried on the breeze.

Leaning back, ignoring the way the metal digs into my back through the blanket, I exhale slowly up into the crisp night air above me. The clouds part and reveal a slice of moon and stars. In front of me, the fog blows away, revealing the spires of Saints Peter and Paul Church across the park.

The distant bellow of a foghorn is comforting, but it fades as

I'm back inside the church, as if it were yesterday. On tiptoe, I peer into my sister's coffin, staring at her in the white communion dress she never had a chance to wear. I'm yanked back from the coffin by my aunt, who rushes me back down the aisle, where I'm forced to sit with my two brothers in their too-tight black suits. I can almost feel the scratchy crinoline of my dress, the one we picked out for me to wear to Caterina's first Eucharist.

Every time I see the church spires, I'm taken back in time. They aren't always bad times. Sometimes they are happy memories of playing in Washington Square Park, across from the church. My mother sitting with the other moms and laughing. My brothers playing bocce, imitating the old guys at one end of the park. Caterina sitting with the older girls, giggling and ignoring me when I try to get her to play with me. She's too cool for her younger sister, even though we are only a year apart. Over the past few months, memories of my dark past have been pushed down as I deal with my new, private grief, but they always linger there under the surface.

A gust of wind sends a chill through me, and the night grows darker as clouds cover the moon and stars.

Chapter 11

WHEN I WAKE, the sunlight streaming through the windows helps me momentarily forget my nightmare from last night, and my anger at Donovan has lessened some.

Donovan left hours ago, even though it's Sunday. That's the thing about dating a cop—there is no such thing as a weekend for him. Ever since we met, he's angled to get Sundays off, because he can't pass up the after-party at my nana's house, when everyone gathers to eat after Mass. But this weekend, the first forty-eight hours of a homicide take precedence.

Before my moka pot percolates, I speak to Kellogg and Mrs. Castillo, Maria Martin's mother.

After I pour my coffee, I open the breadbox to fish out the remains of a sourdough loaf. Along with the bread, I spot a tiny white box with a red ribbon on it. It's signed with a D.

Inside is a religious medal. St. Gerard, it says. I finger the miraculous medal of the Virgin Mary on my neck as I turn over the newer, shinier medal in my hands, looking for some clue as to why Donovan gave me this. I know a lot of saints, but this one escapes me. On my bookshelf, I take down the bright yellow spine of my *Book of Saints for Children* and flip through the pages.

St. Gerard is the patron saint of expectant mothers.

The realization makes me slump onto the couch.

I read on. When I get to the prayer to St. Gerard, it makes more sense. Donovan wants me to wear this when I get pregnant again.

This one line says it all: " . . . shield the child which I now carry, that it may see the light of day and receive the lustral waters of baptism."

Reading this makes my arms feel so empty. Donovan is so confident that I will get pregnant again. Me? I'm convinced something is wrong and I'll never be able to have children. If only I had his faith.

When I strip for my shower and see my flat stomach in the mirror, it sends me spiraling back in time to another day I can't forget, when the doctor told me there was no heartbeat.

"I've been doing this for twenty-five years," she said. "In that time, I've told hundreds of women the same thing, and within a year, I've delivered their baby."

Although I never told Donovan what the doctor said, I clung to those words like a lifeline: *Within a year, I've delivered their baby.*

Later, I asked my regular obstetrician when we could start trying again. He must have heard the desperation in my voice.

"It's safest to wait until you've had at least three more regular cycles again."

Three months.

It has now been four.

The chart I have taped to my bathroom cabinet marks every day. Last month, the first month we could "try," I read every book on conception I could find and began taking my temperature and charting my cycle. I quit drinking and smoking. The night I told Donovan "it was time," I was so excited. That disappeared two weeks later when my period came.

Last night would have been another chance to try. I swallow back the disappointment and anger. The last thing I need is to resent Donovan and his job. But deep down inside, I know it's too late.

Chapter 12

TERESA CASTILLO LIVES in San Juan Bautista. Kellogg reluctantly gave me the thumbs-up for the trip because it will be the first interview with a family member of the victims. He made a point to remind me that covering the Mission Massacre was still Nicole's job, but that it'd be okay if I wrote this one story, a profile piece of Maria Martin. Gee thanks.

The trip will take most of my day. I'm missing Sunday dinner at Nana's. But I'm slightly relieved I can postpone facing my family and all their questions about the Mission Massacre.

And I'm doubly glad I don't have to see Donovan today. While I know it's not entirely his fault and that I'm being childish, I'm still furious we missed our window. Part of me wishes I would've pushed him and said, "Come on, let's just have a quickie!" Nothing wrong with that. Instead, a tiny nugget of resentment against him forms.

The sun is creeping over the Gabilan Mountains in a misty haze when I zip past San Jose. The light this morning is amazing, golden and hazy, mingling with lingering coastal fog.

I know I'm close when the car fills with the pungent smells of Gilroy's garlic fields. I pull over at a roadside stand, where I grab a latte and a braid of garlic for my kitchen.

It feels great to fly down the freeway with my windows down, cranking The Cure's "Just Like Heaven," buzzed from the caffeine in my latte. Even though I'm filled with disappointment, a tiny part of me is relieved that I don't have to worry about getting pregnant for another month. The feeling of a weight being lifted combines with a pang of sadness that my body will go even longer without a baby inside it.

I make great time, so when I pull into San Juan Bautista, I'm forty minutes early for my meeting with Mrs. Castillo. After cruising past her tiny bungalow so I know where it is, I park a few blocks away and head for the mission. I've seen it in movies so many times that I'm anxious to see it in real life.

A small line is formed in front of what must be the village bakery. The smell of fresh bread reminds me I skipped breakfast. I'll stop in the bakery after I visit the mission.

At the chapel, a crowd pours out after what must have been the 10:00 a.m. Mass. I creep inside and genuflect before kneeling toward the back.

Closing my eyes, hands clasped, I pray. The wood kneeler digs into my bare legs.

I pray for Lucy. A lurid image of the death scene in that apartment rushes back. I press my eyes even tighter, my face scrunching up. I pray for my own baby. And pray for the chance to get pregnant again.

I know I don't deserve it, but I want to be a mother so badly.

I think about Caterina, and for once, I don't pray to avenge her murder.

Father Liam once told me to try praying for Caterina's killer. I don't know if I will ever be capable of that. Right now, I fear I would pray for his long, painful death at my own hands.

But thinking of him has stopped my thoughts of my dead baby. Pushing my hair back, I look up. The church has nearly emptied.

A dark head is bowed in the front pew.

The altar's bright colors draw me closer. The woman in the front pew briefly looks up, and her eyes brighten when she sees me. She gives me a small smile and nod, and bows her head once more.

I pause in front of the altar. There are six cubbies, lined with red curtains that contain intricately painted statues. I recognize the one that is most prominent, John the Baptist, but the others I'm not sure about.

When I turn to ask the woman in the front row, I realize she must have silently slipped out a side door, because the church is empty.

A FEW MINUTES later, I knock on the door to the bungalow. Small yellow flowers in terra-cotta pots flank the entryway.

Soft singing from inside the house filters out an open window, and a moment later the door opens. It's the woman from the church. Her black hair is cut in a Louise-Brooks-type bob, with a silver streak down one side. She wears blood red lipstick on her full lips and a black turtleneck with black Capri pants.

A small smile spreads across her face, but her gray eyes are possibly the saddest eyes I've ever seen. The loss of her daughter weighs heavy in them, but the warmth in her smile is genuine, and I can't help but return it. I thrust a warm loaf of rustic bread at her.

"This smelled too good to pass up."

"*Gracias*. We'll have some with our coffee." She opens the door wider so I can enter.

Inside, the main room is nearly empty. A small wood table pressed against one wall holds an old-fashioned stainless-steel percolator and two coffee mugs. The main feature of the room is a large easel with a seascape partially completed. Stacks of finished canvases lean against the lower parts of the white stucco walls. Most of them appear to be Mexican landscapes featuring tall, soaring cactus with purple and red flowers against a cobalt sky.

"You're an artist?"

The woman gives a graceful shrug. "It pays the rent."

She has a thick accent, but she obviously learned American colloquialisms quickly. I wonder how long she's lived here.

"Excuse me, why did they say your daughter didn't have any other family in America?" I say as I take the cup of coffee she hands me.

"Let's go out to the patio."

A small door through the kitchen leads to an inner courtyard filled with flowers.

"I am dead to him," she says once we are seated at a small metal bistro table outside. Her tone has grown somber. "A few months ago, I tried to get Maria to leave him. She told him. He forbid her from speaking to me. But she did anyway. I am her mother."

"Her husband? Joey Martin?"

"Yes. He met Maria on leave in Mexico. He wants to 'save' her, he says, he marries her, brings her up here, and leaves. She is so lonely. He brings his parents and sister and nephew to live with her. He is overseas the whole time."

"So, he was gone most of the time?"

"Yes." Mrs. Castillo pours us more coffee.

"How often did he come to visit since they married?"

"Not much. Maybe three times. Only for a day or two."

Long enough to knock her up, though.

"But the last time, Maria asked me to come to stay when he is on leave here." She raises an eyebrow as she says it. The last person I would want around when my husband was home on leave from overseas would be my mother.

Mrs. Castillo butters some bread and hands me a thick slice. I take a bite, chewing. Despite the smell, it tastes like everything else I've had to eat lately—cardboard. Even so, I am halfway done with my piece while she gingerly nibbles on the crust of hers.

Maria asked her mother to stay in her small apartment when her husband was last home on leave.

"Why did Maria want you to stay?"

"She was afraid." Mrs. Castillo says this matter-of-factly.

"But she was never really alone, was she? You said his parents were up there, and his sister as well, right?"

"Yes, they live in the same building as Maria. They watched baby Lucy for her sometimes."

They lived in her building? Did the police search their apartment, as well?

"Do you remember what apartment number?" I keep chewing the soggy piece of bread, which is lasting an eternity in my mouth.

"312. I remember it because it is the same as my birthday—three, twelve—March twelfth. Maria spent a lot of time there, too. She liked his parents." Her bright eyes blink back tears.

I finally swallow the bread.

"There was also his friend," she says, and I wonder why she is bringing this friend up. Is there a reason? "He was always around. Wish Maria would have married him. Much nicer. Good family," she says and takes another tiny nibble of her bread, running a fingernail around her mouth to make sure her lipstick hasn't smeared.

"What friend?" Why does she want me to know this? What is she trying to tell me?

I wait as she finishes chewing. "Army buddy. Nice boy."

"Do you remember his name?"

Mrs. Castillo looks off into the distance as she tries to remember.

"Marnie? Arnie? Maybe something with an A, but some type of girl name. On a boy." She says this as if it's a travesty. Fingering her chin, she gives a big sigh. "It will come to me. One of these days."

"Can you call me if you remember that friend's name?"

She nods, absentmindedly handing me another slice of bread she has buttered.

"Do you have a picture of Maria I could borrow? I could make a copy and mail the original back today."

The screen door slams behind her as she heads inside. I lean back, looking up at the blue sky for a few seconds before I take in the morning glory flowers snaking up a trellis beside me.

When Mrs. Castillo returns, her eyes and nose are red, as if she was crying and blew her nose because she didn't want me to know. She hands me a glossy five-by-seven picture. It's a wedding photo.

It is a candid shot of the couple walking on the beach. Maria wears a white gown that is severely buttoned up to the neck, which somehow highlights her voluptuousness. He is dressed in his army uniform. Only his profile shows as he looks at Maria.

Maria's face is lit from within. She is laughing merrily, hair slightly mussed, holding his hand in a way that looked like they had been swinging their arms. Tucking the picture into my notebook in my bag, I ask about Maria's childhood.

Mrs. Castillo tells me how Maria grew up on the family ranch in Mexico, helping her father with the horses and cows. How she rode the wildest horses, taming them, having them eat out of her palm. And how shortly after her father died, she met Martin. He was visiting a friend on a nearby ranch, and he saw her riding bareback in a dress with her long hair flowing behind her. He decided right then she would be his wife. He was charismatic and handsome, and Maria told her mother it was love at first sight.

Glancing at my watch, I realize I've skirted around the issue long enough. "Why did you want to speak to me in person? Why do you want to stop Lucy's father from getting her?" I take another sip of my coffee.

"He is so crazy about her, he wants to be with her all the time. He was so angry he had to go overseas. His own fault. He signed the papers. Twelve more years."

Twelve more years enlisted? That's a serious commitment. She stands and begins puttering with her plants, stroking the leaves and checking the soil for moisture. She's avoiding my eyes. I see her swipe at her eyes when her back is turned.

"Mrs. Castillo? I know this is difficult for you, but you haven't answered my question. You called him a monster. Said you would rather die than see your granddaughter end up in his care."

She gives a nervous laugh and doesn't look up from an azalea plant. "I don't know. Sometimes I say crazy things."

Why is she backing off now? What has changed? I can't figure it out. I stand and set my coffee cup down. I open the door to her bungalow, and she follows.

"You told me on the phone that more than anything else, you

needed to stop him from getting your granddaughter," I say once we are inside, standing near the front door. "You need to explain that. I didn't drive down here for the coffee."

When she looks up at me, I see the answer in her eyes. Mingled with the sadness is a look of terror.

"You're afraid, aren't you? You're afraid of whoever killed your daughter?"

She acknowledges my words with a nod so slight it could be imagined.

"Lucy will not be safe if he has her. . . . That little girl is all I have now. All I have of my Maria . . ."

She trails off.

"Why won't you tell me why you're afraid? You called me down here for a reason. Why won't Lucy be safe with her father? Please tell me."

She shakes her head no.

Something dark and unfathomable stirs inside me for a second. She looks up and takes my hands in hers.

"Can you save Lucy?" Her sharp fingernails, painted the same blood red as her lipstick, dig into my hands.

"Tell me what you're afraid of."

She won't look at me. Her demeanor conveys a desperation that doesn't match her words. I sense her fear, shooting through her hand into mine.

"He is here. He has been here. He was here the day Maria died."

"What? The police said he's thousands of miles away in Iraq. What are you trying to say? Are you saying he had something to do with your daughter's death?"

"Can you stop him from getting Lucy?" she repeats, her hands clutching mine so tightly that it hurts.

"Not unless you cut the bullshit and tell me what you really know. What do you mean, he's here?" Infected with her fear, I lash out, in a harsher tone than I intended. I tear my hand out of hers, open the front door, and step outside.

Instead of answering, she pulls back and closes the door on me as if I've slapped her. I pound and pound, but she doesn't open the door. Finally I stop and put my mouth near the door.

"If you can't convince me, you'll never convince the cops."

The door slowly opens. Only wide enough for her face to peer out.

"In her apartment. In her closet, there is a steamer trunk. Underneath is a loose board. There you will find her letters. If they are not there, check in the in-laws' apartment. In the linen closet. She said she will hide them one of those places. They will explain everything. You have to believe me when I say Lucy is in danger.

"He is here."

Chapter 13

As soon as I'm in San Francisco, I find myself missing my exit for the Embarcadero and taking the next one. Before I know it, I'm parked in front of the apartment building in the Mission, peering up at the lighted windows of the four-story structure. Several windows are dark, including the corner apartment on the second floor, where Maria lived, and one on the third floor—the one where her in-laws lived? Is Mrs. Castillo crazy with grief, or is Lucy in danger? If the letters are there, I'll believe her. And if she's telling the truth, the cops need to know. I just won't tell them exactly how the letters ended up in my hands. A minor detail. Besides, none of what Mrs. Castillo says is going to matter if we can't prove it.

It only takes me a few seconds to decide. I'll need to swing by my apartment first. Donovan left a message earlier saying he was going to try to sleep a few hours at his place before heading back to work.

At my place in North Beach, I rummage on top of my cabinets, where I keep things hidden: mace and my lock pick set. I have one canister of mace on my keychain, but I like to have an extra one hidden in my apartment. I grab my lock pick set and tuck it into a small bag I sling crossways over my body.

Once I'm in front of the apartment building, I wait until the street is quiet before I get out of my car, closing the door softly and not setting my noisy car alarm.

At the front door of the building, I look both ways down the street before slipping inside, my heart pounding. I jog up the small flight of stairs to the second floor. At the end of the hall, the door to apartment 210, Maria's apartment, looks normal. Once I'm in front of the door, I try the handle. Locked. I take out my lock pick kit. My hands are shaking, and my palms grow sweaty and slippery even looking at the door. I'll start at the in-laws' apartment upstairs. It has been a few months since I picked a lock.

Lopez gave me the lock pick kit in August for my birthday.

He spent an entire afternoon showing me how to pick different types of locks. Armed with a set of picks and a tension wrench, we practiced on dead bolts, combination locks, pin tumbler locks, and regular doorknob locks at his family's homes.

"Get that torsion wrench in and hold it with a light touch with your thumb. Very little pressure. Now, take your pick and hold it like a pencil. Use your wrist, not your fingers, to move it . . . push it up and down gently. Feel the pins?"

I'd shake my head no, but he never lost his patience.

"Don't push the pick all the way to the back. Do you feel a pin that is stuck? Yes? Apply a little pressure. You can tell every time you unlock a pin, because you'll feel it in the wrench and the plug will move a little, got it?"

I'd nod excitedly when all the pins were unlocked.

"It's all about the touch, man," he kept telling me that afternoon. "The biggest mistake people make is they think they need to crank on that thing. When you pick a lock, a light touch is what works."

Lopez always treats me like another one of his little sisters, and that day was no exception. He got so excited for me when I finally figured it out. "High five, man. You got it!" The rest of his family seemed to think this was a normal birthday gift and a perfectly reasonable way to spend our Saturday afternoon. His sister cooked a feast, and we stayed for the best tamale dinner north of San Diego.

Even though I pretty much have the hang of it, it takes a lot longer for me to open a door than it does Lopez. He's promised to make me a bump key—a key that can open most locks—but hasn't yet. A lock pick kit is better, he says, because you can sneak in and out without any trace, and bump keys sometimes ruin locks.

"Do burglars know about these?" I asked him.

"Fuck yeah, home skillet. 'Course they do."

Great.

Upstairs, at room 312—Joey Martin's parents' apartment—I kneel in front of the door and work on the lock, remembering what Lopez taught me, but I am jumpy, worried every time I hear a small sound from neighboring apartments. Beads of sweat are dripping down my brow by the time I hear the last click and the door swings open.

Inside, I close the door behind me and lean against it in the dark, catching my breath. My blood is racing through my veins, pumping loudly in my ears. I did it. I am officially a burglar.

Moving carefully in the dark, I reach for a light switch.

The apartment is simple, like Maria's down below, but it seems more cheery, homier. It also is impeccable. Is there a chance the cops dropped the ball and didn't search this apartment?

There is a colorful afghan blanket thrown over the couch. I smell something that reminds me of my uncle Sal, and it makes sense when I see the small ashtray that contains a tiny, half-smoked cigar.

A Formica dining room table is spotless, and a morning paper is neatly stacked on one corner. I glance at the date. The morning Maria called me.

Everything is in its proper place. Dishes from breakfast are clean and resting on a dish rack to dry. Towels on the counter are perfectly stacked.

I glance around the bedroom. The bed is neatly made.

The few clothes in the small closet are neat. Shoeboxes contain well-worn and cared-for shoes. The bathroom, also, yields nothing. It smells like bleach. But it looks like the cops haven't searched it. I wonder why not.

Holding my breath, I crack the linen closet in the hall and rummage around. It only contains neat stacks of towels and sheets. No letters. I scan the rest of the apartment. I'm not sure what I thought I could find. Maybe it's what's missing that tells me something. There is only one picture on a small end table—of Joey Martin's mother and father taken years ago. Maybe their engagement picture? Or wedding picture. He wears a dark suit. She wears what appears to be a pale jacket over a high-necked blouse. Her hair is clipped neatly back away from her face. They are smiling.

But there is not one single picture of Joey. Not a baby or school picture. Not a wedding picture of Joey and Maria.

Before I leave, I give one last glance around, trying to memorize it and take it all in, just in case I missed something. I can't believe the police searched this place and left it so undisturbed.

Back on the second floor, I pause, looking down the hall at Maria's apartment, but I can't make myself go in there. Not in the dark. Not by myself. No matter how hard I try, I can't help but see the apartment in vivid Technicolor, full of bloody, chopped-up bodies. Their ghosts surely must haunt that tiny space.

But I owe it to Maria to look for those letters. I owe it to her and her baby. She turned to me for help. Someone killed her before she told me her secrets, but maybe I can help her now.

In front of apartment 210, I press my ear to the door. The only sound is my heart thumping loudly in my ear. I know I'm overreacting, but I get the overwhelming feeling that a tangible evil is emanating from the apartment. My mouth grows dry, and the hairs on the back of my neck stand at attention. I wipe my palms on my pants before I try the doorknob to make sure it's still locked. I get out my lock pick kit. It takes a little less time than before. I stand back and gently kick the door open. The apartment is dark. A noise down the hall that sounds like a door opening sends me scurrying inside, pushing the door closed softly behind me. I reach off to the side for the light switch, but when I flick it, the room remains black.

My heart races, and even in the dark, I see bloody faces in corners, my imagination running wild, mixing with my memories of the massacre. The apartment seems alive even though I know all the bodies are long gone. A lingering evil presence remains. With shaking fingers, I fumble in my small bag for my flashlight. I'm about to turn it on when a floorboard across the living room creaks and I hear a breathy sound—like someone exhaling with scuba gear.

I am not alone.

Chapter 14

I FRANTICALLY CLAW for the doorknob behind me, but it's too late. A weight slams into me in the dark, crushing me back against the wooden door. A gloved hand closes over my mouth, stifling my scream. My hand is on the doorknob behind me, and I have it twisted. If I can get our weight off the door, I can open it.

Clawing for the eyes, my fingernails scrape against bare cheeks. I bite through the gloves and meet flesh at the same time my knee connects with the man's groin. He grunts and yanks at my hair, tugging so tightly that tears spring to my eyes. As he yanks me away from the door, my hand is still grasping the twisted doorknob. The momentum of him pulling away as I hold the doorknob sends the door careening open. The scream building inside me lets loose at the same time light from the hall illuminates my assailant's face. Bushy eyebrows and full lips. Eyes narrowed with hate. The same face I saw in the wedding photograph with Maria.

Joey Martin.

His eyes widen as my scream goes on and on. Within seconds, doors down the hallway are opening, and he has scrambled off me and is gone. Without thinking, I clamber to my feet and chase him, heading straight to the bathroom. I climb in the tub and peer out the window in time to see a stocky figure in black leap off the bottom of the telephone pole beside the building. Something drops from his waist, but he doesn't seem to notice. Instead, he gives one glance up and darts around a small fence, right when the sound of sirens fills the air.

Then I'm down in the alley, searching in the leaves.

I find a small, metal, pointy thing.

It's like a metal stick with a sharp end like a stake. The gunmetal gray has ridges in it, like a piece of bamboo. The entire object is about the shape and size of a marker. I tuck it in my pocket as the police come charging around the corner with guns drawn.

KHOURY SITS ACROSS from me at her desk. She is not amused.

I'm not under arrest, but she wanted me to come down to the station to tell my story.

I already told her the whole story earlier, when she first showed up at the apartment. I told her how Mrs. Castillo thinks Joey Martin killed her daughter and that he is in town, not in Iraq. For a short time, she believed me enough to order an officer to pry up the floorboard in the closet. When the officer lifted the board, we all leaned down to see.

There was nothing there.

Now, back in her office, I can tell that Khoury won't believe anything else I have to say.

"It was him, I swear. It was Joey Martin."

"He's in Iraq," she says in a monotone.

I have one chance left to convince her. Digging in my bag, I hand her the piece of metal.

"He dropped this when he was running away from the apartment. I know I've probably corrupted the chain of evidence, but if it has his prints on it, will you believe me?"

She doesn't answer, just puts on gloves and drops the metal stick in a plastic bag, which she seals.

"The fact that it was outside their apartment is not incriminating in itself. He did live there, right? It wouldn't be unusual to find one of his possessions either in the apartment or outside it, right?"

My excitement fades. She's right.

"But he attacked me."

The look she gives me tells me she is not convinced.

"You're lucky I believe you were attacked, because I hate to break this to you, but you're not looking so squeaky clean yourself right now."

My eyes widen as I take in what she means. "What are you trying to say?"

She clears her throat. "You found the bodies. You were in the apartment again tonight. You found some so-called weapon. Your prints are all over the crime scene and now on a potential weapon."

Weapon?

"The only reason I'm entertaining any notion that you're telling the truth is because you're Sean Donovan's girl and he did something for me once. I owe him—and you get to benefit from that."

She pushes a stack of four-by-six photos toward me. "Prove you saw Joey Martin there."

All of the photos are of men in army uniforms. I find him immediately. The blood rushes to my face, and my fingers shake as I pick up a photo of a man with full lips and bushy eyebrows.

"This is the guy who attacked me."

She nods. She believes me.

"Has anyone shown you a picture of him before?"

My heart sinks. The wedding picture Mrs. Castillo loaned me is still in my bag.

"Yes."

She presses her lips tightly together. "I don't know who you saw, but Joey Martin is in Iraq. He's coming home a week from Friday on leave so he can get his child out of CPS care," she says. "She'll be with family again instead of strangers. You should be happy to hear that."

I shake my head. "He's here. It's been three days since the murders. He could have flown home by now. And if you ask his mother-in-law, she'll tell you he was here at the time of the murders."

Her eyes narrow. "So you're not only saying the U.S. military is lying to the San Francisco Police Department but that Joey Martin killed his entire family?"

"Maybe."

We have a stare down. She squints, as if she can see into my soul, before leaning back in her chair and exhaling.

"I'll play devil's advocate here for a second, and let's suppose that you are right. Even if you are, there is nothing we can do about it. He's heavily alibied. He was overseas. Iraq. The U.S. Army is vouching that he has been in Iraq since March."

"The military is lying." My voice is shaking.

She studies me for a few minutes. I wonder if she's remembering how I refused to turn over Lucy the first time we met. Does she think I'm too stubborn to listen to reason? Leaning forward, she shuffles some papers on her desk without looking away from me.

"The military is not going to lie about this, Ella." I cringe at her using my nickname, reserved for family only. The look Khoury gives me is a combination of pity and condescension. It makes me wonder what she knows about me. What she's heard. I stare at her until she speaks again. "I'm sorry. I know you personally want this case solved, but you can't want it any more than I do."

"What if he was actually here during the murders, despite what the military says? Would he be a suspect then?" I don't blink, and her gaze doesn't falter.

"Mrs. Castillo may hate her son-in-law, but that doesn't make him a murderer." She waves her hand, dismissing my words.

"What if she's right?"

"You mean what if some elderly woman is right and the U.S. military is wrong? Well, that would be interesting, wouldn't it?"

I give her a stony stare and stand to leave.

"Are you guys even going to search his parents' apartment?"

"My men already did."

But I see a flicker of doubt cross her brow. She's not sure they did, is she?

In my car, my cell rings. I don't recognize the number.

"Giovanni," I say.

"Give me motive," Khoury says. "Why would Martin kill not only his wife but his parents, his sister, and his nephew as well? Give me one reason, and I'll shift gears."

"I'll get back to you," I say quietly and hang up.

Driving home, I pound the steering wheel in frustration.

I know what I saw. Joey Martin is here. He was in his apartment. What was he doing? What was he looking for? The letters under the floorboard? Did he get to them first?

The military is lying for him. To protect him? His own mother-in-law called him a devil. She said she would give her life to prevent Lucy from ending up in his hands. I believe her when she said the baby is in danger. And there is no doubt that Mrs. Castillo is afraid, terrified.

I worry I've ruined my credibility with Khoury. Now I've got to find proof of my own.

Because a week from Friday—in twelve days—they are turning Lucy over to a man who might have massacred five people, including his own parents. Meanwhile, that little girl has been with strangers in a foster home for the past three days and will end up spending two full weeks there. The realization hits me that staying in foster care might now be the safest place for her.

Chapter 15

LOPEZ MEETS ME at Peet's Coffee on Lakeshore Monday morning near Donovan's apartment. I called Donovan to see if he wanted me to bring him a coffee, but he was already at work and too busy to talk, asking if he could call me back.

I'm a little relieved. I don't want to hear his reaction when I tell him I was attacked last night at the Martin apartment and had to go to the cop shop to give a witness statement that was barely believed.

Lopez and I park ourselves on the bench in front of the coffee shop. I hand him the double espresso I sprung for to get him out of bed so early. Lopez usually sleeps in late after staying up most of the night listening to the police scanner.

He takes a long gulp of hot coffee that would burn anyone else's throat and drums his fingers on the back of the metal bench.

"What's up, man? Let's see it?" The foot in his steel-toed combat boot taps the ground.

I sigh with frustration. "I turned it over to the cops." I describe what it looked like. "Seen anything like that before?"

Lopez lights up. “Kubaton.”

“God bless you,” I say.

“It’s a weapon. A martial-arts weapon. You can jab it in the neck or rib cage, but you also can take a little fold of skin between the metal and your thumb at the armpit or throat or inner thigh, and it feels like a little electric shock. Bring a big dude to his knees.”

“Nice.” I have new respect for that tiny scrap of metal I found. “Where can you get one of these?”

“A dojo.” A martial-arts studio.

“Know any dojos around here that might carry one like this?”

“Sure, man.”

He reels off the names of several dojos in Oakland and San Francisco.

“Think it’s worth checking every one?” I ask.

He grabs his phone. “Stand by.”

Within about ten minutes, he’s narrowed it down to four in Oakland and two in San Francisco that might sell kubatons.

We split up. He has to shoot the San Francisco Giant’s game this afternoon, so he offers to take the San Francisco dojos. My job is Oakland.

Before he leaves, he hands me a key. A bump key he made for me by carefully sanding down the grooves. Now I really am a burglar.

The first dojo is on fancy, yuppie Piedmont Avenue, across the street from the famous Fentons Creamery. The woman who runs this dojo knows exactly what I’m looking for, but she says she hasn’t seen one for years, not since she was in Japan.

The next stop is on the border of Berkeley and Oakland. The

kid inside takes my card and says he'll have his father call me. The third dojo has a FOR LEASE sign in its window.

My fourth stop is at the dojo in Oakland's Chinatown. A small door has the dojo's name on it—Kocho Bujutsu Dojo—but the door is locked, and nobody answers when I punch the doorbell ringer a few times. The street is busy with people chattering as they go about shopping and taking lunch breaks.

On the sidewalk out front, an odd-looking chair on wheels sits next to a pile of trash. It smells like rotten produce from the shop next door. And stale beer. On the other side, braids of bread hang in the front window of a bakery called See Yee Yum.

The screen door clangs shut behind me as I enter. The ripe smell of the street is replaced by something sweet and fresh. A long, narrow walkway borders bakery cases that almost extend the length of the shop. At the far end sits a single bistro table and a refrigerator full of American sodas. Inside the bakery cases are all sorts of unidentifiable pastries. Even though I'm not hungry, the bakery smells amazing—a combination of fresh baked bread and barbecue.

A small woman in a crisp white shirt with rolled-up sleeves looks up at me without smiling.

"Can I help you?"

"What do you recommend?" I ask, while the woman busies herself rearranging pastries with a pair of tongs.

"Pork bun," she says matter-of-factly without looking up.

"I'll take two."

While she packages them up, I ask about Kocho Bujutsu Dojo. She tells me the dojo is on the second story, above her bakery.

"Do you know what time it opens?"

The woman looks over my shoulder, as if she is thinking. "Sometimes not till five, but most of time, they are open by two."

It's noon. I'll come back later.

"One dollar." She hands me a white bag with the top neatly folded shut.

I rummage around in my bag and extract a wrinkled dollar, which I try to smooth out before I hand it to her. "Best deal in town," I say.

Finally she cracks a smile. "You try first."

Outside, I cross the street and eye the bank of windows above the bakery. It could be my imagination, but for a split second, I think I see a shadow move in front of the window.

I stare for a few seconds longer before I head to my car.

Chapter 16

I'M FINISHING UP my profile story about Maria Martin when Liz, the news researcher, comes over to my desk. In my story, based on what Mrs. Castillo told me, I've painted a portrait of a sweet woman who studied nursing in the hopes of living a life devoted to helping others. Now she's dead.

Liz watches as I swallow my last bite of pork bun. A small paper bag holds another pork bun. I was crazy to think I could eat two of them. Last year, I would've been able to scarf six of these puppies down in the blink of an eye. Now, I'm forcing myself to eat.

Liz smiles. Her soft brown eyes twinkle behind her purple eyeglass frames. She wears her signature long flowing skirt and Birkenstocks, like a real Berkeley hippie should.

"You kill me," she says. "The way you love food is practically pornographic."

Guilt streaks through me. She doesn't know my appetite flew the coop after my miscarriage. I hold up the paper bag. "You're in luck. I was saving this pork bun for the best news researcher west of the Mississippi."

Her smile fades. "I haven't found anything recently on Frank Anderson. I know you told me not to look anymore, but I can't help it. I can't give up. I have to check at least once a week."

"Thanks, Liz." I grow quiet for a moment. The pity and warmth in her big brown eyes make me slightly weepy. I change the subject. "You're going to love this!" I wave the bag.

"Sugar, you know me. I never pass up pork buns." She takes the bag from me with a smile.

"That's because you're my type of woman."

I start to open my e-mail in-box. She remains standing there, so I look up. "I'm sorry," I say. "I thought you were just coming by to say hello."

"This probably doesn't mean anything . . ."

I wait.

"I heard something on the scanner this morning when I was walking by. I couldn't tell what department it was, but it was talking about a DOA, and I'm pretty sure they said something like it might be connected to the Mission deal."

"Thanks. I'll try to track it down."

She walks away. Another body connected to the massacre four days later? And it might be connected? Maybe the killer committed suicide? Or did the killer knock off someone else? And is it Joey Martin? Is he the killer?

Before she turns to leave, I dial the cell phone number for Brian, my source at the morgue.

"May the force be with you."

"You working the morgue?"

"You will find that it is you who are mistaken . . . about a great many things."

"What? Is that another *Star Wars* quote? I told you I don't remember that movie. So you're *not* at the morgue?"

"Search your feelings."

"Heard something about a DOA that might be connected to Mission Massacre? Is it in your county?"

"These aren't the droids you're looking for."

"I'm going to assume that means no. Can you find where it is? Will you try to help me?"

"Try not. Do . . . or do not. There is no try."

I say thanks and hang up.

A few seconds later, my cell phone rings. I rummage around in my bag. It's Donovan.

"Hey." His voice is low and warm and comforting.

"Hey yourself," I say in a whisper. "I never got a chance to thank you for the medal."

He waits a moment before answering. "Sorry. This murder has been brutal."

I don't answer.

"Do you like it?" he asks.

"It's beautiful."

"I think we got a lead on the killer. I know we're close." he says. "My sister, Mary Jo, said she wore a medal like that after her . . . you know. And that it comforted her and she wore it the whole time she was pregnant with Ben."

I press my lips together. "Thanks."

"Listen, I've got to run. I'll try to be home early tonight."

"Wait," I say, before he hangs up. "Have you heard anything about a DOA that might be connected to . . . the Mission slayings?"

"Sorry, I've been feet on the street tracking leads. I can ask around."

I disconnect, but hug the phone to my chest for a few seconds before placing it in its cradle.

Glancing at the photograph of my sister on my desk, I feel guilty that I've been thinking more about that black-eyed baby than her.

I was only six when Caterina, older than me by fourteen months, was kidnapped out of our front yard. Her body was found eight days later, in a rural area, by off-road bicyclists. My father never got a chance to learn this—he dropped dead of a heart attack three days after she disappeared. The doctor blamed it on the stress of my sister's kidnapping.

My world dimmed the day my sister was kidnapped. I've fought my entire life to press back the dark shadows that have hovered around me ever since. It has only been in the past few years that I've faced my sister's death head-on and tried to move past it. Donovan has helped. In so many ways. Not only by being a solid presence in my life, supporting me at every turn, but also by investigating her murder.

Last year we got a lead on Caterina's killer that pointed us to a man named Frank Anderson. This man bragged to another inmate in prison that he had killed my sister. By the time we found out, he'd been paroled. We found him by searching the property records of his girlfriend. Both him and his girlfriend were on the lam, but when we arrived at the house, traces of him squatting there were obvious. It is so frustrating to think I was within a hairsbreadth of finding him—I walked into an empty house seconds after he escaped out a window. He's been underground ever since.

Now that he's loose on the streets, he's in my sights. I'm not done with him yet. Even though I told Donovan I'd let go of actively investigating him, I can't stop thinking about it. I'm relieved that Liz hasn't stopped, either.

Losing the baby sent me plunging back into the despair that has haunted me every so often in this life. I'm often able to set it aside, but there have been a few times I've been immersed in the darkness and barely escaped with my life.

The last few nights were the first in months that I didn't fall asleep thinking about Caterina.

Now all I can think about is Lucy in the arms of a killer.

Chapter 17

EVERY TIME MY cell phone rings, I jump, hoping it's Brian with info on that DOA, but the first time, it's my mom, and the second time, it's my therapist's office reminding me of my appointment. I let both calls go to voice mail.

The afternoon is spent working on a story about a school principal arrested for stalking. Cops are playing coy about telling me who he was stalking. I work with the education reporter, Brent, on the story.

Finally, we reach a parent who tells us off the record that the principal was stalking another school employee—the school librarian. It's not a student, which was what we feared, but still not good for the fool. He can kiss his career in education good-bye even if he gets off.

I hand over my portion of the story to Brent and decide to visit the Oakland dojo on my way home.

Right before I pack up, my desk phone rings.

It's Brian from the morgue. He's dropped the *Star Wars* shtick, thank the angels and saints. "Alameda."

"That's where the DOA is?" I pause, shrugging my bag onto my shoulder.

"Yup. Sliced and diced. Maybe samurai sword."

"Mother Mary."

"She had nothing to do with it."

"Male? Female?"

"Male. Twenty something. Lived alone. No sign of forced entry."

"Got an address?"

"That is negative."

"Thanks, Brian. I owe you."

"So, what do you think? You think a princess and a guy like me . . ."

And just when I thought he was over the *Star Wars* stuff. He's about to hang up, when the big-screen TV across the newsroom shows some footage of the Iraq War.

"One more thing. Can you give me a heads-up if you guys get any soldiers on ice? I'm looking specifically for active duty. Maybe home on leave from Iraq."

"I suggest you let the wookie win."

"Thanks."

I hope Brian's *Star Wars* obsession doesn't last as long as his Abba music phase did. For about six months, every time I called I had to listen to practically an entire Abba song before he would let me talk.

I rack my brains. Do I have any sources with the Alameda Police Department? Nope. Moretti works Oakland, which is just on the other side of the tunnel from the island. I make arrangements to meet him after I visit the dojo.

When I get there, the dojo's door is still locked tight, and nobody answers the doorbell. The woman in the bakery shrugs when I mention this.

When Moretti pulls up in the parking lot of Children's Fairyland, which lies on the side of Lake Merritt opposite the bakery, I hand him a hot cup of coffee and the bag full of pork buns as I slip into the passenger door of his unmarked Crown Vic. Nearby, kids are squealing with delight as they play on the rides at Fairyland.

"What's happening, kiddo," he says, taking a sip of his coffee and digging into the bag. "Pork buns! From See Yee Yum?"

"Seems everyone in the world knew about this place except me."

"That's affirmative." He mumbles around his first bite. He doesn't come up for air until the entire pork bun is gone. He flips down his mirror and checks for crumbs in his moustache before he rummages in the bag for his second one. "Love these things. Kate only lets me have about one a year. She says they're pure heart attack MSG food, but I don't care. If I'm going to go, I want to go out eating pork buns and manicotti!"

Moretti is small, slim, and fit, but he's already had one heart attack.

"Uh-oh. Give me that bag," I joke, reaching for it. "I don't want Kate mad at me."

"Won't happen, kiddo. She loves you like a daughter." He nods vehemently. His slicked-back black hair doesn't move when he nods.

I can't help it, but my cheeks grow warm. I'm so lucky to be friends with the Morettis. They've invited me to every big family event they've had in the past five years I've known them —baptisms, kids' birthday parties, first communions.

"So what's up, kiddo? This anything to do with that Mission deal? Saw you on TV."

Who didn't? Thanks, KXYZ.

As he scarfs down four pork buns, I fill him in on the last few days and include the part about the Alameda body. Steely Dan is playing on his radio, interspersed with police scanner traffic.

Every time I lean over to lower the volume on the music, he immediately turns it back up with the controls on the steering wheel.

"Wait a sec," he says when I finally finish getting him up to speed. He extracts his cell phone from his blazer pocket, turns down the volume on Steely Dan, and dials.

"Moretti here." The voice on the other end of the line comes across as a deep rumble. I can't make out the words.

"Yeah, yeah. We're all busy. That's why I called. Think it's connected to the Mission Massacre? Where was it? Okay. Yeah. Thanks." He clicks his phone shut.

"They think it's the same perp, don't they?" I say.

"Yep. Cut up the kid same way that family in the Mission was killed. This guy knew his victim. He opened the door for him."

"Address?"

He rattles it off.

I leap out of his car before he's done. "Thanks, Moretti. I owe you."

He waves his hand at me and cranks up Steely Dan.

"Pork buns," he says. "I now accept all repayment of favors in pork buns."

Chapter 18

CHINATOWN IN OAKLAND is the only way you can get to and from Alameda Island from the northwest. I take the Webster Tube, a tunnel that goes underneath the Alameda-Oakland Estuary to the island. It was the tunnel used in a scene of *The Matrix*. Driving through the lighted tunnel under God knows how many bazillion pounds of water above doesn't bug me—in fact, I find it exhilarating—but it gives my best friend Nicole hives. She refuses to take BART from the East Bay into the city because it goes 135 feet under the Bay for more than three miles.

Once I emerge, I drive through the quaint downtown area to get to the address Moretti gave me. People are window-shopping at the antique stores and boutiques, and a few classic pastel-colored cars are parked early for a car show advertised for the next day. Passing a parked squad car, I ease up on the gas pedal. With twenty-five-mile-per-hour speed limits, the entire island is a speed trap.

I had to do a report on Alameda when I was in grade school. It's fine, as long as you don't have to visit any place on the island in a hurry. Out of its twenty-three square miles, ten are underwater. Even as a fifth-grader, I found this annoying. Why do you count the ten miles underwater, anyway? What's the point? And besides, the island is really two islands, with a lot of one of them taken up by the former Naval Air Station, which was important during the Cold War.

The apartment building I'm looking for isn't far from the former naval base. In fact, it looks like the back side might even have ocean views. Not too shabby for a twenty-something kid. Dead kid, but still. How can a kid afford a place in the Bay Area with water views?

I pass the building three or four times before I find a parking spot. I remember why I actually dislike the little island of Alameda so much—not only the ridiculous speed limit but also because the island is so crowded it's impossible to park. I have to deal with hellish parking in my own neighborhood in North Beach. I should be used to it, but it makes me hate parking problems during my workday even more.

I end up parking six blocks away from the address Moretti gave me. Keeping to the opposite side of the street, I approach the building, eyeballing it to see if it will give me any clues about the murder. A sprawling, two-story brick building, it doesn't look like much. A wooden sign out front says THE WILLOWS. The building is set up a bit like a motel in a big U shape, with a walkway in front of all the second-floor apartments. Bonus—the apartment numbers are visible from the street.

Moretti said the apartment was number 230. Standing by a big palm bush across the street, I sort of shrink back into the leaves and dig my mini binoculars out from my bag. No way to scope it out without being obvious. I count. It's five doors in from the right and four from the left. I walk about half a block more before crossing the street. A few feet away is an opening to what appears to be an alley. I hurry down the passageway. Bingo. Ocean view.

There is a road between the complex and the beach. Wooden walkways lead to the water. Within a minute, I'm behind the apartment building. By counting balconies on the back side, I find apartment 230. A woman holding an aluminum watering can comes out of the sliding-glass door of the neighboring apartment. She holds it over a window box attached to the balcony railing. It's filled with begonias. Her blond hair is neatly tied back above a string of pearls peeking out from her white blouse, which she's paired with crisp black slacks.

"Excuse me?" I say. She looks down at me, startled, and spills a little of the water down the side of the balcony. I jump out of the way. "I'm sorry to scare you. I'm with the *Bay Herald*. Do you have a moment? I'd like to ask you about your neighbor in number two thirty."

"What do you want to know?"

"Can I come up?"

"Apartment two twenty-nine."

When I get back to the front of the apartment building, the door to 229 is ajar. When I pass 230, the curtains are closed in the big front window. No gap to peek through.

"Hello?" I nudge the door open slightly.

"Come on in. Shut the door behind you."

Inside is a spare, modern apartment with a big white sofa, abstract art, and a black laminated armoire. Across from the living room stretches a long bar and the kitchen. The woman points to a bottle of alcohol. "I've had a long day. I'm having scotch. Care for one?"

"Sure." At the counter, she hands me a drink.

"I'm Sue."

"Gabriella Giovanni."

"You're here about Javier?" She opens the sliding-glass door to the balcony and gestures for me to go out first.

I take a seat in a comfy chair with a red cushion, and she does the same, putting her drink on the table between us. I set my pen and reporter's notebook innocently between us on the table.

In front of us, beyond her flower boxes, the frolicking water in the Bay reflects the sunlight, like shards of glass, as the sun dips behind the San Francisco skyline.

"Your view sucks," I say, gesturing at the water with my tumbler.

She darts a glance at me and smiles. "Yeah. Buying this place made my divorce all the sweeter. Eat your heart out in Stockton, you husband-stealing bitch."

"Sorry."

She downs her drink in one gulp.

"Don't be. I've never been better . . . well, except for what happened with Javier."

I sit up straight. "So you do know him." I'm perfectly aware that I'm using the present tense. God knows I never want to be the first person to use past tense about someone.

"Know him? Not really. I mean, we never talked much. We were too busy doing other things."

My eyes widen, and I try to close my mouth, which has dropped open. She's got to be in her late forties, maybe even early fifties.

"Don't judge me. I'm not a perv, just get lonely sometimes."

A small tint of pink has flushed her cheeks, and I notice that her eyes have some crow's-feet. She watches my reaction.

I hold my tumbler up. "More power to you. Twenty is a consenting adult."

She squints her eyes shut tightly. "Goddamn it. Why did someone have to kill him? That kid didn't deserve that. The cop I talked to said it was . . . bad."

Nobody deserves to be murdered. Well, very few people, at least. "Did you tell the cops about . . . you know . . . your relationship with Javier?"

I try to pick up my notebook without making it too obvious.

She scoffs. "Relationship? From the beginning, it's been about the sex. We met at the pool one night. I'd been drinking. Divorce papers came in the mail that day. He got out of the pool with water dripping off him. God, what a specimen. I smiled at him—the next thing we were in my bed. Now, whenever I have a hard day, I just knock on the wall between our places and he comes over. No strings attached. The perfect arrangement." She holds her empty tumbler up to her lips, trying to get the last drop, and shrugs, putting it back on the table. "Boy, did I need that. Bad day at the J-O-B."

She stares into the setting sun for a moment and then turns to me. "He could make me forget any bad day I had."

"Did you ever go to his place?"

Her eyebrows draw together. "No, never invited me over. And the one time I rang his doorbell, he stood in the doorway, sort of blocking my view." She gasps. "Do you think he was hiding something? Or someone?" Her eyes widen.

"I don't know." To my left is his balcony. "Did he ever come out on his balcony?"

"No. Isn't that funny. I mean, here I am trying to spend every waking moment out here, looking at the view. God knows I pay enough for it."

"Javier is pretty young to afford a place like this. Do you know what he did?"

Her look grows sly. "He was a DJ at some sex club. You know one of those places where you have sex in different rooms and stuff? He wanted to take me there one day. He said it was totally hot. God, these young guys know about everything."

"Do you remember the name?" I scribble "sex club" in my notebook and circle it.

"Don't think he ever mentioned the name," Sue said, eyes looking off into the distance. "It's in Oakland, though, I think. A bad part, too."

"Anywhere else he liked to hang out?" I ask.

"The only other place I think he went was his dojo over in Chinatown."

My scalp prickles. "Dojo? Do you know the name of it?"

"He never said. But it's only a block or two from the tube."

I mull that over. It has to be the connection. I try to hide my excitement. I have a few more things to do here before I head for the dojo again.

"How did you hear about Javier?"

"The cops said it happened on Saturday. I was in Napa over the weekend and then this morning went straight to work. When I came home, found a card on my door from a detective. I called and he told me a little about what happened. I guess the downstairs neighbor heard a racket Saturday night but didn't call until this morning. When the cops got here, all they found was Javier." A tear slips out.

Eyeing the balcony rail, I turn toward Sue. "I got an idea."

I swing a leg and, with little grace, scramble onto Javier's balcony, landing in a heap on my hands and knees. Sue giggles, waiting on her own balcony.

Putting my hand on the handle of the sliding-glass door, I make the sign of the cross. Sue raises her eyebrows. I tug. The door slides open. Pushing away the heavy drapes, I peer into the dark apartment. It smells like pizza.

Sue is silent on her balcony behind me. Any and all giggling is over. Her face is pale, and she tightly crosses her arms across her chest.

"Wait here." My tone leaves no room for argument. Not that she would probably hop the balcony like I did, anyway. The heavy swoosh of the drapes closing behind me is the only sound as I step fully into the apartment. My eyes adjust.

I lean over to a table and switch on a light. The living room is as bare—besides the bloodstain—as a hotel room. No decorations. No books or magazines. A couch and love seat. No TV.

The front door is across the way. A black trail of dried blood leads from the front door into the living room. The killer must have started attacking right when he opened the door. Javier probably backed up to try to get away and ended up in the living room, where the biggest pool of dried blood is.

That's one thing they never tell you. Cops don't clean up the blood. They investigate the death and then—good-bye—they leave the bloody gore for someone else to deal with. They do give family members resources to call—people like my friend who owns Crime Scene Cleanup and charges a pretty penny to scrape brains and guts off walls and ceilings.

The bathroom and kitchen refuse to yield any clues. The refrigerator has some fresh fruit and vegetables and leftover pizza slices in a cardboard box. The cupboards have some rice and canned beans.

In the hallway leading to the bedroom hangs a black-and-white photograph of a twenty-something man with his shirt off, leaning against a wall in a dark room. His skin is smooth and perfect. He looks like a model for men's underwear.

In the bedroom, I see the same young man hugging two women in another photograph. Both are scantily clad, and he has his hands on both of their bottoms. Another picture shows him with yet another bombshell woman in a bikini.

"Looks like you were quite the player, Javier," I murmur.

All the dresser drawers are open. Obviously the cops searched the room. Javier was apparently a minimalist. His closet has half a dozen dress shirts, identical except for the colors—purple, navy, burgundy, black, gray, red—and identical black pants. I peer at a label. Armani. Not bad for a kid.

On the other side of the closet are martial-arts looking duds.

I check the pockets of all the shirts and pants. Nothing.

On the top of the dresser in the bedroom, a polished metal tray holds a Rolex watch, a wad of cash in a silver clip, and a slim enamel cigarette case. I tuck my fingers into the long sleeve of my shirt so I don't leave fingerprints, then pop open the cigarette case. It has a few sepia-colored cigarettes and a matchbook slid into the other side. I slip the matchbook out.

The cover features a picture of two men and a woman engaged in a ménage à trois. I squint at the man in the back, whose face is slightly obscured. Is it Javier? Could be. Inside the matchbook is the name of the joint—Fellatio. No subtlety there. The address is in Oakland. It must be that sex club. Was he more than just a DJ? Maybe a high-class prostitute? This apartment and designer duds make more sense.

I slip out the front door, duck under the crime-scene tape, and, without saying good-bye to Sue, head for the dojo.

Chapter 19

THE SUN IS setting as I pull into Chinatown in Oakland. By the time I park, the windows of the dojo are lit up. Kocho Bujutsu Dojo is open for business. I'm tempted to buy another pork bun, but I head for the door to the dojo.

Although my finger presses down on the white button, I can't tell if it's ringing inside or not. I wait to the beat of ten and try again. Nothing. After I press it for the third time, I run across the street to see if I can catch anyone peeking out the windows to see who is calling below. But I don't see anything.

That's okay. I'm patient.

After fifteen minutes of waiting by the door of the dojo, I'm growing sleepy and hungrier when the door swings open so quickly I jump back.

A man in dark sunglasses, dressed all in black, flies by me on the stairs. A sliver of light shines down from a crack in the door. Trying not to step on every squeaky stair, I make my way up and knock on the door, which is partly ajar.

"Hello? Anyone home?"

I can hear heavy breathing. I nudge the door open a bit more. I take in a flash of someone in white flying across bare wood floors at the same moment a cold, hard piece of steel is lodged under my throat.

"Don't move."

The words are whispered in my ear, accompanied by warm breath. The man in white comes to a halt and smiles.

"You were so focused on me, you didn't see him behind you."

The blade is removed. I clutch at my throat, expecting it to be wet with dripping blood.

Turning, I see a man all in black, with only his eyes showing.

He's dressed like the man who flew out the door downstairs, except this man's face is covered. He bows to me and walks over to a table, where he lays the blade on a black velvet cloth among several other swords. My eyes widen as I spot other weapons— flat metal stars and kubatons laid out on the other side of the cloth in different types of metal and sizes. I try not to make it obvious I'm interested in them.

The space is wide open, with bright lights high in the tall ceiling, illuminating polished floors. Besides a half dozen chairs against one wall and the small table with weapons, the room contains no other furniture.

"Your first time." It is not a question. The man in white takes a towel and wipes his brow before chugging on a bottle of water, keeping his eyes on me.

"What's up with the swords?" I say, trying to shake off my unease and sound confident.

"Along with military-style Budo, we also teach the art of samurai bujutsu—the ancient art of swordplay."

"Gee, what a coincidence," I say, walking over to the window and looking down at the Chinatown streets teeming with shoppers and people on their way home from work. "A few people have died from a sword in the past few days."

As I say this, I turn to see the man's reaction. His smile has faded.

"Yes. So I've been told."

"Any of your students gone missing?"

"The police came to us to tell us about Javier. It is a shame. He was a promising student."

A promising student? Is that all he was?

"Did you know him well?"

The sensei shakes his head. "No, sadly. He kept to himself."

He said the detectives came to the dojo a few days ago—Saturday—when they found Javier's body. I wonder if they connected his death to the Mission Massacre. I wander over to the table with the swords and stars and kubatons. "What are these?" I point at the star.

"We are the only dojo in the state that fashions these ancient fighting stars." The man in white fingers them lovingly and holds one out for me to take. "Careful. The blade is extraordinarily sharp. They are called shurikens. We are also the only dojo in the United States that teaches students how to use them. They are a ninja art."

I finger the blade lightly. "Do many of your students train in the use of these?"

"No," he frowns slightly. "It is a lost art. We only have maybe twelve students who use these."

"What about this?" My hand hovers over a pink kubaton.

"A kubaton."

"May I?"

The sensei nods his approval. I reach to pick it up.

"You like that one? Would you like a demonstration? We sell more of that style than any other. Women attach it to their key ring. It is an extremely effective form of self-defense if used properly." He nods, and the man in black appears before us.

Without explanation or conversation, the sensei and the man in black demonstrate how a well-placed thrust of the kubaton can easily take down an assailant. At one point, the sensei uses it to split a chunk of concrete.

"Impressive," I say. "What about this one?" I finally point to the one with the dagger-like tip that matches the one I handed over to Khoury. "This one would cause more injury, right?"

His expression does not change. "Yes." He says it in a low voice.

My heart speeds up. How far should I push this?

"Have you sold any exactly like this one?"

It is almost unnoticeable. His back stiffens and his eyes slightly narrow, but his voice remains flat. "Yes." His words are careful and measured.

"How much for this one?"

"Twenty dollars."

I hand over a twenty and tuck it into my bag.

"Do you keep a log of your sales?" I hold out another twenty.

The doorbell interrupts us, and he leans over, pressing a small button. Within seconds, the sound of male voices and laughter drifts up the stairs. He remains silent.

Feet pound up the stairs, and a group of men enters the room, greeting the sensei.

"Here is my card." I lay it directly on top of the twenty-dollar bill and leave.

Downstairs, the air is chilly as I emerge onto the sidewalk. I cross the street and look up at the window. A dark figure stands there, watching.

I duck into the bakery and pick up a few pork buns. When I come out, there is a piece of paper under my windshield wiper. When I unfold it, I see a list of names under the words "Bought kubaton." Sure enough, one name stands out: Joey Martin. I dart a glance up at the windows of the dojo but only see shadows flitting back and forth.

Chapter 20

THE ADDRESS FOR Fellatio, the sex club on the matchbook cover, is in an Oakland warehouse building near a back entrance to the Bay Bridge. This is the part of town that has given Oakland a bad rap over the years.

I pull in front of the address and look around, wishing I had asked Lopez to come with me.

Trash lines the gutters, and people cluster in groups in empty parking lots or gather around bus stop benches under billboards, staring down anyone who drives by. A group of young men across the street stops talking and watches me park. A few lean back on a small stone wall and smoke, talking and gesturing to my car. A fight breaks out nearby, and they turn their attention to that. One man punches another man, knocking him down and then kicking and spitting on him.

For a second, I debate calling 911, but the man on the ground gets up, holding his palms out, and backs away. The other man gets in his face, until finally someone whistles and the attacker turns away.

I dig the kubaton out of my bag and clutch it in my palm before getting out of my car. Pulling my shoulders back, I head toward the steel door with Fellatio's address on it, keeping the group of young men in my peripheral vision. I push all the doorbell buttons and wait, glancing back over my shoulder. The group has grown larger, milling around. Like the little piece of metal in my hand will help me. I don't even know how to use the thing. My heart is racing. It's stupid to be here alone. This is not a part of town anyone should come to alone.

I pound all the doorbells again but don't hear the click of the door opening. Probably too early in the day for the wild sex I saw on the matchbook. I head back to my car, eyeing the group across the street and slamming the lock as soon as my legs swing inside my car. Across the street, a parked motorcyclist I didn't notice before revs his engine. The rider is dressed all in black, with the black visor on his helmet pulled down over his face. I can't tell for sure, but it seems like he's looking my way.

Clutching the steering wheel, I scold myself. Young men gathering in a bad part of town doesn't equal criminals, does it? I've interviewed crazy killers in jail, ridden along with girl gangbangers for three weeks for a story, sat in on autopsies, and I'm intimidated by a group of punk kids on a street corner? I'm a shame to the cop reporter profession.

I unlock my door and unfold my legs from the car. As I do, the man on the motorcycle roars off. Standing, I pull my shoulders back and assume my most badass demeanor. Stalking over to the group in my girlie high heels doesn't help much, especially when I stumble a little on a pothole, but when I walk up to the group, I look them all dead in the eye, one by one.

"My name's Gabriella Giovanni. I'm a reporter with the *Bay*

Herald, and I need to ask you about that building." I throw my arm behind me without turning. "What can you guys tell me about it?"

Leaning back on the wall, a bigger kid with a skullcap pulled low to his brow glares at me and spits. "What makes you think we know anything?"

"You know every single fucking thing that goes down on this block," I say without blinking. "Don't tell me any different."

A teenager in the back chuckles.

The bigger kid straightens up. "What you gonna give us if I tell you?"

I square my shoulders. "I'm a real reporter. Not some TV bimbo or crooked fuck at the *National Enquirer* who pays for her stories." I fold my arms across my chest and wait.

"I could talk to her." A smaller kid with a baseball cap on sideways says this and gives me a shy smile.

"Shut the fuck up," the bigger kid says. "I'll tell her. Listen, lady, there is some funky shit that goes on there. I'm talking sex stuff. You come here at eleven at night, this whole street is full of cabs. Everyone who gets out looks like they're starring in a fucking porno or something with big old leather straps up their ass and stuff." His friends all chuckle. "Some come straight from out of town in those airport vans. They got little suitcases on wheels and shit. I don't know what happens inside. Ain't never been invited in."

His friends laugh.

"Do you know what time the place opens or closes?"

"Some people never leave. I think there are rooms there. Sometimes in the morning people come down and go over to the minimart there and buy milk and smokes and shit and go back in. It's some crazy-ass shit going down inside there, I know that much."

When he's done, I nod my head and start to leave, but I turn back to the teen in the skullcap.

"What's your name?"

"Tre."

I hand him one of my cards. "Thanks, Tre. You did me a solid. I won't forget that."

"Stay cool, Lois Lane." He tucks my business card into the edge of his hat.

Chapter 21

Sometimes I wonder what I ever did to deserve Donovan. I'm not an easygoing, even-tempered type of girlfriend. I come with a little more baggage than most.

I am passionate about . . . everything. What I like and don't like. There is little gray in my preferences. I either love or hate. It sometimes is exhausting. Sometimes my passion gets too intense even for me. I blame it on my Italian blood.

Tonight, when I get home, my studio apartment is lit with glowing candles, and U2's "Walk On" is coming out of the speakers. I throw the bag of pork buns on the counter, and we head straight for my bed.

But something is off. I can't figure out if it's him or me. Deep inside, I know it's me. I have a kernel of resentment that is slowly growing. All I can think about is how right now I can't get pregnant, so what's the point of even having sex. I know this is totally crazy thinking, and it fills me with guilt.

Lying in bed later, Donovan traces his finger around my breast and says, "You've lost a lot of weight, haven't you?"

I shrug. "I don't own a scale, remember?" I don't mention that most of my pants are sagging off my hips.

"That's what I love about you," he says, starting to kiss my hip bone. "A woman who isn't obsessed with her weight."

He scoots up and props himself on one elbow. "I think you are incredibly sexy whatever weight you are, but this"—he gestures at my naked body—"it worries me. I mean like I said, you gun my motor no matter what, but I like my women with a little meat on their bones."

"Gun your motor? How you like your women? Meat on the bones? When did Mr. Macho Cop show up?" I say, teasing.

His words are interrupted by Dusty's meowing from the bathroom. I've started locking him in there during sex because he freaks Donovan out with his staring. It is sort of unnerving.

"I'll go let the cat out," I say, getting up.

We eat a European, snack-type dinner, breaking off hunks of baguette and shoving slices of Gruyère between us, munching on green grapes as Donovan polishes off an old bottle of cabernet sauvignon. I manage to swallow a chunk of bread and several pieces of cheese and feel better. We have pork buns for dessert, and I eat every bite of mine.

I didn't like it when Donovan pointed out I was losing weight. I'm a girl who loves food. I love my curvy body, and I love to eat. It's something that until recently has always brought me pleasure. A small part of me worries over my lack of appetite lately, but I brush it off. I'll never be a toothpick girl on a date, moving around the lettuce on her plate. God forbid. Give me a big plate of pasta, some bread slathered in butter, and a glass of wine, and I'm a happy girl. Maybe not right now, but that is who I am at my core. That can't change. At least I hope it can't.

After we eat, we plop on the couch and watch an old Alfred Hitchcock movie, *Vertigo,* which we've seen at least three times together already.

I know Donovan usually prefers movies with happy endings, but he indulges my love for this movie. I sit up straight when James Stewart (Scottie) and Kim Novak (Madeleine) arrive at the mission in San Juan Bautista. Next time I go there, I'll see if I can get up in the bell tower. I kick myself for not trying when I visited Mrs. Castillo.

Right after the end credits roll, Donovan turns to me.

"How are you?"

"A little sleepy," I say and yawn.

"No," he sits up. "I mean, how *are* you?"

I swallow. I know what he means. I've been avoiding this conversation for some reason. I'm not sure why. It's only been a few days since I stumbled onto that scene of carnage, yet it is hard to remember my life before that. So much has happened, and because of Donovan's homicide investigation, we've spent much of the past few days apart. I fill him in on what has happened, including my visit to Mrs. Castillo and being attacked in the Mission apartment. I tell him my theory that Martin is the one who attacked me, that he's supposed to take custody of Lucy a week from Friday, and that I have to stop him. I hold my breath, waiting for his reaction.

His brow furrows. "You were attacked? Jesus Christ, why didn't you tell me earlier?"

I swallow my guilt. "I asked Khoury not to call you. She wanted to. I didn't want to worry you." It's true. I didn't realize it until now.

"You can't do that to me. You have to tell me what's going on."

"Okay." I don't argue. It's something I know I need to work on.

"You really think the military is lying?"

"I know what I saw. It was him."

I'm instantly defensive, expecting him to tell me my judgment is skewed because of my miscarriage, but he surprises me and leans into me, breathing into my hair.

"Promise me something?"

I pull back and look into his eyes.

"Promise you'll be extra careful investigating this. If the military is lying . . . there must be a reason for it. Something they are trying to hide. This is a dangerous game they're playing, and you might want to consider staying far away."

I don't answer. I can't promise, so I'm not going to lie.

Later, when we go to bed, I can't fall asleep.

In the dark, I can still feel Lucy in my arms, how she clung to me and wrapped her fingers in my hair. Holding her made me ache with longing for my own child.

Shortly after I found out I was pregnant, I began thinking about my baby girl—I'm convinced it was a girl—constantly. I couldn't help but imagine my child's entire lifetime played out in vivid Technicolor. In my mind, I saw her birth, I saw her birthdays, and I imagined her as a young woman graduating from college. This unborn baby had taken on an entire life before she drew her first breath. There were so many hopes and dreams wrapped up in her that I felt her presence in my life even though I had never actually met her.

The life inside me might have been too small to see with the naked eye, yet I'd already seen that child's lifespan from birth to death in my hopes and dreams for her. And when that vision was ripped out of my arms, my world dimmed. And those shadows cling to me.

It's also not the first time this has happened. When I lost my sister and father both in one fell swoop, it took a long time for the colors to return to my world.

It was so easy, stupidly easy, to get pregnant.

But keeping the baby wasn't.

I can't help but worry I'll never be able to have a baby. That I'm being punished for taking a life. Taking two lives.

For long, dreary days, the only light at the end of the tunnel was hitting that three-month mark—the time my doctor said we could try again. And my lifeline was clinging to what the doctor said that day in the office. " . . . *I've told hundreds of women the same thing, and within a year, I've delivered their baby.*"

Last month, my scientifically proven method of getting pregnant should've guaranteed a pregnancy. But it doesn't work like that, does it?

Or maybe it does for everyone but me. Maybe it does for women who are not killers.

Despite what Father Liam says, I will never be able to forgive myself for taking a life. And worse, I'll never be able to forgive myself for knowing that if I had the chance, I would do it again.

Chapter 22

I'M RUNNING LATE to work the next morning, so I punch the gas along the Embarcadero toward the Bay Bridge. I have a lot to do before I attend the massive memorial service later today for Maria and her in-laws. I cut up to a residential street, hoping to save time. I'm swerving around slower drivers when I see red and blue lights behind me. Damn.

My heart is racing as the officer walks up. I'm digging through my purse, but I can't find my wallet. I see the blue uniform out of the corner of my eye at the same time the officer knocks his flashlight on my window. Before I can turn to respond, there's a flurry of movement, and he's shouting.

"Get out of the car with your hands up!"

Turning, I freeze when I see his service revolver leveled at my face.

"Take your hands slowly out of your handbag."

My heart is up in my throat as I remove my hands and hold them up. I see passersby on the sidewalk nervously glancing over their shoulders at my car.

"Put them on the steering wheel. Eyes straight ahead."

I'm staring at the street in front of me, which all of a sudden is disconcertingly empty of people and cars. I hear, rather than see, the cop tug open the door. There is a blur of a young guy with a crew cut, sunglasses, and bulging muscles, and I'm yanked by the front of my shirt out of the car and slammed face-first along my trunk.

"I was looking for my license."

"Uh-huh," he says, patting me down.

I start to get angry.

"I didn't do anything wrong. I was reaching for my wallet. My purse is a black hole. I swear I wasn't doing anything bad."

He ignores me and holds my hands behind my back with one of his hands.

"You've got to be kidding me." My mouth grows dry as sawdust as his other hand pats me down again, but this time he starts at my chest, wrapping his big paw around my breasts and fondling them, pressing his body against me and breathing in my ear, "You say one fucking word, and . . ." He punctuates his point by shoving his knee into my tailbone. I wince, but stifle my cry.

"My boyfriend is a cop. You're going to regret this." I practically spit the words out.

He leans down and puts his mouth to my ear again. "I know who your fucking boyfriend is. He's not here to help you now, is he? Remember that. It's not always daylight. There won't always be people around to save you." A chill races through me as I realize I've never told him my name and never got a chance to get my license. How does he know who my boyfriend is? Who the fuck is this cop? What is he talking about?

"Let me go. Now." I grit the words out at the same time he

presses his groin against my backside and yanks me up from the trunk by my hair. "You will regret this." I spit the words out, channeling some Italian Mafia ancestor I'm sure I have somewhere in my background.

I'm filing a complaint as soon as I get to the station. He will not get away with this. This is fucking madness. He must hate Donovan. Maybe he's friends with that moron, Detective Jack Sullivan? That guy hates me so much, but even I wonder if he would stoop this low, getting other cops to harass me.

Feeling humiliated and afraid and utterly helpless, I try to blink back hot tears spurting into the corners of my eyes. I won't let this bastard see my cry.

A cell phone rings, and I hear him mumble something. Seconds later, he's thrown me to the sidewalk. As I scramble to my feet, I hear an engine start and see his car peel out. I squint to see his license-plate number, but his car is too far away. At the opposite end of the street, two squad cars come flying around the corner, with lights and sirens blaring. I slouch onto the curb and put my face into my hands.

A few seconds later, the sirens cease, and I see polished black shoes in front of me.

"Ma'am, are you okay? We got a call about an assault in progress. Someone in one of these apartment buildings called in. Described a victim in a red blouse."

Yep. That's me.

"It was one of your own," I say.

The officer scrunches his features in consternation when I explain what happened.

He tilts his head and speaks into the walkie-talkie clipped to his shoulder before turning to me. "We didn't have anyone over here on the east side. And none of ours called in a traffic stop. Are you sure it was a San Francisco police officer? Any chance it was BART police or something?"

"I don't know." And I don't. It was a black-and-white car, but I don't remember a number or shield on the side. I don't remember a badge number or name, either. I didn't get a chance to look at the cop or his car. I don't know if he actually is a cop. But I do know that I was just given a warning.

"Do you want us to escort you home?"

I decline. As the two officers wait for me to get into my vehicle, I peer up at the tall apartment building. I mouth a silent "thank you" before I drive away. A few curtains fall shut as I do.

Chapter 23

STEPPING INSIDE THE dark church, I'm struck by the Virgin de Guadalupe shrine to one side of the altar. It is so bright with silver and gold that I can't stop staring. How can this tiny church be so amazingly beautiful? The altar itself is lit from above. Sunlight streams down from a skylight and bathes the simple stone altar, which is covered in white cloths and dozens of white roses.

I take a seat in the back. I'm still shaken up from my encounter with the fake cop. I called Donovan on the way over here, but I left out the part about the fake cop's beefy hands touching me. When he heard what happened, Donovan swore and said in a dangerously low voice, "I'll handle this."

I'm worried about what he has in mind. He has a temper that sometimes gets him in a heap of trouble. I remind myself to concentrate on this memorial and paying my respects. I know I never met Maria Martin in person, but she turned to me for help. And I failed. I was too late. Whatever she needed to tell me is going to the grave with her.

The five coffins at the memorial are almost too much to take in. The altar is covered with more flowers than I've ever seen in a church in my life.

Mrs. Castillo won't return my messages, and I don't spot her in the church. For a second, a flicker of fear shoots through me. What if Joey Martin went after her? Is that why she's not answering her phone? She seemed so afraid the other day.

As I scan the heads in the church, I spot Nicole's blond bob toward the front. In her big Sunday story about the massacre, Nicole wrote about a brouhaha in the church over the memorial service.

Some people wanted to wait to hold the service until Joey Martin got home, but others said he didn't want them to wait. Apparently a military official told one of them that Joey Martin gave his go-ahead to have the service early, since he wouldn't be home for another ten days.

Nicole is trying to track down who this "military official" is. Right now, she's getting the runaround. Each time she's referred to a person who spoke to the military official, they say it was someone else. It sounds bogus. Everything about Joey Martin seems suspicious to me now.

I'm darting glances at the people around me, when my scalp tingles, as if someone is staring at me. I'm in the back row, so I don't know who it can be. I turn in time to see a man with full lips, bushy eyebrows, and a baseball cap pulled low slip out the back door.

Joey Martin. I leap from my feet and brush past people in my pew, leaving them mumbling irritably in my wake.

Pulling the heavy doors open, I squeeze through and look both ways.

The streets are empty. In the distance, the growl of a motorcycle grows fainter.

KHOURY SEEMS LESS than enthused that I've had another Martin sighting.

Even on the phone, I can hear her exasperation. I'm pacing on the church's stone steps, wishing I'd been quicker to spot him and react.

"Don't take this the wrong way." She pauses before continuing. "Have you seen anyone about what you saw? You know, talked to someone about it?"

She means a shrink. She goes on.

"Even the most hardened cops on the force go talk to the department's psychiatrist about these types of things." She waits in silence for a few seconds. "I had a case once. A really bad one. Dead kid. Didn't handle it well. It helped to talk to someone."

She is opening up to me, telling me things she doesn't have to so she can help me, but I can't go there, so I change the subject. "I found this dojo that sells kubatons." I wait for her to tell me to quit butting in. She doesn't, so I go on. "It's the same dojo that Javier went to. I talked to this sensei. He gave me a list that shows Joey Martin bought a kubaton there."

"Hmmm." She actually sounds interested. "Can you get me that list?"

"Of course."

"And do me a favor?"

"Yes?"

"Next time you stumble onto something like this list or this sensei, please give me a call and let me handle it. It's my job. This isn't a game."

Anger flares through me, but I choke it down. I need her on my side.

Before I hang up, I have another question for her. "Who told you Joey Martin was in Iraq and on his way home?"

She breathes heavily before she answers. "First off, I don't have to tell you any of this. I'm doing you a professional courtesy because your boyfriend stuck up for me once at a training deal. I like him and I owe him. Otherwise, I'd never be talking to you, got it?"

Feeling chastised, I mumble, "yes."

"One of my men talked to a local recruiter about Joey Martin. I don't have time to find the guy's name. And I don't mean to be a hard-ass. I get your personal involvement and sense of responsibility in this case. That crime scene was hard even for those of us who routinely investigate homicides, but you're going to have to let us do our job here. I need to devote every waking second to finding that killer, not digging through paperwork looking for phone numbers for you."

I'm about to hang up when I remember. "By the way, you might want to check on Mrs. Castillo. She's not returning my calls."

"She's fine."

"How do you know?"

"Spoke with her a few minutes ago. She's fine. Don't take this personally, but did you ever think that maybe some people just don't want to talk to reporters?"

I hang up without answering.

Chapter 24

"MAMA?" I'M WALKING down Columbus Avenue in North Beach when my mother answers my call. It's hard to hear her over the booming music filtering out of the street's restaurants and clubs, a mix of opera from the Italian restaurants and hip-hop from the strip clubs. I'm trying to hit a quick chess game on Market Street before it gets dark. I have so much anger ready to burst out of me that I need to do something besides sit in my apartment. I've fallen into a funk since Donovan left a message telling me he's working late—on the verge of an arrest for the weekend's homicide.

I planned on making gnocchi with Gorgonzola sauce for him and sharing a bottle of wine. Now I'm all alone. Again.

I try to focus on my mother's words through the phone.

"Thank God you finally called back. I saw you on the TV news. Are you okay?"

"I'm doing alright." I wait for a second before blurting out, "Mom it was awful." My mother is the first person I've said this to. I don't tell her about my appointment with my therapist. My mom doesn't approve of me in therapy. It is something to do with her old Italian roots, something she likes to call "*omerta*," which is basically the Italian tradition of the Mafia not talking to the cops, but which my mother likes to interpret as not sharing the family business outside the family.

"*Dios mio*! It sounds . . . horrific . . . like a horror movie."

A bus passes me and pulls to a stop about two blocks up. I debate jogging to hop on, skipping the longish walk to Market Street. After people file out of the bus, a man with dark sunglasses consults a piece of paper. He looks vaguely familiar. I can't place him. As I come up on him, he turns, and I smile absentmindedly as I pass.

"Honey?" My mom's voice in my ear is nearly drowned out from the sounds of cars honking and music blaring out of the strip club I'm passing. Two guys smoking out front make kissy faces at me. One gestures and grinds his hips and comes dangerously close to getting a kick in the crotch.

"Murders don't usually bother me, Mama. But there was so much blood . . . so many bodies right there in front of me, where I could reach out and touch them . . ." I say it looking directly at the guy who had his lips puckered at me. He draws back, his lips baring his teeth, his eyes wide, backpedaling to get away from me now. His friend mutters something that sounds like "*Loca chica*"—crazy girl.

"I don't know why you don't quit that job." My mom knows quitting is not an option. "That poor baby. She was clinging to you for life."

"I know. They pawned her off to CPS. Her whole family was killed in front of her, and they handed her over to strangers."

"Now, that's not fair. You know your cousin Tricia works for

CPS. She's been there about a year now. She says it's the best thing for kids in most situations."

"Tricia works there?" I pretend to be surprised. But that's the main reason I called her back. "You got a number for Tricia? I might ask her about how it works. Might make me feel better."

"Sure, honey. Just a sec." I hear her flipping through papers in her flower shop and humming to Maria Callas singing in the background. "Here we go."

She gives me the number.

"Thanks, Mama."

"See you Sunday at Nana's house. We missed you this week. Tell Donovan I'm making cannoli."

"Will do."

By now, I'm in the heart of Chinatown. A few blocks ahead of me are the ornate green gates that lead to Market Street. Strolling under red, green, and blue paper lanterns strung across the street, I pass a tiny bank with an elaborate red-and-green pagoda storefront. One store window is full of hanging meat, what looks like chickens, and ribs, and turkeys. Walking through Chinatown, with all its brilliant colors and plethora of trinkets to buy, always sends me to the edge of sensory overload, but I can't resist.

Tricia answers on the first ring.

"Hey, it's Ella." I stop and finger a soft turquoise cashmere pashmina on a table outside one shop. I'm dressed in my chess battling clothes: old jeans, combat boots, and a hoodie, but the fall air has chilled. Now the scarf seems like something I need.

"Ella! Geez, cuz, I haven't seen you since, what was it, Uncle Robert's wedding?"

I pick up the scarf and loop it over my shoulder, peering in a mirror hanging outside the shop.

A woman with an enormous bun comes out and smiles. "So pretty on you. Color is good. I give you big discount. You lucky. I give it to you for twenty dollars."

I gesture that I'm on the phone. The woman nods and moves away.

"I know, Tricia. We only live about a mile apart. What's up with that? When you going to make it to Nana's on a Sunday? We all miss little Federico."

"Soon. Not tomorrow, but soon. Raul keeps telling me his mom will lie down and die of a heart attack if we don't come to her place for Sunday suppers, but I miss seeing all the Giovannis and Nana. It's not the same. They don't have pasta. Mama Ruiz makes a killer carnitas taco, mind you, but I am craving some manicotti, you know? One of these days. Freddy just started walking, keeping me crazy busy plus my new job. You know how it is."

I don't, so I just murmur appreciatively. The woman in the bun has returned outside. She holds up a piece of paper with "$18" written on it. I clear my throat. "Tricia, did you hear about those horrible murders . . . in the Mission?"

"Christ on a cracker, I did!" she says. "Saw it in the paper. They said you were there. I don't know how you do that job of yours."

"Did you see the picture? Me holding that baby?"

"Yeah, she was a little sweetie. Reminds me a little of what Freddy looked like as a baby."

I'm looking down, fingering different colored scarfs, when I notice someone beside me. It's that man in the sunglasses I saw consulting a piece of paper a few blocks away. Damn. I should've never smiled at him. Of course, it's feasible he was heading into

Chinatown the entire time, but I don't like his sudden appearance beside me. Besides, it's getting dark for sunglasses, and I'm still wary, because although he's familiar, I can't quite place him.

"That one's pretty," he says and points to a pink scarf. I point to my phone. He nods, puts his finger to his lips, and mouths, "Sorry." A group of boys practicing for a parade come around the corner. Each one has a piece of a colorful dragon costume. The first boy's holding the head. Two boys with drums follow.

I duck into the little shop so I can hear better, then say, "They had to turn her over to you guys—CPS—because most of her family was in that apartment."

I peer out the front window through a rack of clothes. The man smiles, hands twenty dollars to the woman in the bun, and walks off with a black scarf tucked under his arm. He never looks inside where I am, so I relax, but I keep an eye on his retreating back for a minute to see if he's going to turn around and look for me. He has short-cropped hair and a dark suit. He never turns to look back and soon disappears in the crowded street.

"That poor baby. Why did the killer let her live? Do you think she was asleep and he thought she was dead, like in that one case in Colorado?"

"Maybe. I don't know. It's hard to believe someone who could slaughter an entire family would have enough of a conscience to not kill a baby. Who knows why she was spared." But in the back of my mind, I remember the UPS box outside the apartment. Maybe the killer was interrupted?

The woman with the bun comes inside. She scribbles on another piece of paper: "$15."

Tricia continues. "Well, she's in the right place, then."

"Huh?" I'm not sure what she's talking about.

"CPS. She's in the right place. They'll find her family."

The woman in the bun follows me as I pace the store. I wait the beat of ten before I answer Tricia.

"Well, Tricia, this is what I'm wondering. I know there are privacy restrictions on kids in CPS, but I . . . need . . . want to find out what happened to her. I mean, maybe if the dad isn't around or something, I could maybe take care of her."

Again, I wait, making the sign of the cross and closing my eyes. The woman in the bun throws up her hands in exasperation.

"Well, that privacy stuff is to keep some abusive parent or something from finding a kid taken away for their own safety, so that doesn't *really* apply here. Still, I'm not supposed to do this . . . but I'll see what I can find out."

Score.

I thank her and hang up.

"I go to dinner now," the woman says offhandedly while folding and refolding some scarfs that are already neatly stacked. "This is my final offer. You very, very lucky I give you this price. This is very good deal. Twelve dollars."

I walk out with the turquoise scarf looped around my neck.

As I pass through Chinatown, I remember where I first saw the man in the sunglasses. Coming down the stairs at the Oakland dojo. Did he follow me to San Francisco? How did he know I would be walking in Chinatown? The coincidence is too much and sends a chill down my spine. The sound of a motorcycle nearby sends me darting into a doorway, but the growl grows fainter. I duck into doorways every once in a while and peer out to see if the man in the sunglasses is following me. I don't catch sight of him again, so I continue on to Market Street, where I play chess until the sun sets. The Bulgarian who runs the chess games eyes me as I leave, pockets stuffed with forty bucks in winnings.

"Natasha, you are wasting away." He clucks at me with concern.

He's called me "Natasha" for years. I've never bothered to correct him. She has now become my alter ego—Natasha, a motorcycle-boot-wearing chess master who is not the sister of a dead girl.

I shrug and turn away. Natasha is a woman of few words.

But he's right. I hitch up my jeans as I walk. I need to eat more. If only to keep up my energy so I can do the things I need to do. Time to focus my energy less on my sorrows and myself and more on someone else—helping figure out who murdered Lucy's family.

I round a corner a few blocks up from Market Street and leave the noise and bustle behind. The sudden quiet and dark make my heart beat faster. I look behind me every few minutes until I spot a cab and flag it down. I can't usually afford to take a cab for a distance I can easily walk, but after realizing the man with sunglasses from the dojo might be following me, I'm willing to fork over whatever it takes to get off the deserted streets tonight.

When Donovan gets home at 2:00 a.m., he crawls into bed and says he has to be at work in three hours. He turns his back to me and immediately begins to snore. I lie awake, staring at the ceiling, once again feeling the seed of resentment inside me grow bigger.

Chapter 25

When Donovan kisses me good-bye this morning, he seems distant, distracted.

Glancing at my calendar, I note that Joey Martin will take custody of Lucy in less than ten days unless I do something first. I also see that I'm not ovulating again for three weeks. Vaguely, I wonder if abstaining will increase our chances of getting pregnant. I frown. I don't remember reading anything like that in the stack of books on my nightstand. They all promise to hold the key to getting pregnant. I cling to the small tendril of hope that grew with the doctor's words: "*. . . I've told hundreds of women the same thing, and within a year, I've delivered their baby.*"

Donovan has to be patient with me. The only thing I can focus on, the only thing I have energy for, is proving that Lucy's father murdered her mother. That way, she won't end up in a killer's hands.

I'm the first one in the newsroom, and I'm already halfway through typing up some press releases from the police department about minor burglaries and stickups, when a new one comes across the fax.

It catches my eye because it has a surveillance picture of a man in a convenience store above a photo of a cute, fluffy white poodle.

Thirty minutes later, I've talked to the cops and the owner of the poodle. Apparently the dude thought it would be a good idea to steal the poodle, which was tied up in front of the convenience store, while its owner, Josie Bartholomew, was inside buying a half gallon of milk for her Poopsie. No, you can't make this up. Poopsie.

What kind of jerk steals an old woman's dog? And what kind of woman names her dog Poopsie?

People will be up in arms over this story. Nothing enrages readers more than someone messing with an animal. Kidnapped and murdered kid stories don't stand a chance. It still ticks me off, but I'm resigned to the fact that people are more outraged about mistreated animals than mistreated people.

This is front-page material for sure.

With the adorable pictures of the mutt and the not-supposed-to-be-funny-but-hilarious quotes from the cop—i.e., "Our main priority right now is to reunite Poopsie with her owner"— TV will have a field day with this one.

I'm just about finished writing my story, which I gleefully slug "Poopsiepinched," when the phone rings.

"Giovanni."

"Hello. I'd like to report a hole-in-one."

Call sports. "Hold, please."

I stand on tiptoe. Nobody in sports yet. A few people have trickled into the newsroom, so I shout, "Hey, this guy wants to report a hole-in-one, who should I transfer him to?"

"Tell him one-eight-hundred-call-your-mama!" someone hollers from the copy desk.

My other line rings.

"Cripes." Instead of getting back on the phone, I send the golfer up to Jan at the reception desk. She'll be able to figure out where to transfer him. Then I remember Jan is on vacation and there is a temp worker. Not her or his fault trying to figure out where all the crazy, random calls go.

At least they aren't for me today.

I scrabble to answer when my cell phone rings. It's my cousin.

"I think I found her," Tricia says. "She's with a real nice foster family in Noe Valley. They take in kids all the time. Her file says that her biological father will be back in the country next week and pick her up."

The baby has been in CPS care for a week. I suppose another week won't hurt her. And I have a feeling that if Mrs. Castillo is right, any place is safer than with her father.

"Noe Valley, huh?" I ask. "What part? What's the address? I know a yummy Chinese restaurant there." I try to make my question as casual and matter-of-fact as I can.

Tricia is silent for a minute. "Even if I had the address—which I don't, they don't even put it in the file for confidential reasons—even if I had it, I'm not supposed to give it out. Even to family."

I swallow hard. I don't mean to put Tricia on the spot or try to make her jeopardize her job.

"I'm sorry. I understand. Thanks for telling me what you did." I try to lighten the mood. "And you guys better get over to Nana's. I need a Freddy fix soon."

"Deal. Love you."

I'VE MISSED MY appointment with Marsha and feel a mixture of guilt and relief. I call to reschedule before leaving work early. Because even though I don't want to talk to my therapist, there is someone I do want to speak with.

Thirty minutes later, I'm knocking on the door of the rectory to St. Joan of Arc Church in Oakland. Father Liam answers the door himself. His bright blue eyes are sparkling, and his full head of dark hair, swept back away from his face, is just starting to become fringed with gray.

"What a lovely surprise. It's my entertaining hour. Would you care for a drink? Or possibly a spot of tea?"

Sometimes I forget that although he's half Italian, he's also half Irish. Do the Irish prefer tea to coffee, like the British?

"Just water, thanks. Do you have a minute?"

"I always have time for you," he says. I follow him upstairs to the study. He's dressed casually, in pressed designer jeans and a button-up top with a soft cashmere cardigan and loafers.

He busies himself at the bar, and a few seconds later, he turns and hands me a Pellegrino with a small slice of lime on the edge of the glass.

"Thank you." I take a sip.

"The pleasure is mine," he says as he folds himself into an armchair. He crosses one leg over the other and takes a sip of his Bombay gin and tonic.

In between sips of my water, I tell Father Liam about the massacre in the San Francisco apartment and how I feel unusually attached to the child I held in my arms.

"I did see that—and you—on the television. I wouldn't wish that on anyone, finding something like that. But with that said, your attachment to that child appears to be a normal reaction for someone who has been through what you have," he says.

Maybe I should fire my expensive therapist and turn to Father Liam exclusively. I brush that thought aside. I came to him for a more spiritual reason today.

"Do you think you could bless this for me?" I hold out the medal in my palm.

He takes it from me. "Ah, St. Gerard. Is there something I should know?" His eyes twinkle, but his brows crease in consternation when he sees the answer on my face. He quickly amends what he said. "Well, it never hurts to pray, my dear. I'd be happy to bless it."

I'm afraid to meet his eyes and see the sympathy in them, so I stare at the round heels of my pumps. Father Liam lifts my chin with two fingers until I meet his eyes.

"Now, now."

"I know you said it's not true, but—"

"It's not true. I told you that's not a possibility. And it's not up for discussion." His clipped accent puts an end to the conversation.

He's sick of hearing it, and I don't blame him. I've told him several times that I'm convinced my miscarriage and inability to conceive is my punishment for killing two people.

He will have nothing to do with that idea.

I leave a few minutes later with the medal tucked into the neckline of my blouse, nestled against my miraculous medal. I finger them both as I drive toward San Francisco. As Father Liam said, "It never hurts to pray."

Chapter 26

ONCE I PULL into North Beach, I'm restless. Donovan is staying at his own place tonight whenever he gets home. This homicide he's working is all consuming. We've been together two years, so I should be used to it, but for some reason I've found I'm less and less understanding.

The thought of sitting in my apartment alone is stifling.

Within twenty minutes I'm cruising the placid streets of Noe Valley, a family-friendly neighborhood in the city, chock full of row houses and small stores on its main road. I ignore the alarms going off in my head warning me that looking for Lucy is bordering on crazy town.

I drive past Eric's Chinese restaurant on Church Street and glance into the window of a little Santeria shop that sells potions and candles. For half a second, I'm tempted to stop and see if they have any spells for baby making, but imagining Father Liam's face when I confess this keeps me driving.

At one point, passing a woman with several kids, including a baby in a stroller, I slam on my brakes and wait for them to walk past, even though cars are honking behind me. When the woman gets close, I can see that the stroller holds a little boy in a baseball cap. After a few more false alarms like that, I finally admit I'm acting irrational and head back to my part of town.

Back in North Beach, I park and hit the streets, wrapping my new turquoise scarf loosely around my neck.

October is usually my favorite time of year in the city. It's a little-known secret locals don't like to divulge—summer in the city is the pits: rife with tourists and bitter-cold fog and wind. Mark Twain got it right when he said, "The coldest winter I ever spent was a summer in San Francisco."

Fall in the city is the best time of year. It's when the fog clears and the warmth of the sun's rays soak into bare skin. But this year it seems like a shadow of its former self. The East Bay is unseasonably warm, and the city is abnormally cold.

Tonight, even with the chill in the air, the streets of North Beach are teeming with diners and shoppers and strollers taking their *passeggiata*—nightly stroll—before dinner. In the old country, even in the smallest villages of Italy, whole families dressed to the nines and strolled the promenade or the town plaza, catching up on local gossip, news, and admiring one another before a late dinner. Romances and business deals alike were made during *la passeggiata*.

It is a chance to see and be seen, to create *la bella figura*.

In San Francisco, some of the old-school Italians still stroll, but mainly the old-timers plant themselves at sidewalk cafés to chitchat while nursing a beer or glass of wine. Usually this makes me smile, but tonight it just makes me jealous, seeing everyone greeting one another as I walk alone. Although I often see friends, today all the faces I see are those of strangers.

I stop at Molinari's deli, where I fill my market basket with some rotini pasta noodles, a small, expensive tin of Donovan's favorite amaretto cookies, and an Italian sub. At City Lights bookstore, I pick up the latest Anna Gavalda book and head home.

Sitting out on my balcony, I put my sub sandwich on a china plate and one of my nana's handmade, rose-patterned cloth napkins in my lap, and pour myself some cabernet sauvignon. One glass of wine won't hurt, since I'm not pregnant this month anyway. Unfortunately, the sub tastes like cardboard in my mouth, and I work hard to chew some and swallow. I'm tempted to give up, but I take another bite instead and wash it down with wine. Take another bite, wash it down. Repeat. The only thing that goes down easily is the glass of wine. I didn't realize until now how much I missed drinking wine while trying to get pregnant.

On the drive home across the Bay Bridge, I vowed to myself that tonight I would pamper myself, relax, not think about saving Lucy from her father, not obsess about finding the man who kidnapped my sister, and ignore the aching hollow in my midsection that once held a life.

But after refilling my wineglass a few times to get the sub down, all bets are off.

I'm at my computer looking up Joey Martin's name, but I find nothing.

After using all the search engines I can, I give up. I have a call in to Liz, the news researcher at the newspaper, to see if she can dig up any dirt on him.

Maybe she's found something new. I check my work e-mail. Nothing from Liz, but my heart starts to beat wildly when I see an e-mail from Anderson: FA2858.

This time, the subject line says, *An eye for an eye?*

Why the question mark? I click it open.

This time the Bible verse is Romans 12:17–19.

"Repay no one evil for evil, but give thought to do what is honorable in the sight of all. If possible, so far as it depends on you, live peaceably with all. Beloved, never avenge yourselves, but leave it to the wrath of God, for it is written, 'Vengeance is mine, I will repay, says the Lord.'"

Is he warning me not to seek justice for the Mission Massacre, or not to seek justice for Caterina's murder? It doesn't matter. Before I die, I will seek justice for both. I still don't know how he found me, but I vow to make it his downfall if I can.

I forward the e-mail to the detective. A tiny flicker of guilt zings through me as I remember Donovan's happy face asking me to let it go and concentrate on being pregnant. I flick it aside. I'm not pregnant anymore. There is no reason not to go after Anderson with everything I've got.

I search through the trash file on my computer to find the old e-mail he sent me with the subject line *Thou Shalt Not Kill.* This time nothing will stop me from reading it.

Again, inside the e-mail there is nothing but Bible verses. This time three of them:

> James 4:2—You want something but don't get it. You kill and covet, but you cannot have what you want.
> James 5:6—You have condemned and murdered the innocent one, who was not opposing you.
> John 3:15—Anyone who hates a brother or sister is a murderer, and you know that no murderer has eternal life residing in him.

It's as if he knows me, and knows how the weight of the men I killed weighs so heavily on my soul. At first the verses send a chill through me, but then I grow angry. How dare he? How dare he, who is a murderer, judge me?

I shoot off an angry e-mail to the detective assigned to Caterina's case.

What is going on with my sister's case? I haven't heard from you in months. I've sent you three e-mails now, including the one I sent a few seconds ago. What are you doing about them? This is the man who killed my sister, and he's taunting me. If you won't do something about it, I will.

Feeling a bit better, I hit send. If he doesn't respond, maybe I'll show up in person.

Looking over my shoulder—even though I know I'm alone—I punch in Frank Anderson's name and hit search. Guilt streaks through me, but I brush it off. When nothing comes up online about Anderson, I grow weary. My eyes are heavy. My legs feel like lead, my mind, dull and gray.

I close my computer and crawl under my covers.

But as soon as I get in bed, I'm wide awake, my mind whirring along, analyzing the e-mails.

I bet the detective isn't convinced the e-mails are from Anderson. How can I prove it? I know the initials "F.A." stand for Frank Anderson. But what does "2858" stand for? I've racked my brains for the past two months trying to figure out what it might mean.

I switch my light back on, take a small key, and unlock a drawer in my desk. Inside, I unearth a worn manila folder. It contains all the information about Caterina's kidnapping and murder. I've looked at all the documents so many times I nearly have them memorized. In fact, I just read them two weeks ago, but I pick them up again and reread them.

On the third time skimming the documents, I pause on an arrest record for Anderson, when he got caught sneaking into a little girl's house and masturbating in her room. Her dad came home early and beat the crap out of Frank until the cops showed.

Reading the arrest record makes me the tiniest bit happy. I like reading how the father beat Anderson to a pulp. I think he even had to have reconstructive surgery on his face. Good. He tried to sue the father for assault, but a judge threw the case out. Are they going to side with a veteran? Or a pedophile?

Starting from the top, I read every box on the arrest report. At first, I skip right over the box marked "birthdate." 2-8-1958, which can also be written 2-8-58. FA2858. It's him. It is a message. He wanted to let me know that it *is* him.

After I find myself falling asleep sitting in front of the computer, I crawl back into bed. Before I turn out the light, I study the picture of Caterina on my nightstand. Each night her picture reminds me that her death remains unavenged. For now.

Chapter 27

"ANGEL OF DEATH?"

It's Brian at the morgue.

"Pretty ironic, coming from the Grim Reaper himself," I answer. "Did you trade in your light saber for a scythe? I barely recognized your voice, since it wasn't quoting *Star Wars*."

"Got a soldier on ice," he says.

"I'll be there in a few," I say and hang up.

Brian is one of several sheriff's deputies assigned to a two-year stint at the morgue. They are called out to any suspicious death or car crash fatalities and have to take photographs of the death scene, do the initial investigation, bag the bodies, and transport them to the county morgue, where a forensic pathologist does the autopsies. Because death doesn't punch a time clock, they take turns filling the twenty-four-hour shift, sleeping alone on a cot in a creepy, windowless room. The last place I'd want to stay the night alone, with about a dozen dead bodies chilling only a wall away.

When I get to the morgue, Rita at the front desk is on the

phone, so she buzzes me in and waves me back instead of us catching up with our usual chitchat about her grandchildren and recipes we've tried.

Brian greets me in the back offices with a folder he plops into my arms. With his blond crew cut and ripped forearms, Brian is built like a linebacker, so it always strikes me as funny how nerdy he actually is. He once told me his wife encourages him to collect figurines from *The Simpsons* TV show. I keep meaning to get him some for Christmas.

"I've got a bad feeling about this." He points me to a chair. "You will never find a more wretched hive of scum and villainy . . . We must be cautious."

"Got it," I say.

I open the file, and on top of a stack of documents lies a vivid picture—a close-up of a guy with half his head blown off. I've seen worse in person at the morgue, but this one is particularly gruesome. Brian hovers over my shoulder, so I don't react. I'm sure he'd stop letting me see the complete autopsy files if I'm a wimp about it. Other pictures show the man sprawled on the floor of a garage. His body is near the tire of a silver vehicle. A gun lies nearby. I scan the cover page. His name is Richard Abequero.

"Suicide?"

"Guy ate his gun." Brian leans against the cubicle wall, flipping through a stack of photos he took out of a large envelope. "Been back from his tour of duty about six months. Lives in Oakland."

"Iraq?"

"The force is with you . . . but you are not a Jedi yet!"

"Thanks."

I study the picture closer. Above the bloody mess that used to be a face I can see a close-shorn haircut.

"Married? Any kids?" I ask.

"Married."

Brian pulls out a chair across from me. He takes out his Death Book and adds new pictures to it, carefully using a glue stick to adhere them to the professional-style scrapbook. I know later he will take a fine ink pen and mark poignant details. For instance, on one he wrote, "Father of four. Asphyxiated from sinking into silo bin full of grain."

Along with photographing the scene officially, he takes snapshots "unofficially" and keeps them in his Death Book, his morbid account of his time at the morgue. And he calls *me* "Angel of Death."

I continue flipping through the file until I find contact information. His wife. Her name is Carol Abequero.

"They pick him up yet?"

"Yep. He's over at Dunwoody Funeral Home. Viewing is tonight. Seven p.m. Closed casket. Ugh. And I thought they smelled bad on the outside."

Closing the folder, the image of the soldier's mangled face is seared on my mind. "I'm sure."

I pick up my bag. "Thanks again, Brian."

"The circle is now complete."

"Um, okay. See you."

IN THE CAR, I start making calls. First, Liz in news research.

"Hey, sugar," she says, and I can tell she is smiling.

Liz should work for the CIA or FBI. She could unearth Jimmy Hoffa's body if she set her mind to it.

"Got a name for you, Liz. Carol Abequero. Looking for an address." The best way to get someone to talk is to show up in person. Anyone can hang up the phone. And they often do.

"Will do, sugar."

Next, I call Detective Khoury.

"I don't have anything new for you. They'll look at that weapon you gave me, but there is a backlog of evidence they're working." She says it before I can ask a question.

"Any chance I can get that recruiter's name yet? I want to know who says Joey Martin was in Iraq."

"I got some bad news for you. It's more than just the recruiter. My lieutenant apparently talked to a general over there. The big guy is vouching for Joey Martin. That gives the husband the best alibi I've heard in a decade," she says. "Wait, I take that back. There was a better one. The suspect who was already dead in the cemetery had the best alibi I've ever run across. Even so, his neighbor was convinced he killed her husband. Asked me if I'd ever heard of zombies."

"I would've liked to have written that story." I'm impatient with her tangent, but trying to humor her.

"The San Jose paper had a field day with that one."

"I know you're busy, but I was wondering if you had a name or number for Martin's general."

I want to hear out of his mouth that his soldier was overseas the day his family was massacred.

There is silence for a few seconds. "If I give you a name, will you back off?"

I hear the rustling of papers and know I'm close, but I'm also not going to lie and say what she wants to hear.

"I can't guarantee that." The noise of the papers stops. There is silence for a second. I stare out at all the red lights of cars slowing in front of me.

"I haven't had time to look up the recruiter's name. It's buried somewhere in all this paperwork on my desk, but Martin's commanding officer is General Craig Hightower. At least, he's the one who faxed a letter to my lieutenant confirming Martin's return date."

She hangs up before I can say thank you. I take the exit for Oakland.

"I DON'T KNOW General Hightower, but I know the man directly under him," Moretti says, narrowing his eyes at me and running a hand over his slicked-back hair. "You really need to talk to someone in Iraq? And it has to be a lieutenant general who is currently overseeing a war in a theater overseas?"

"The higher up the better." Moretti has bragged about his connections with the power players in the Iraq War; now I'm calling him on it.

He gives me a fake glare. I know his resistance is all an act. At least I think it is. I eye the photo of Moretti and another man in fatigues with their arms around each other in Vietnam. I meaningfully push the bag of pork puns from See Yee Yum across the desk toward him.

In an instance, he's snatched the bag and dropped it in a desk drawer.

"Well, here goes nothing," he says and pulls his phone toward him.

"What? It's not like you'll get in trouble for calling him."

"Listen, kiddo, let's just say, it's not going to make me his best friend, putting a reporter on his tail." He swings his short legs off the desk and leans forward, flipping through his Rolodex.

He's going to do it. I try to hide my excitement. He pauses. "On one condition."

I nod.

"I'll do all the talking. What's this yahoo's name?"

I scribble "Joey Martin" and push the scrap of reporter's notebook paper his way.

Lighting a cigarette, one practiced hand holding his silver Zippo, he squints at the Rolodex card and punches in some numbers on his phone. I plug my nose and wave my arm widely, as if I'm clearing the smoke from the room.

Even though he's had one heart attack, he continues to smoke. It drives me crazy.

"Lieutenant General David Cooper, please. Tell him it's Michael Moretti." He hums and taps the desk with his fingers, waiting.

I try not to look impatient. He whispers to me, "You know, this guy is a big deal. He'll probably take over the war soon, because rumor has it Hightower is running for president next year. This better be important, kiddo."

"It *is*," I hiss back.

"Yes, Coop, it's Moretti," he says and laughs at something the other man says. "Kate is fine, thanks for asking. Yep, same with the kids. Janie is at U.C. Berkeley now. No, Tommy is still 'finding himself,' whatever the Christ that means. Tempted to ask you to find a place for him in your outfit, but I wouldn't wish that kid on anyone."

More words on the other end I can't hear. Moretti clears his throat.

"I've got a question for you. I've got this pesky friend of the family. A reporter. Gabriella Giovanni. Seems she's covering a murder in San Fran that affects one of your soldiers."

He glances down at the piece of paper I gave him. "A Sergeant Martin, Joey. His wife and his parents were killed this week."

A deep voice rumbles on the other end of the line. What is he saying?

"Yes. Yes. It's a damn shame. Wanted to check and see if Sergeant Martin was on base at the time?"

"Sure, I'll stand by," he says. Leaning back in his chair, he exhales perfect smoke rings above his head, giving me a wink.

I cough loudly, exaggerating, and wave my hands to clear the smoke, which is nowhere near me.

He pushes the silver cigarette case my way. "You want a cancer stick, too?" he whispers, holding his palm over the mouthpiece.

For a second, I see myself reaching for it, but I resist. He snatches it back. I make a face at him. Of course I want one. But I want to be pregnant more. No more smoking for me.

The lieutenant general must be back on the line, because Moretti sits up and grabs a pen and pad of paper. "Well, that is interesting. We've been told he's coming home next Friday on bereavement? Yeah. A week from tomorrow. I know. National security and all that. We're good. She just wanted to verify he was on base during the murder. She's as trustworthy as they come. Thanks, Coop. Stay safe over there, my friend."

He hangs up.

"He doesn't exist."

"What?" That doesn't make any sense.

"Coop told me this because we go way back. This is off the record—Martin is Army 'Combined Applications Group.' Do you know what that means?"

"Not a clue."

"Some call his unit 'Delta,' but there isn't an official name.

Once you get picked up by CAG, you don't exist anymore. The only people who know you exist? President. CIA. Maybe FBI."

"I don't get it."

"Officially, he's not there. Not anywhere. There is no record of him. Until the other day. Now, here's the interesting part. Even though he's not supposed to exist, nobody is supposed to say his name out loud. Coop just got a memo the other day saying if anybody asks about Martin, he's been on base since April and will be home on leave a week from tomorrow."

"But he hasn't been there, Moretti. They're covering up his murder spree. I'm not making this up." I tell him about getting attacked at the apartment. "I also saw him at his wife's funeral. Or rather, I saw him run out the back door of the church at the funeral."

Moretti's forehead crinkles. He believes me. But he's not sure how it's possible. Welcome to the club.

I don't get up to leave but sit fiddling with my notebook and pen.

Moretti fills the silence, just as I expect. "I'll make a few more calls. If you say you saw him, then maybe you did. Even Coop seemed surprised by his orders."

I stand to leave.

"Kiddo?"

I pause.

"I think you should consider backing off this. Talking to Coop has me a bit worried that you're poking around in something this big. If the military is lying, they probably got a pretty damn good reason for it and you should stay the hell away."

Chapter 28

I HAVE EIGHT days to prove that Joey Martin killed his wife, or that he had something to do with it. Otherwise Lucy will end up in the hands of a man his mother-in-law called "the devil."

She belongs with her grandmother. I picture the baby girl a little bit older, dressed in a blue dress and black shiny shoes, her chubby hand in her grandmother's wrinkled one as they walk to Mass at the San Juan Bautista mission.

Back at my desk, I make my "cop calls"—the long list of calls to police departments I make twice a day to see if they have any newsworthy crimes to report. My tenth call is to Amy Morgan, the Walnut Creek public information officer. Amy is a former reporter, who worked at our paper before my time. She is easy to work with and always returns my calls. Today, she picks up on the first ring.

"You'll like this, Giovanni."

"Do tell."

"Bank robber."

"Go on." I wait.

"Wrote his demand note on . . . guess?"

"A withdrawal slip with his bank account number on it?"

"Close. The back of an envelope that contained his electric bill. With his name and address on the front. Detectives picked him up five minutes ago. He had all the bait money on him. Open and shut. I'll have a press release out to you in a few minutes."

"This will be a fun one to write," I say.

"Thank God for dumb crooks."

I write up a short story about the dumb bank robber, then make a series of calls. When I have about three pages of notes, I ask for a minute of Kellogg's time.

I need an excuse to pursue the Mission Massacre story without Kellogg realizing I'm doing so. Earlier, I thought about the phone call I received from the woman who complained about how the military is shortchanging soldiers who've returned from the war. I realized it gave me the perfect cover to continue investigating the Mission Massacre.

Kellogg and I settle into two old, creaky chairs in one of the empty conference rooms. I lay it all out for him—too many soldiers are coming back from Iraq with post-traumatic stress disorder. Some of them are killing themselves. Others are beating up their wives. Others are overdosing. From what that woman said on the phone, the soldiers are having a difficult time assimilating back into life in the U.S. and may not be getting enough—or any—support from the military. I explain all this to Kellogg, who raises his eyebrows. He's interested.

He leans forward. "This is definitely different than what we saw in the Vietnam War. This is a different type of war. There are different types of issues the soldiers are facing. Could be a Sunday piece." He strokes his beard. "Be sure to focus on a Bay Area angle."

While the story *is* fascinating, my goal is to be able to work the Lucy story in under the radar. If my research on the vets pans out right, the story can be a sidebar to my scoop on Joey Martin being the killer.

"I'll start by talking to my sources at the morgues and find out if they've had many veteran suicides," I say, not mentioning I already have one—the Abequero suicide. "I'll see if the military has any stats and what kind of resources they're providing. They might be doing something, but from what this woman says, it doesn't seem like enough."

"I think you're onto something here, Giovanni," he says as he stands and waits for me to follow suit. Turning toward the door, he says over his shoulder, "Glad to see you're letting the Mission Massacre story go. Those are the kinds of stories that will fuck you up."

Guilt swarms through me as I nod, afraid to speak.

On my way home, I swing by the sex club. This time there aren't any kids hanging out on the street. Probably too early in the day. I'm parking, when a car pulls up in front of the door. A beautiful woman wearing Chanel gets out of the backseat. The windows are tinted dark, so I can't see inside. She touches a doorbell, and the steel door opens automatically. She doesn't break stride, just pulls the door open and disappears. I rush over and tug on the handle, but it's locked again. The big black car beside me starts to pull away, and I jump in front of the hood. The car stops on a dime, touching my hip. The driver is a young woman with a buzzed head and a suit jacket. She glares at me, and I give her a big smile.

Keeping my fingers trailing on the hood of the car, I make my way over to her window. She makes a face but lowers the glass.

"I'd like to talk to your lady friend, the one you just let out."

"Miss Sabrina doesn't talk to people she doesn't know." The woman says the words in a snotty voice.

"She might want to talk to me," I say. I lean in a bit on the lowered window. The woman glances down, and I realize I'm giving a free peep show. My face warms as I stand up and tug my top up higher. The driver snickers.

"Listen. I'm trying to find out about someone who worked here. A kid named Javier. You know him?"

I watch her eyes dart to the side when I say the name. She knows him, alright.

"I'm trying to find out who killed him. Maybe Miss Sabrina or you could help."

"You the po-po?" She leans away from the window and puts her hand on the button to roll it up.

"No, I'm not a cop."

She studies me for a minute and bites the inside of her lip as she speaks.

"Javier was okay," she said. "I don't know anything about what happened to him, though."

She's telling the truth. I lean back down one more time.

"I'd like to get in there and talk to someone about Javier. Can you help me out?"

"Listen, lady, I have never even been in there. Miss Sabrina has me drop her off and calls when I'm supposed to pick her up again."

I press my lips together. If that is true, then how does she know Javier? This isn't working. I fish out one of my cards and hand it to the driver. "Can you give Miss Sabrina my card?"

She doesn't answer, just nods and rolls the window back up. Within thirty seconds, the car is gone.

Before I drive away, I cross the street and look up at the windows. They're all covered with thick curtains. I try knocking on the door and ringing the doorbell one more time before I give up and head to Donovan's place.

DURING DINNER—ENCHILADA takeout from one of my favorite Oakland restaurants—I go over my day with Donovan.

We both have the night off, and we decided to eat at his place. He's hinted a lot lately, especially when I first got pregnant, about me moving into his apartment on Lake Merritt, but I've been reluctant to let my place go. My studio apartment barely fits me alone. I use the excuse that the deal on my rent-controlled apartment is just too good, but I know it's more than that.

I know when we get married one day, my life in San Francisco will be over. But I'm not willing to do that yet. And so far, I haven't managed to convince Donovan to move into the city.

His apartment has an actual bedroom. With a door. And it does have spectacular views of Lake Merritt and the downtown Oakland skyline, which is so cheery at night, all lit up with the fairy lights surrounding the path around the lake and sometimes little glowing lights from people taking nighttime gondola rides on the water.

And we can walk most places we want to go, like the Holy Land deli, La Casita for enchiladas, and now even See Yee Yum.

But. It is still not San Francisco.

When I finish telling him about my day, I take a deep breath and tell him my idea about working the Mission Massacre story under the guise of doing a story on soldiers coming home traumatized from the war. "I mean, I'll do both stories, of course, but this gives me the excuse I need to be out talking to generals and recruiters and whatnot."

When I finish, he doesn't say anything. He looks worried.

I poke around at the food on my plate, forcing myself to take another bite. I chew and chew and swallow and he doesn't answer.

"It's not like that," I finally say.

"Just be careful. This might be another case that will end up unsolved."

"Another case? What do you mean?" My voice rises in outrage. Is he referring to my sister's murder?

"San Francisco doesn't have the best clearance rate. They are overwhelmed and underfunded. You know how it goes. I don't want you to be crushed if this remains an open case."

"I'll only be 'crushed,' as you put it, if they give that baby to her murdering father."

"It's more than that," he says. "If the government is covering something up, I want you to stay far, far away."

I appreciate his concern, so I try not to make a face. But his next comment sends a ripple of irritation down my back.

"And you're sure you saw him?"

"Are you joking?" My voice is steel.

"You need to be open-minded to what I'm going to say next," he begins, and I close my eyes in annoyance for a second. He waits for me to open them back up before he continues. "Is there any chance that the strain of what you've gone through—"

"What *we've* gone through," I interrupt. I stand and clear my plate, scraping the remains of my enchilada into the trash.

"What *we've* gone through—is there any chance that you might have been seeing things? With the strain and lack of sleep. I mean, those things could be hallucinations." He says all this to my back as I rinse my plate at the sink.

"You've got to be fucking kidding me." I turn toward him, feeling as if lightning bolts are shooting out of my eyes. "I'm ninety-nine-point-nine percent sure he was the one who attacked me and that he's the one I saw at the funeral," I say as calmly as I can.

He watches me for a long moment. "Okay. I believe you saw Martin," he says. He starts cleaning the dishes from the table but stops. "Are you carrying a gun?"

"No." I scowl. "I don't own a gun. You *know* that."

"Yeah, but you could take one of mine. I've got plenty. Unless you want me to follow you around all day, because I can do that, too."

I laugh. "I promise I'll be careful."

We stand at the sink and do the dishes together, like we always do, but this time there is little splashing or flicking bubbles at each other.

When we are done, I dry my hands and head for the bedroom. My eyelids are heavy, and all I want to do is curl up in a warm bed and sleep for two days.

Caterina's unavenged murder, my miscarriage, the two men who have died at my hands, the fate of Lucy—sometimes I don't want to think or feel anything anymore.

In the bedroom, I'm so exhausted that I shrink away from Donovan when he turns and wraps his arms around me. I keep my back to him, and before I know it, I fall into a dark pit of unconsciousness.

Chapter 29

My phone rings in the middle of the night.

"They've made an arrest." It's Khoury.

There is something in her voice.

"What do you mean, 'they'?" I ask.

Even over the phone, I can tell it pains her to say the words: "They punted the case. Took it out of my hands yesterday and last night arrested an East Bay woman."

I sit up and flip on my light.

"Who took the case? What woman?"

"My lieutenant handed the case to another detective, and he made an arrest last night. Woman named Carol Abequero."

My eyes narrow in suspicion. "What detective?"

"Jack Sullivan."

"That prick." Donovan rolls over and sits up, squinting at these words.

"Uh-huh." Khoury obviously agrees with my assessment of Sullivan.

I'm still stunned by what she said. An arrest. And who they arrested: Carol Abequero.

"Her husband just committed suicide," I say to Khoury. "What's the connection with Martin? I don't get it."

"This will be in the arrest report. They think she was in love with Joey Martin, and when he scorned her, she lost her mind and sought revenge by killing everyone he loved," Khoury says. "Martin and her hubby were in boot camp together a few years back."

I squint at my clock. It's early Friday. Joey Martin will take custody of Lucy one week from today.

"Her husband, Richard Abequero, is scheduled to be buried later today," I say. Donovan lies back down and puts his arm over his eyes.

Khoury says the funeral has been changed to a memorial service without a body. "They're taking his body back to the morgue. Making sure he was a suicide."

"No way. I don't believe it."

"Me either, kid." Kid? She can't be that much older than me, but it also makes me wonder if she likes me a little.

"I'm sorry they took the case away from you."

"Yeah, me, too."

"What will you do now? Are you going to back off?"

"I'll keep in touch."

As soon as the jail opens, I fax over a request to interview Carol Abequero. An hour later, I get a fax back. "Interview denied."

Chapter 30

FOR ABEQUERO'S SERVICE, the second memorial I attend in a week, I wear the same black dress and patent-leather pumps to the small chapel on cemetery grounds in Colma. I sneak in the back and try to be inconspicuous in the last row.

I bury my nose in the program but look up when I sense someone watching. A man in uniform. What looks like a high-ranking member of the military. I don't know what all the stripes and badges mean, but this guy is no slouch. Even without the uniform, he's obviously a man of authority. He has that aura, that presence, head shaved, shoulders back. More than just the way he holds himself erect and makes eye contact with me without flinching. He is turned around in his pew, surveying the crowd and his gaze has stopped on me. He watches me until a woman touches his arm and he leans down to hear what she says.

I realize the woman is probably Abequero's mother. She wears a black dress with a tiny hat and veil. He turns back toward her, takes her arm in his and pats it gently. He's forgotten about me.

All of his attention is on this woman. I let out the breath I didn't realize I was holding.

I stare at the back of their heads for a while. Is he her husband? No. He is so formal with her. Does she believe her daughter-in-law killed all those people? I'm tempted to ask, but now is not the right time.

Something about his mother, maybe the shade of her hair, reminds me of my own mother at Caterina's funeral. I'm thrown back in time to that day. When everyone stands for a prayer, I push that memory aside. I don't have time for my own grief, I remind myself.

Thinking of Caterina makes me remember the e-mails from Frank Anderson. The secrets I'm keeping from Donovan feel like a towering mountain of deceit. I haven't given up my hunt for Anderson, and now I'm worried that doing this behind Donovan's back will drive an invisible wedge between us.

I slip out before the service is over.

Joey Martin will be home in one week to claim Lucy. I'm running out of time to prove he had something to do with the murders. And now, even with proof, I'll need to convince the cops, who are already happy to neatly wrap up the murder case with Carol Abequero's arrest. Thank God Khoury seems to believe that Joey Martin is not the innocent husband the military would like us to believe.

On my way into the newsroom, I stop at the sex club again. This time my knocking is answered. The steel door swings open. A short guy with bad teeth and a flannel shirt steps out and leans against the building, eyeing me as he lights a cigarette. He inhales deeply and doesn't say anything, only watches me.

"I'm here about Javier. Heard he worked here." I stand so I'm about a foot in front of him.

"What about him?" the guy says, blowing smoke in my face and looking over my shoulder warily. I turn to look, too, but there is nobody there.

"Any idea why he's dead?"

He sneers at me and scoffs out a "no."

"What did he do here?"

"You could call him a handy man." He chuckles.

"You know if he knew a dude named Joey Martin?"

For a second, his eyes darken. He knows Martin.

"You know Joey Martin, don't you?" My voice rises excitedly, but he's already stepped on his cigarette and with a flick has the door to the club open.

"Wait," I say, but the door closes. Angrily, I jerk at the handle, but it's locked once again.

ONCE I GET into the office this afternoon, my first call is to the VA. It takes me about twenty minutes, but I finally get transferred to someone who can help me. Sort of.

"I'd like to find out some statistics—say, the number of soldiers who return from active duty overseas and seek counseling for mental and physical issues."

"Medical records are private."

"I get that. I just need some numbers. I don't need to see actual files from individual soldiers."

"I'm going to have to get back to you."

She takes my name and number. I don't hold my breath. Instead, I immediately fill out a Freedom of Information Act form and fax it to her office, to her attention.

Before I log off, I check my e-mail. My fingers freeze on the keyboard.

Another e-mail from FA2858. Subject line: *He does not hear you.*

Inside, the e-mail reads, *Isaiah 59:2—But your iniquities have separated between you and your God, and your sins have hid his face from you, that he will not hear.*

My heart pounds loudly in my ears. My fingers are shaking as I forward the e-mail to the detective. If I don't hear from him by next month, I'm going to stake out his office until he gives me some answers.

I FILL UP my gas tank and point my car south.

Khoury hasn't gotten back to me with the name of the recruiter who called her, but Liz says the main recruitment office for San Francisco is south of the city, in Mountain View. It's a pain in the ass to get there, but worth a shot. I'm afraid if I just make a phone call, I won't get anywhere. Better to ask the tough questions in person.

The office is crammed in between a video game store and a dry-cleaning business in a strip mall, of all places.

It's 2:40 p.m. Of course there is a little clock on the window saying they will return at 3:00 p.m. I pull out my reporter's notebook and start listing everything I know about the Mission Massacre and questions I have:

Carol Abequero is arrested for Mission Massacre.
Joey Martin attacked me in his apartment.
Saw Joey Martin at wife's memorial service.
Sensei acting hinky, seems afraid to talk.

Dojo and sex club connect Javier and Martin.

Javier's death was done in same manner as Martin family.

Is the kubaton Martin dropped actually evidence?

Mrs. Castillo thinks Joey did it.

Maria was afraid.

Who else would know Martin?

The military is lying for Martin. Why?

I look at the list and feel overwhelmed and hopeless—it's a bunch of unrelated facts that don't seem to add up to anything.

I call Lopez to pick his mind about how to cajole information out of a U.S. Army recruiter.

"You're S.O.L., man. They aren't going to tell you jack."

"You don't think I can sweet-talk him?"

"Giovanni, you could probably convince a dead man to start dancing, but this is a whole different animal."

I chew on that for a few seconds. Great.

Right before three, a car pulls up. A big American car with shining hubcaps, exactly what I'd expect a recruiter to drive. But the driver is not someone I expect to see. It's the man who was comforting Abequero's mom at the funeral.

"Whoa." I breathe the word into the phone as an exhalation.

He walks by, glancing around. I slouch down in my seat for a few seconds until he unlocks the door, takes down the clock sign, and turns on the lights.

"Whoa what?" C-Lo asks.

"Is it normal for a recruiter to attend the funeral of some soldier he recruited?"

"No way, man. All we are to those bozos is a number, a quota that needs to be filled."

A quota. "Would it be normal for him to make arrangements for a soldier to come back home on leave from overseas?"

"Man, why don't you sit tight? I'm on my way. Sounds like that recruiter is going off the rails. That's not something he'd even *be able* to do if he wanted."

"I'm in Mountain View. By the time you get here, I'll be done. But thanks anyway. Call you when I finish." I click off. It's not like the guy will hurt me in broad daylight in some strip mall. The buzz of a helicopter sounds overhead, but when I peer out my windshield, I don't see anything.

I count to ten and open my car door. *Let's do this.*

The door chimes loudly as I enter. I give the guy a big grin, as if he never gave me the stink eye at the funeral.

"Good afternoon!" I chirp.

His face is deadpan.

"How can I help you?" He eyes my high heels. Definitely not G.I. Jane material. Better cut to the chase.

"I'm Gabriella Giovanni with the *Bay Herald* newspaper. We're working on a story about soldiers who return home from Iraq." I pause. "I've heard you really care about the soldiers you recruit." His expression does not change. "I'd like to ask you a few questions."

I pause again. He continues to stare.

"Soldiers returning home from Iraq are facing some unique challenges," I go on. "They leave a highly charged environment, where they are essentially forced to be on high alert nearly twenty-four hours a day, to come back home to, in some cases, a wife and children in a serene subdivision. I know there are services out there to help these soldiers, and I'd like to do a story about those, but maybe also we can bring light to the fact that additional services and resources are probably needed."

I come up for air after my spiel, and Rambo hasn't even blinked.

"Some of these things which the military might be a bit hesitant to bring to light might find support and funding if the public puts pressure on the politicians." I know I'm babbling, but I go on. "In other words, Mr. . . ." I squint, trying to see his name on a pin. ". . . Johnson?"

"Sergeant Jameson," he says stiffly.

"Mr. Jameson, if I put it in the paper, it can help your boys."

It's the longest speech I've given since college. The room is silent. I hear the gurgling of the water cooler and the hum of a tiny refrigerator in the corner. He sits as still as stone.

Crossing my arms across my chest, I wait for him to respond. He's a tough nut to crack, but I'm good at this game.

We stare at each other. I raise one eyebrow and give the slightest nod. *I can do this all day, buddy.*

Finally, when I'm nearly about to throw in the towel, he clears his throat.

"Mrs. Genovese—" I can see by his smug smile that he knows he has my name wrong and he knows that two can play at this game.

"Giovanni. Miss."

"Miss Giovanni, as I'm sure you must realize, my hands are tied. While I appreciate your . . . concern . . . for our soldiers, I am not authorized to speak to the media. We have an entire division dedicated to this. In fact, we probably have some of the best-trained media experts in the country. I know they would be happy to help you."

"Yeah, I have a Freedom of Information request in. What I need to do is talk to you about our local soldiers and what you've seen here in the Bay Area. I'm sure you have more authority than you let on."

Okay, I admit I'm slightly buttering him up, appealing to his vanity. But it doesn't work.

He gives an exaggerated sigh. "I wish I did."

I'm tired of acting like we didn't see each other a few hours ago.

"I saw you at this morning's funeral— Abequero's. Is it normal for recruiters to comfort the grieving family of the soldiers they recruit?"

"Ah." He leans back, as if that explains everything. "That was an unusual situation. Abequero's mother and I went to high school together. The least favorite part of my job is hearing about the deaths of the men and women I recruit. I deeply regret when circumstances turn out this way."

"What do you think went on there? Did you know his wife, as well?"

"I can't comment on that." I remember that as far as the public is concerned, Abequero committed suicide.

"What about Abequero's death," I say. "It seems that other soldiers returning from Iraq have suffered from depression and committed suicide. Can you tell me what type of screenings, mental, physical, and otherwise, people go through before they enlist? It sounds like they don't always pick out issues that might surface later? Does this system need to be improved?"

The annoyance that flashes across his face is quickly masked.

"That is a question that has been tossed around for years in the branches of the military. We keep trying to refine and perfect the screenings, but alas, sometimes people who are clever at taking the tests slip through. Not often, though. I'd say that Sergeant

Abequero was an anomaly. I've known him since he was in grade school and never would have expected this."

Of course that's how he'll play this. An anomaly. A fluke.

"What about these cases in Kentucky? Suicides? Domestic violence? Maybe even a homicide?"

His eyebrows knit together in a concerned frown. "Not familiar with those. I tend to focus on my own recruits."

"Would it be possible for me to look at a sample of some of the screenings and tests potential recruits must go through?" I don't blink, waiting for his answer.

"Of course." He reaches down into a drawer. I can't help but be suspicious. How come he'll turn this over so easily? I'm not surprised when he draws out a sheet and hands it to me, along with his business card.

"Here's a list of the people you could contact to send your FOIA requests to. And here's my card if you have any follow-up questions."

I clear my throat as I stand. As a reporter, you learn to lob the soft balls early on and save the tough questions for last.

"How did you know Joey Martin was coming home from overseas if you are only his recruiter? Is that a special case, as well?" It's a gamble. I don't even know if he's the man who recruited Martin.

His eyes turn steel gray. I wonder if I imagine the dangerous glint I see, because it so quickly disappears as a huge smile spreads across his face.

"That's confidential. I'm restricted from speaking about that particular situation, miss. You must excuse me now. I am expecting an important phone call."

His smile disappears as he watches me leave.

Chapter 31

Getting onto the 101 Freeway, I'm stuck in traffic, at a dead stop. Several squad cars zip by me on the shoulder with lights on. Must be a crash. I flip on my police scanner to the CHP channel and dial Lopez. "He totally shut me down." I tell him about my conversation.

"Man, you think you can go up against the U.S. Army?" C-Lo says. "I know you're a tough one, but this is a little out of your league."

"I don't know what to do." I close my eyes. I want to keep this girl from going to her dad.

The line is silent. From the scanner, which is turned on low, I can hear the CHP talking in the background about a minor injury crash on the freeway that they are about to clear, opening all traffic lanes.

"Whatever you do, I got your back, man," C-Lo said.

"You rule."

"Later."

THE REST OF the afternoon drags. I try calling Mrs. Castillo but always get voice mail. After leaving three messages, I don't bother leaving any more.

For a split second, I worry that she isn't answering her phone because something bad happened to her, but she probably is just ignoring me, since I'm not helping her get her granddaughter. It sounds like Khoury is keeping tabs on her anyway.

Feeling like it's useless, I fax another interview request to the San Francisco Jail. I'm sure the San Francisco police threatened Carol Abequero, telling her that if she spoke to me, things would be much worse for her. Not that they could get much worse. Accused of murdering a family of five pretty much tops it.

I wait until dark to visit the dojo because the sensei obviously doesn't keep banker's hours. I'm supposed to meet Donovan at my place in an hour to go to dinner.

This time when I ring the doorbell to the dojo, it clicks open immediately.

My body is hyper-alert as I trudge up the stairs, and the hairs on the back of my neck are tingly in anticipation of what awaits me at the top. The door into the dojo easily swings open. I look around to make sure Ninja Dude doesn't ambush me again. I can still feel the cold steel on my neck. Instead, I'm greeted by a class practicing.

Fluid movements seem synchronized as the lines of men in black thrust and kick and bow. It is poetry in motion.

At first I stand, but then I sink into a chair, mesmerized. Their movements are pure art. Their bodies flowing so smoothly, even their falls, are artful, a graceful roll and an easy leap back to their feet.

I'm so caught up in watching that I don't realize a man is by my side. The sensei.

"Maybe you should try? Our beginner's class meets on Monday nights. These are the black belts."

"How long does it take to achieve this level of expertise?" I ask.

"It depends on the student and level of practice, skill, and commitment. Some . . . never. Others, within four to five years. A few? In eighteen months."

I turn and stare at him. His eyes are deepest black. They are shining passion. But I'm not here to talk about martial arts.

"Joey Martin was in town when his family was murdered." At those words, his eyes grow flat again. I push on. "I've seen him. The question is whether you have? If you have, you are protecting and covering up for a murderer. A man who slaughtered his entire family."

He acts like he doesn't hear me. He turns away, addressing the members of the class, who are wiping their faces with small white towels and chatting in small groups. "I'm canceling the free time for tonight. I forgot I have an appointment, so I'll be closing up in the next few minutes."

Irritation swarms through me. He's trying to avoid this conversation, isn't he? He's kicking us out? Well, I'm not leaving that easily. To emphasize my point, I remain sitting. Reaching for my bag, I take out a nail file and start working on my nails, ignoring everyone around me. Vaguely, I notice the students leave, filing by me, speaking in low voices. Finally, it is silent. When I glance up, the sensei is watching.

"Now we can talk," he says. "Would you like some tea?"

He gestures toward a small doorway. I nod and stand.

"He is a dangerous man," he says, handing me a steaming mug of green tea.

"Anyone who kills his wife and parents probably isn't Mister Rogers. And I think he killed your student, Javier."

I take a sip of my tea, watching his face. We are sitting at a small wooden table in the tiny kitchen. Another door must lead to his bedroom and bath. He said he lives here at the dojo. A vase contains some long, thin pussy-willow branches.

He plucks some out, wraps the stems with a small piece of leather, and hands them to me. "It is good luck to keep these in your home."

"Javier is a bit interesting to me," I say. "Young kid with a nice pad in Alameda who worked as a DJ, but dressed like a Hong Kong executive and liked to hang out here in his free time. Am I right so far?"

His nod is nearly imperceptible.

"Anything else I'm missing?"

He looks around, as if he's afraid someone might be crowded in the small room with us, eavesdropping. He even stands and pokes his head out the door to the dojo before sitting back down and saying so low I nearly miss it, "They were friends."

Friends? Javier and Martin. Bingo.

"How did they meet?" I push on.

"That is all I know. He brought Javier here one day last year. But I didn't really get to know him—Javier. He kept to himself. Came to class late usually and left early, before anyone else."

"Joey Martin." I watch him quickly take a sip of his tea. "You might be the only one who can prove he was here. The United States Army—heck, a general, for God's sake—claims Joey Martin was in Iraq the day his wife and parents were murdered. You and I both know that isn't true."

I pause, trying to gauge his reaction to this. His face is stone. I try to appeal to his sympathies.

"You can help protect that child. She'll be turned over to him a week from today. You have to stop it. You have to help me. You have to tell the police what you know."

"It is not for me to say."

"That's a total cop-out." I narrow my eyes at him.

He presses his lips tightly together.

"Why won't you admit it? He was here. I saw him. Why can't you just say that?"

He looks away, and I see something in his eyes. Shame.

"You're afraid." I know I'm right, because I see his Adam's apple as he swallows. He's making a decision.

"I have a niece," he says after a long pause. His eyes meet mine. He folds and unfolds a small napkin as he speaks. "She is the most precious thing in my life. Her father, my brother, is dead. Drug overdose. His death is my fault. I should have taken better care of him."

"Taken care of him?"

"I am older by only two years. But I raised him. We came from China as parachute children when we were ten and twelve."

"Wait," I interrupt. I remember reading a book by crime writer Denise Hamilton about wealthy Chinese kids raised by nannies while their parents remained working and living in Hong Kong and China. "You were a parachute kid?"

He nods solemnly. "My brother went wild. He got into drugs. Then he met his wife. The love of his life. When she got pregnant, he straightened out. Went into rehab. But the pull was too strong. One night he went looking for more meth and got some bad drugs. He died from it. I am now the closest thing my niece will know to a father. She is the only piece of him I still have. I failed him. I allowed him to get addicted to drugs. Now, because of me, he is dead. I owe him this much. I have devoted my life to her now. His only child."

His guilt hangs in the air between us.

"It's not your fault," I say. "You shouldn't have been expected to raise a child when you were a child yourself."

He waves away my sympathy. "It is not relevant. What matters now is my niece and her well-being."

"Are you worried that if you say something, Martin will come after you or your niece? Maybe the police can do something to protect her?"

He shakes his head, and his eyes are filled with hopelessness. "They cannot."

"If he's locked up for the rest of his life, he can't hurt her, right?"

"It is not that simple."

The words sink in.

"Who does Martin know? Who *is* he? Why is he so dangerous? He's just a man, right?"

The sensei shrugs and looks out the window.

"Right?" I repeat.

"I need to go—I am expected by my sister-in-law and niece for dinner soon."

I understand the fierce need to protect family, especially a vulnerable niece, but the sensei might be the only way to prove that Joey Martin is a mass killer. I scribble my cell-phone number on one of my business cards. "If you change your mind, call me. And you should know, I have to tell the detective what you've said. That you know Martin was here but are too scared to say anything. I have to."

"Do what you must. Follow your heart. I cannot tell you otherwise." He says it so quietly that I almost don't hear him.

I slip out the door, shutting it softly behind me while he stays staring out the window at nothing.

Chapter 32

WHEN I UNLOCK the door to my apartment, the first thing I see is the look on Donovan's face. He's sitting at my kitchen table, drumming his fingers on the wood. A tumbler full of golden liquid sits next to the bottle of bourbon. He downs the glass while I watch from the doorway. He doesn't wait for me to set down my bag or take off my jacket. I prepare myself for something I won't like.

"I'm worried about you," he says.

He doesn't look angry, just sad. Disappointed.

"I try to give you your space, let you do what you need to do, but I'm worried you are becoming obsessed." His voice is gravelly, as if confronting me is costing him. Or that maybe his disappointment in me is painful. I swallow what seems like a wad of cotton stuck in my mouth.

"I understand you need answers to what happened to your sister. I get that. But I also don't want it to interfere with you being able to live a normal life."

I collapse onto the couch. Dusty hops up with me, but I push him away. How does Donovan know I haven't given up searching for Frank Anderson? He would never go into my computer. I trust him to respect my privacy. But he is a detective. He must have found out somehow. I think about what he said: "a normal life."

"I'm sorry, Sean. I don't know if I can live a normal life."

He runs his fingers through his already messy hair. "Fine. But you can at least try to live a healthy life. One where you are eating and sleeping and not trying to destroy yourself with your obsession."

I sit up straighter. "I admit I have been doing a little digging every once in a while to see if Anderson pops up somewhere. But just a little. I promise you that I'm not manic about it." *Like I was.* "I am keeping feelers out to find him. I'm not convinced that detective is doing a damn thing."

"I'm not, either," Donovan says in a low voice.

"Donovan, I am still hunting Caterina's killer. I'm not sure I can ever stop doing that."

Saying it and meaning it and laying it out there like this feels good. I lift my chin as I say it. *This is who and what I am. Take it or leave it.* And as the words stream through me, I am certain of them. I can't change who I am for someone else. I wanted to—I wanted to be a normal girlfriend. But I'm not normal. My sister was kidnapped and killed by a monster. I can't deny that. Or forget it.

"You're right about the detective," Donovan says. "I'll check into it."

He pours another two fingers of bourbon and downs it without speaking. I can smell the alcohol from here. He stands. Is he leaving? A chill runs through me that has nothing to do with my open balcony door—it's sadness and resignation. I can't change my history.

"There's something else." He shrugs on his jacket.

My face flushes.

"I believe you when you say you are only 'keeping feelers' out on Anderson." I'm holding my breath, waiting for his next words. "You may not realize this yet, so this might sound blunt: Your obsession with Frank Anderson? You've surpassed that."

Donovan is at the door now, his fingers turning the doorknob.

My forehead scrunches in confusion.

"Now you're obsessed with getting pregnant *and* that baby on top of everything else," he says.

But he's wrong. I'm not obsessed. When I was covering the Jasmine Baker kidnapping and murder, I drank myself silly every night and even lost my job. I've got it together now. I'm even covering other stories at work. And just because I take my temperature every day does not mean I'm obsessed with getting pregnant. But in a dark recess of my mind, I know he's touched on something I don't want to admit even to myself.

"Look at yourself. Take a good, honest look at yourself." He points toward the mirror by my door. "Your clothes don't fit. You've had dark circles under your eyes for weeks. You don't even seem to like food anymore. . . . You're not yourself. You are not the Gabriella I met two years ago."

He's not done.

"And, frankly, our sex life . . . the last few times, well, it leaves something to be desired." He looks away after he says it.

I sputter to respond, jumping to my feet, indignant.

"What are you talking about? I want to have sex all the time." *When I'm ovulating.* "You're the one who keeps turning me down. How do you think that makes me feel? Not attractive, that's how it makes me feel. My fiancé doesn't even want to have sex with me, so how am I supposed to feel?"

"It's not making love."

I squint at him. What?

"It's like anyone will do. You've turned it into a clinical, cold, scientific procedure. It is not working for me. At all. I'm not just some sperm donor."

"I never said you were." As soon as I say it, I realize he's right. Our lovemaking has turned into a task for me and—worse—a chore for him. Is it because I've let my resentment toward him grow until it has blossomed into a prickly wall between us?

And I don't know what to do about it. I stare at him, horrified.

"I'm only bringing this up because I'm worried about us," he says. "And I'm worried about you. I'm worried that this time—with everything that has happened recently—I'm worried that this time your obsession will do you in. You aren't yourself, and you're flirting with danger.

"You are pushing me away—right when I think you need my support the most. I need to be part of this and part of your life, and that means you need to include me in what you do. Don't hide shit from me. I'm not stupid, and I'm not naïve. I know that things haven't been perfect, but you have to let me in. I'm on your side. Don't fucking treat me like a child. I'm your partner, your equal, and you need to treat me that way if you want this relationship to stand a chance."

He opens the door and walks out, leaving me alone.

After staring at the wall for two hours, I finally dial his number and confess to him my furtive searches for Frank Anderson and the e-mails I've received. And he tells me how he found out I haven't given up my search for Frank Anderson—Liz called.

"Your phone rang. I didn't pick it up, but I heard the voice message. Liz from the newspaper. A hit on someone who might be Frank Anderson. You'll want to give her a call."

He hangs up without saying good-bye.

Chapter 33

"It's him."

Khoury doesn't need to identify herself. It's early, and I'm still in bed, putting off getting ready. Tossing and turning over my argument with Donovan last night did not bode well for an early start. He's angry, and I don't blame him. But I'm angry, as well. I can't change for him. He knew what he was getting into when we started dating.

"The prints were a match," Khoury says. "And the kubaton has blood spatter from his wife, his father, and his nephew. All on that little piece of metal. I think it might have been attached to his belt during the attack."

Blood spatter? She tested it for blood spatter. Not just fingerprints. And found evidence. She believes me. "Thank God," I say, hopping out of bed. I begin filling my moka pot with water and ground coffee. "So, he *was* there. He *was* in town. I did see him. But how do we prove it?"

She graciously ignores me saying "we."

"I'm officially 'off' the case since the arrest," she says. "But I haven't let go of it for one second—something about Carol Abequero struck me as wrong from the beginning. She didn't kill all those people. My gut tells me that, even though the evidence is so strong against her."

I don't know why I'm so relieved to hear it. It would be better for Lucy if her father *were* innocent. Holding the phone between my ear and shoulder, I rummage in my breadbox for some leftover baguette. "What evidence?"

"Something solid on her. But I think there is a good chance she's being framed. It was almost too damn easy."

"Can you tell me what they have on her?" I hold my breath, but I know she's going to spill it, because somewhere along the line it became "us" against "them."

"I'm not even supposed to talk to the press. I sure as hell can't give you confidential police information that will make or break a case."

"Oh, come on." I slam the breadbox shut. "Who are you protecting? You know you need me on your side. When this whole thing is blown out of the water, you'll be the hero. I'll splash your picture all over the front page."

It almost sounds like she laughs. "The sword."

"You're shitting me."

"In her backyard. Buried in the dirt. Her fingerprints were the only thing found on it besides the victims' blood."

"How the hell would they plant evidence or fake that?" I stick a slice of bread in the toaster oven and pour some milk into a pot on the stove.

"Believe me, they could do it," Khoury says. "Think about it. Whoever can get the U.S. Army to lie to the police department can surely plant evidence pointing to her. Here's the thing.

There is some blood on it—still determining whether it is the victims' blood—and her prints, but the thing is brand new. It had a sticky spot, like there had been a price tag recently removed. I don't think it's the same sword that killed the Martin family."

In the kitchen, the water is percolating. The apartment has that fresh coffee smell I love so much. I pour myself an espresso and add the hot milk. Now that Khoury believes me and is on my side, I tell her everything, including what Moretti's friend in Iraq said—how Martin was part of the most elite military organization the country has and that he was supposed to be *persona non grata*. "But Lieutenant General Cooper was told to tell anyone who asked that Martin was on base," I finish.

"Motherfucker." She clears her throat. "It all makes sense. My father is ex-Army. Big shot in the Army. He made some calls. His buddies were afraid to talk, but finally he got a hold of one, who said that Joey Martin has been AWOL since before the murders."

"Is this on the record?"

"I'm afraid not. I'm looking into it more. I have no idea why I'm telling you any of this. You're the media."

Instead of answering, I rinse out my coffee cup. I know why she's telling me. She needs someone on her side. But I don't say this. Instead, I make light of it.

"I'm not *the media*. Do I have big hair, stilettos, and a truckload of makeup on? No? Those are the TV reporters. I'm newspaper. We have ethics. Haven't you heard about reporters going to jail to protect their sources? Well, you're one of my sources. You're good."

"Still." She is quiet for a second, probably mentally kicking herself for talking to me at all. "And I'm not telling you all this because I want some glory in the paper when I'm proven right. I'm trusting you because of Sean."

I'll take it.

"And you should know Sean called me. Whoever pulled you over that day wasn't one of ours. Somebody has something to prove with you. So why don't you let us do our job?" She doesn't say it in a mean way, either.

But I don't need her advice.

"Thank you for your concern, but I can handle myself." I change the subject. "What next?"

There is silence for a few seconds.

"Arrest the real killer."

My first stop in the newsroom is Liz, who usually works Saturdays. Donovan is working today, and there's no way I can stay home when I know Joey Martin is going to take custody of Lucy in six days unless I do something about it.

"Hi, sugar," she says, peering at me over her glasses. "So, got this hit on what might be Frank Anderson. It was in L.A.—woman and her boyfriend came home early from a trip, dropped off their luggage, and went out to dinner. When they came home, saw someone standing in their kitchen window. Her boyfriend freaked out, screaming, and the man slipped out the back door. But in the bedroom, they found a bunch of her underwear missing. Here's a copy of the police report. He didn't leave any prints, either, which makes it seem like he's done this before, so it might be Anderson even though the victim wasn't a child and he didn't do his . . . you know . . . usual thing."

Masturbating on the panties.

"Thanks, Liz."

"Not so fast," she says. "I couldn't find a damn thing on that Carol Abequero, though. It would help if we knew her maiden name. Looks like she married in Mexico, but there's no record of her under her married or maiden name."

Damn.

My next stop is Kellogg, who doesn't usually work Saturdays but is busy overseeing coverage of game six of the World Series while the sports editor is at the ballpark. If the San Francisco Giants win today against the Anaheim Angels, it's all over.

"Got a sec?"

It takes him a minute to look up from his green screen. "Yeah, sure."

"Can we talk in the conference room?" He reluctantly eyes the big-screen TV. It's only pregame coverage. He has another hour before the first pitch.

The desk creaks as he pushes his chair back and stands, grabbing his cup of coffee and some papers. My heart is pounding for no reason, and I sense eyes boring into my back as we walk.

I shut the door. He relaxes into a swiveling chair at the head of the table and starts pivoting in his seat. He's anxious to get this over with, I can tell.

"Sorry for the dramatics, but I don't want anyone else to overhear."

"They can't help it. Reporters are naturally nosy." He raises an eyebrow. "Not excluding present company."

Fair enough.

"I might have a lead on the Mission Massacre killer."

He stops swiveling. "Go on."

"I think it's the husband."

"They made an arrest, Giovanni." He gives a big sigh but hasn't stood up yet. He strokes his beard and continues. "Let me get this straight. We're talking about the same husband, right? The one alibied by the military?" Anyone else would have said it with a heavy dose of doubt and sarcasm, but Kellogg says it plainly, and this encourages me to go on.

"Even the lead detective says this might be the tip of the iceberg. That the military is lying for some bigger reason." Khoury didn't say that *exactly,* but that's where she was going. He waits without fidgeting. "And there is evidence. I found this thing, this military weapon, called a kubaton. She ran it for prints and blood. His prints. His wife, nephew, and father's blood."

"This is good stuff, Giovanni. What's next?" He takes a sip of his coffee and glances at the clock on the wall.

"We wait to see what Khoury does with this evidence. Meanwhile, how will I go after the military?"

He squints and frowns. Finally, he shakes his head. "I don't know. But I think your instincts are right. If they are lying for this guy, there is probably a reason, a reason that could get you killed. Didn't the sheriff grant you a permit to carry and conceal last year?"

"Yes." But I'm not carrying a gun ever again if I can help it. If you have a gun, it means you're willing to kill someone.

"Well, you probably want to be packing," he says. "I don't like any of this, and I don't know exactly what to do about it right now."

I was afraid he'd say that. I was hoping he could give me some direction. Unlike some editors, Kellogg rose up from the trenches of cops reporting after years of covering corruption in South Central L.A., where he grew up. If anyone could come up with a good idea to prove the military wrong, it'd be him. But he has nothing.

"And really, when you think about it, going after the military on this will be the cops' job, as well," he finally says. "The most you can hope for is to be on the inside, to be the first reporter to get the scoop."

"Yeah," I say, but I'm disappointed. I want more than just the scoop. I want to prove the military lied to the police, and I want to know why.

Chapter 34

THROUGHOUT SUNDAY DINNER at Nana's, I catch my mother looking at me across the crowded table. Her forehead is crinkled with worry. There are about twenty of us sprawled at the tables stretched under the grape arbor and nestled along the patio. My mom and I are at different tables, and despite the uproarious laughter and conversation, I can tell she is not happy. Every time our eyes meet, I smile and look away and take a bite of my pasta or bread. But I'm not fooling anyone.

By the time the tiramisu and cannoli have made the rounds, I'm a bundle of nerves, anxious for the showdown with my mother. I pick at my mom's chocolate chip cannoli, something I normally eat with relish. When we're in the kitchen cleaning up after the meal, Donovan darts a glance at me and catches me sliding the cannoli into the trash.

Most of the afternoon is spent huddled around the TV watching game seven of the World Series. When the Giants lose, the mood grows somber, and the men all gather to inspect Nana's house.

Every year, my uncles and brothers and cousins weatherproof Nana's house for the winter. Nana has lived alone here for years and does quite well on her own in the sprawling stone house surrounded by vineyards. She spends her days tending her flowers and giant backyard vegetable garden. Every fall, family members show up on a certain Sunday to rake leaves, clean her gutters, and do any necessary upkeep and handiwork. It's an annual October tradition.

After most people have gone home, my sister-in-law Sally and I finish washing and drying the dishes. Nana hovers so she can oversee where everything goes. Giving her a supervisory role is the only way we can stop her from doing the dishes herself. She already spends every Saturday making giant vats of sauce. It was only a few months ago that we finally talked her out of making the meatballs herself.

Now, several of us grandchildren take turns spending Saturday afternoons forming ten pounds of beef into dozens of meatballs to feed the family. It has quickly become a tradition that the kids in the family love. Not only do they get to spend a few precious hours alone with Nana but she always saves a half pound of the meat to make the kids *polpettines*—mini meatballs that are salted right out of the frying pan and popped into mouths for a delicious treat.

When it's time to leave, my mother follows me out to my car. "Do you have a second?" she asks. I was silly to think I could avoid this conversation. "I'm worried about you." She presses her lips tightly together.

"Mama, I'm fine." I lean back against my car, feeling the warmth of sun-warmed metal against my back.

"That clearly is not true." She flings her arms toward me in frustration. "Have you taken a good look at yourself lately?"

I look past her over her shoulder at some vines creeping up the side of my grandmother's house. She's right. I was in the bathroom a few minutes ago and caught a glimpse of myself in the mirror. My brown hair is lank and lackluster. My skin's sallow, my eyes sunken, with purple bags. My clothes are droopy and ill-fitting. Yeah. I look like shit. What does she expect?

"I'm fine, Mama. I'm just dealing with some stuff." Donovan and I agreed to not tell my mother about the miscarriage. And I'm glad. Her heartbreak over it would have made everything that much worse.

"Dealing with what stuff? If this is what your job does to you, you need to seriously consider changing careers. It's not just about you anymore. You have a man who loves you now, and you need to take his feelings into consideration."

He talked to her about me, didn't he? The heat creeps across my cheeks. I catch a glimpse of Donovan trying to make his way outside Nana's house—one foot inside, one out. When I left, he was politely trying to say good-bye to one of my uncles who was telling a tale about the San Francisco Giants.

"Mama, I'm fine." If I say it enough times, will she believe me?

"I think you need to see a doctor."

"I'm going to see Marsha. Soon."

"I mean a physical doctor. A physician. I'm worried about you. We all are."

Donovan did talk to her.

"Mama"—I turn to her and hold her hands—"I haven't felt like myself lately. But as soon as I find the man who killed that family, I'll be fine. I just need to find who killed them. I just need to make sure that he's punished."

I've said something wrong. My mother draws back with a frightened look on her face.

"Listen to yourself, you—"

"Ma," I interrupt.

"Let me finish." Her voice is firm, and I close my mouth. "Take a minute and listen to yourself. Donovan was right. You are obsessed with this case. You need to take a vacation. If I have to, I'll call your boss."

"Editor."

"Editor. Whatever." She throws her hands in the air. "I'll call him and tell him you need some time off."

A smile grows wider on her face as she warms to the idea. "In fact, that's exactly what you need. I'll call Dina at the travel agency first thing tomorrow. I'm sending you and Donovan on a vacation together. That's what you need. That will do wonders for you. When is the last time you took a vacation?"

I shrug. I know it's useless to try to resist her plans now, when she's on a roll. I'll just let her talk, let her think she has it all figured out, and then be too busy to take the vacation. A small part of me worries that she can convince Kellogg, but I'll try to get to him first.

Chapter 35

My mood matches the gray skies seeping out of San Francisco this morning. And not simply because it's a Monday. The wind is whipping and howling and moaning when I wake, filling me with unease. Even Dusty is acting freaky, sort of like he does before an earthquake, winding himself around my legs and then hiding under my bed.

It's almost as if something evil is nearby. Something isn't right, and some sixth sense is telling me to watch out, be wary. Logically, I know there's nothing tangible behind it, but I've been filled with unease since I woke. It's more than just knowing I have less than five days to keep Lucy out of her father's hands. It's something more—a simmering level of anxiety or foreboding I can't shed. I burn my toast and spill my coffee all over my front this morning and have to change clothes at the last minute.

It doesn't help that Donovan seems like he's avoiding me. We've eased into a truce since we had it out the other night, but things are still a little prickly. He picked up a shift last night and is planning on working another one tonight.

I'm heading toward the Caldecott Tunnel when I notice a helicopter above the freeway. Another one. The thudding of the helicopter sends a surge of anxiety through me. Some of Lopez's paranoia is rubbing off on me. I'm peering out my windshield, trying to see if the helicopter has any identifying information, when my cell rings. C-Lo.

Relief floods me when I see the helicopter has the emblem for the California Highway Patrol, probably monitoring traffic from an accident I passed a ways back.

"Lopez?"

"Yo badness. Where you at?" he asks.

"About to enter the third bore."

"Flip a bitch and head to the city. Got a one eighty-seven."

I frown. San Francisco isn't my beat. But Lopez wouldn't call if it weren't important. A wave of adrenaline hits me as I slam on my brakes and cut off several cars to make the last exit in Berkeley before the tunnel.

"What's the skinny?"

"Vic is five-o." He says it somberly.

A cop. Donovan. My heart leaps into my throat. I pull over on the side of the road as fear spurts through me, causing a wave of cold and dizziness. I press my forehead down on the steering wheel, but at his next word, my heart starts up again.

"SFPD."

San Francisco Police Department. I open my eyes. "What you got?"

"Inner Sunset. Twenty-first Street." *In the Aves.* "Walking her dog. Might have been a robbery gone bad. Bullet to the temple."

We haven't had an officer killed in the line of duty for about a year. And it's rare for a cop to die violently off the job, but it's still a major deal. I can already see the giant police funeral that will take place. What a shame. Now I know why Lopez called; any cop killed is a big story. Especially one who dies as a victim of a crime.

I exit and get back on Highway 24, headed toward San Francisco. The city lies before me. Rays of sunshine shoot up through a low haze of fog that hasn't yet burned off.

The Inner Sunset is an area of San Francisco that is almost always thickly cloaked in fog. It is not uncommon to go days there without seeing the sun. The address Lopez gives me is between Santiago and Rivera streets. I don't know a lot of female cops in San Francisco. Only Khoury. I don't even know if she lives in the city. A ripple of anxiety surges through me. *Don't be ridiculous. There are dozens of women cops in the city.*

THE CRIME-SCENE TAPE blocks off the entire block on both sides. When one of their own falls, the last thing cops want to do is talk to the press, but that doesn't stop at least six news trucks from parking at one end, their satellite antennas extended up into the fog.

As I pass for the fourth time, looking for a parking spot, I see Detective Jack Sullivan's red hair. That guy hates me. The feeling is mutual. He couldn't pin the mayor's murder on Donovan or me last year, and I know it drives him crazy. It made him look bad when we found the real killer, and I'm sure he hasn't forgotten that. I scan the cops for Khoury's petite frame and boyish hair but don't spot her. My mouth grows dry and a wave of anxiety floods me, but I reassure myself. I'm being paranoid.

Finally, I park a block away, near Abraham Lincoln High School. I pull on my gloves while I walk and wind my new turquoise scarf around my neck as the wind whips my hair around my face, stinging my cheeks.

Isn't this supposed to be the best time of year in San Francisco? The air is biting today, and the Inner Sunset, only three miles from the Pacific Ocean, is the worst for bitter cold and chill.

Most of the first floors of the houses contain storefronts, like the ones on this block—a Thai restaurant, a boutique, and an old-fashioned drugstore. The bay windows above are for the second-story flats. All the buildings are painted lemon and sky blue and peach. On the road closed off by crime-scene tape, waist-high wooden flower boxes line the sidewalks near the street, and several European scooters are parked on sidewalks. Despite the gray and cold, this neighborhood seems so friendly, cheery even. So why is there a knot in my stomach?

HOVERING AT THE edge of the crime-scene tape, I ignore all the TV reporters. Some are in their vans, staying warm. One extremely coiffed reporter in stilettos and a pencil skirt is ordering her photographer around, treating him like a lackey. No respect. I see Andy Black, my competition at the *Tribune,* but look away before he meets my eyes. Every time I see him, I regret our one-night stand with all my heart and wish I had been the one who'd given him a black eye that day instead of Donovan.

My cell vibrates in my bag. When I finally fish it out, I see it is Lopez.

"Where are you?" I ask.

"Look up and over at the third apartment building in from the corner."

I squint. Right at the edge of the lingering fog that hovers at the top of the building, I see a lithe figure dressed in black. He gives me a little wave.

"Sweet," I say. I clear my throat. "Can you see the vic?"

"I've got eyes on her." At these words, my heart catches in my throat. She's covered with a tarp, he says.

He keeps talking. "Some pissed-off cops down there. As soon as one notices me, I'm outta here. Today is one day you don't want to be on their bad side."

"No kidding. Have you figured out which place is hers?" I brush off my fear. The body could belong to any of a dozen female cops.

"Yeah. They've been going in and out. It's the dark green three-story."

"'Kay. Call you back in two."

I hang up and dial Liz, reading off the house address. "Can you run this house number and tell me who lives there?"

"Sure thing, sugar. Hold the line." I hear her click-clacking on the keyboard and close my eyes. *Please don't let it be her.*

"Here we go," Liz says. "Amanda Khoury, thirty-five, bought it last month for two hundred and fifty thousand dollars."

As soon as I hear the name, I close my eyes, and my stomach hurts like someone just sucker-punched me. And I know. It wasn't a robbery gone bad. My fingers are shaking as I thank Liz and click off. A wave of vertigo hits me, and I slump against the wall of an apartment building for a few seconds. My fingers are tingly, and the hair on my arms is sticking straight up. Khoury is dead.

What if she's dead because of what I told her? What I gave her? The kubaton? What if the killer is here watching me? Instinctively, I duck behind a TV van and lean back against it. After a few seconds, I peek out, watching the cops circling the crime scene, trying to see if any are paying attention to me. I freeze when I see one cop standing motionless, watching me. He holds my gaze for a few seconds, and a chill races across my scalp.

Finally, another cop is at his elbow, saying something. The first one waits another second before he turns. As soon as I'm released from his stare, I bolt around the corner and press my back against the cold wall of an apartment building.

My phone rings.

"What the fuck is going on?" Lopez says.

"Did you see that?"

"Yeah, man. Lieutenant Stick-Up-His-Ass was staring you down. But what I don't get is why you ran?"

I fill him in.

"Motherfucker. That's some seriously fucked-up shit."

"I know."

"Hold the phone. Two cops just went inside. Let me use my zoom lens. I'll call you back."

After a few minutes, he calls back. "Your boyfriend Sully and the lieutenant are the only ones in the place."

I try to let go of my anger and listen to Lopez. " . . . throwing shit around like they're looking for something they can't find. They've trashed her place completely. I got a bunch of shots of them doing it. Why would they do that, when it was a robbery gone bad? Doesn't jive."

"What else can you see?" I ask.

"Crime-scene investigators just showed up. Hold on. Dude is kneeling down. Okay. He lifted the tarp. Not pretty. Closed casket for sure."

My heart sinks, and I close my eyes. I was just starting to really like Detective Khoury. She didn't deserve to die. Something else occurs to me: the case she was building against Martin—now what? She was the only cop who believed me. Now he'll grab Lucy and disappear, getting away with mass murder. There's no way I can trust Sullivan with what I know. He'd just as soon throw me in jail if I tell him I was in the apartment and found the kubaton.

Lopez's voice interrupts my thoughts.

"Okay. Another dude heading over to the body."

"What's he look like?"

"Six feet something. Good head of hair, brushed back, cop hair. More Ponch than John, though. Close-cut beard. Wire-rimmed glasses. Tall. Lean. Jeans and cowboy boots. Blazer. Got a detective badge clipped to his belt. Talking to the crime-scene guys now. Leaning over. Lifted tarp again. Oh fuck. He's broken up. He knew her. For sure, man. I'd bet ten to one he's the partner. Just closed his eyes for a second. He's pulling it together."

"Let me know when he heads back toward the tape. I'm making my way over there." I start to run, heading down the parallel street, hoping to make it around the block before Khoury's partner is kicked out. Because I'm sure that's what will happen. They will boot his ass out of there. They won't let him stick around and investigate the death of his partner. They'll throw him in counseling or something.

I round the corner, panting. I can see the crime-scene tape a few cars away.

Lopez calls. "He's ten feet from the tape."

"Thanks. I'm here."

The detective ducks his tall frame under the tape. I hear a shout. Someone must have called his name, because he pauses for a second without turning around and then keeps walking. I make my way to the opposite sidewalk and follow him, keeping a few cars behind.

When he stops at a small black sports car that he can't possibly fold his tall frame into, I make my move. I dart across the street.

"Detective?" His face is wary. I wonder what he looks like when he smiles. I speak fast, knowing I only have about thirty seconds to convince him to talk to me. "I'm the one who gave Khoury the kubaton."

"You're that reporter."

I meet his eyes and nod.

Now I will tell if he was on Khoury's side or Sullivan's.

He juts his chin toward his passenger door. I don't hesitate and hop in, slamming the door behind me. It smells like stale cigarette smoke and cologne. He closes the door and leans his forehead on the steering wheel. He grits out the words. "Goddamn it." He lifts his head and squints one eye at me.

"I'm so sorry for your loss." He acknowledges my words with a nod. The pain in his face makes me look away. When I can meet his eyes again, I stick out my hand. "Gabriella Giovanni."

"Scott Strohmayer."

"Thanks for talking to me, Detective Strohmayer."

"None of this adds up." He's tapping his fingers on his steering wheel, staring out the front window. "Why Amanda? No reason to kill her for her cash. She would've just handed over her bag. It'd be no great shakes to her. She's smart—she knows no amount of money is worth losing your life." He shakes his head.

This may be harder than I thought. I'll have to lay my cards on the table.

"Did Detective Khoury tell you she was still working the Mission Massacre? That she didn't think Carol Abequero did it?"

He looks over at me, surprised. "I've been out of town. Annual family vacation to Hawaii. Got back last night. She left a few messages, but we got back so late . . ."

I fill him in quickly, trusting my gut instincts that he's one of the good guys and not part of whatever landed Khoury under that tarp.

Staring out his windshield, he listens without moving. He takes off his glasses and rubs the ridge between his eyes.

I tell him what she told me the other day—that the kubaton had blood spatter from the victims and Martin's fingerprints.

He strokes his beard. "That's good, but that might not be enough. This whole thing is a screwy deal. Now I know why she wanted to meet with me today—away from the station."

He punches the steering wheel. My eyes sting, and I blink back tears. *Pull it together.*

I have one last question for him. "Why do you think Sullivan and the lieutenant are tossing her apartment right now? What are they trying to find?"

His eyes narrow. "Could be her notes on the case. Most of the time if she's working a big one, she carts everything around in that big bag of hers. She's only been here a short time, but everyone knows that Amanda takes her work home with her. It's her whole life. That's the kind of cop she is."

Was.

"If everyone knows she carries the files around, is that why she's dead?" I ask.

"I don't know, but I'm going to find out." His mouth is set in a grim, determined line, and I can tell by the furrow across his brow he's not kidding.

He turns the key in the ignition. That's my cue.

"Need a ride to your car?"

I shake my head no. I open the door and duck down to say good-bye.

He reaches over to his glove box, pops it open, and extracts a small gun, which he sticks in an ankle holster as I watch.

"I'm going to find out what the hell is going on," he says, as if that is an explanation.

I raise an eyebrow.

"Hey, my dad always said you get more with a kind word and a gun than with a kind word alone." He winks and peels out.

Chapter 36

BACK IN THE newsroom, I have a hard time writing the story about Khoury's murder. I want to do her justice, but that's going to have to be in another story. This one is just the facts. And there are so few of them. I didn't stick around for the press conference, but Lopez did and took notes for me. I have so many questions. Eventually I write a story, leaving out everything I suspect about her murder and can't prove.

The military is lying for Martin, and the cops are in on it. Khoury is dead because she was on to them. She must've found something incriminating, and that's why she's dead. Maybe the only thing saving me is my ignorance—the fact that I don't have any proof about Joey Martin or the military lying.

Because the truth is I have no way of proving anything. Khoury might have had a way to prove it, and now she's dead. If they think I know anything, I'm probably their next target.

Donovan asks me to stay the night at his Oakland apartment, saying he's worried that whoever killed Khoury might come after me. For once I don't think he's being overprotective. If the cover-up extends to the cop shop, to the detective who already has it out for me—Jack Sullivan—then I'm also a little apprehensive.

A few hours later, after I finally turn in my story about Khoury's murder and leave work, we are hunched over tzatsiki, baba ghanoush, and tabouli that Donovan brought home from the Holy Land deli. I know he is worried, so I gulp down most of my pita bread, but it tastes like cardboard. He's on his third beer, while I'm still sipping my first.

"If you're right and they took out a cop to protect this Martin guy, there's nothing to stop them from getting rid of you, too." He looks at me over his beer as he takes a long pull. "I didn't think your life was in danger until now. But now I'm not so sure. Whatever the military is hiding must be a pretty big deal for them to take out a detective in the middle of a big case."

"She was taken off the case."

"Gives me more reason to worry."

When Donovan hears about the cops searching Khoury's apartment, the muscle along his jawline starts pulsing, and his eyes narrow.

"Sullivan, huh?"

There is no love lost between him and the San Francisco detective. But I probably despise the man even more.

"That man is like a dog with a bone. He won't let go until he wreaks revenge on you."

I nod. He's right. I make a mental note to ask Liz if she can find out more about the redheaded cop. He's got to have some vulnerability, some Achilles' heel we can find and use to our advantage.

"So, what's this Strohmayer guy like?"

That was out of left field. "Nice guy." I shrug. "He said that everyone knows Khoury took her work home with her. There's motive right there."

"What's Khoury's lieutenant's name again?" Donovan asks.

"I don't know. I think Khoury said Alexander. Does that sound right?"

Donovan nods. "Dennis Alexander. I don't know much about him, only his name."

I'll ask Liz about him, too.

Donovan clears the dishes as I stand and gaze out at Lake Merritt before me. The downtown Oakland skyscrapers soar up into the crisp black sky beyond the lake. The walking path around the lake is strung with lights like a necklace, giving it a fairylike feel from my third-floor perch. I sense Donovan behind me before he wraps his arms around my waist and nuzzles his lips into my collarbone.

I remember what he said about sex being so clinical lately. I close my eyes and try to let my body respond to his touch, but I'm numb. My mind is racing with so many things: Lucy. Her father. Khoury. Sullivan. And underneath it all, lying like a big lump of mud, is the resentment I feel against Donovan for not wanting to get pregnant as badly as I do.

I can't get past it. He must sense my resistance, because soon the warmth of his body leaves mine and footsteps sound along the wood floor as he heads toward the bedroom.

The view of the lake strung with lights is blurry now, just streaks of smeared white.

Chapter 37

Detective Strohmayer calls me while I'm in the newsroom Wednesday.

"I'm in the East Bay," he says. "Got the day off, and I took the twins to Waterworld in Concord. Can you meet me here in a half hour?"

"You're brave."

"Hell, this is the safest waterslide park in the world. Now."

"Right. Now."

A few years ago, a group of graduating seniors from Napa ignored a lifeguard's warning and stormed the seventy-five-foot-tall slide. When they tried to ride down together in a massive pack, the slide collapsed, sending people plunging to the ground below. A seventeen-year-old girl died, and thirty other people were injured. Witnesses said the pool below became red with the blood of those injured.

I agree to meet him and log off my computer. I stop by Liz's desk on my way out of the newsroom. I owe her way more than a box of biscotti. As soon as I have time, I'm taking her out to dinner at Chez Panisse or something.

It's been two days since Khoury's death. Liz did some digging on Khoury's lieutenant.

Unfortunately, Dennis Alexander is pretty boring on paper. Lives in San Mateo. Owns a small house there. Has a wife and two teenage boys. Nothing interesting on him whatsoever.

The paper trail for Jack Sullivan is cold. There is nothing on file for him. Nada. Not even the usual paper trail of a birth certificate, driver's license information, or voter registration. It's like he's a ghost.

For some reason, that makes me worry.

But I'm more worried that Joey Martin is going to pick up Lucy in two days, and right now I don't see any cops trying to stop him.

STROHMAYER IS ON his cell phone by the bottom of the Dragon Tails body slide, a smaller, twisty slide for families. It's ninety degrees out. Unusually warm for October, plus it's a release day for Bay Area schools, so the waterpark is packed. Kids scream and shout, and lifeguards are blowing whistles, reminding people to behave and not run.

Strohmayer is wearing shorts and a bright blue shirt that makes his eyes light up when he sees me and smiles.

He finishes his conversation and clicks off his phone. "Sorry about that. The wife. She's got a roller derby bout tonight and is making sure I'm able to watch the kids."

I don't know why this makes me jealous. That he's married, or that he has kids? Or both?

Two towheaded boys run up. "Dad! Dad! Can we go to Treasure Island now?"

"Yep. Head on over," he says, patting one of them on the head. "I'll follow."

"So your wife does roller derby?" I say as we walk to a picnic table near the Treasure Island pool, a watery playground with tunnels and fountains. "She sounds awesome. Roller derby isn't for sissies. "

"Let's sit here, that way I can keep an eye on the kids. Can't go home tonight and tell Mary one of them drowned, you know. My wife is understanding and all, but that probably wouldn't go over well." He settles in at a table facing the pool. "You're right, roller derby isn't for wimps. The last time I put on skates, it was ass over teakettle. Which, of course, Mary thought was hilarious. Sometimes it's hard to keep up with her. Every year it's something new—this year it'll be jumping out of airplanes."

"That's always been my dream." Of course I don't tell him that I planned on skydiving for my birthday this past summer but put that aside as I sank into a deep funk from my miscarriage.

"Hey, Toby," he says. "Quit splashing your brother." He turns his attention back to me. "Well, she's looking for a pal to skydive with her, but all her friends are chicken. Maybe I should introduce you two."

"That would be amazing." I watch as the two boys wrestle and dunk each other. He turns to me, and I'm afraid to take my eyes off his twins in case one of them drowns or hits his head or something when he's not looking.

He takes out a small wallet-size picture of his smiling wife and twin boys. "Here she is."

I hand it back to him. "I already like her," I say and mean it.

He pockets the photo and grows serious as we settle in. "I

called you because I think you're right," he says, taking a sip from a bottle of water.

"About what?" My cell phone rings. I glance down. Donovan. I mute my phone and ignore the call. There is no way I could hear him over the screams, shouts, and laughter at this waterpark.

"Amanda," he says. "That wasn't a robbery gone bad."

"What changed your mind?" I squint at the pool. For a second I couldn't see one of the boys, but then his head bobs up, like a seal's.

"The evidence is gone."

"What?" My mind goes blank. What is he talking about? I forget about keeping an eye on his twins and turn to face him.

"The kubaton."

Strohmayer explains that when he confronted Sullivan and Lieutenant Alexander, they brushed him off and told him that if he didn't mind his own business, he'd be back to working the patrol shift, nights.

"It's not an empty threat, either." He turns toward the pool and stands. "Matt, get over here and take a time out. I told you not to sit on your brother's head in the water."

Matt gets out and his brother follows. Both boys are crying. They sit on the cement near our feet, both pouting. "Six minutes starting now," Strohmayer tells them and turns to me. "A minute for each year of their life." I don't point out he doesn't have on a watch.

"So, after they threatened me, I figured it'd be smartest to just play their game. Play dumb. I told them I wanted them to find Khoury's killer and to let me know if I could help. Meanwhile, I've been doing some poking around myself. Found copies of most of Amanda's investigation. She must've known something was up, because she stashed a bunch of copies in a file we share for Fantasy Football. Smart lady. I got all the goods on the case except the results of the blood-spatter analysis and fingerprints."

My heart sinks when he says this. He doesn't appear to mind talking about blood spatter around his boys, who are now giggling and talking to each other.

"Six minutes up. Get on out of here and behave!" he says in a mock mean voice. Patting both boys as they run off, he winks at me. "So I thought I'd get the kubaton and requisition the work myself. Went in to ask for it, and bam, the kubaton was gone."

"I don't understand." My phone vibrates, and I look down. Donovan calling again. I ignore it.

"She checked it out the night before she was killed." The smile I saw earlier is gone. "Damn it, Amanda," he mumbles, wadding up his napkin. "What did you get yourself into?"

"If she checked it out, then she had it with her or at her place," I say. "It has to be somewhere, right? Unless another cop took it."

"Yep." He says it and is quiet, as if he's thinking about this.

"What?"

"Or what if she never had it in the first place? I can't see Amanda checking out evidence and bringing it home. Especially when she knows it's a lynchpin in her case. Doesn't make sense."

"If it didn't get checked out, where is it?" I can't wrap my mind around the idea that police evidence can just disappear.

A bloodcurdling scream from the pool makes me jerk my head to look. I immediately spot both boys' blond heads bobbing close together as the twins dip and swim, spitting water out of their mouths at each other.

"It got checked out, alright," Strohmayer says. "Just probably not by her. I think someone else forged her name after her death."

I tap my fingers on the white plastic picnic table. Evidence is missing from police custody.

"So, what now?"

"I don't know, but I'm going to find out."

"He's going to pick up Lucy on Friday. In two days." He knows I mean Joey Martin.

"I know."

"If evidence is gone, then that's proof this whole deal is an inside job, right?" I ask. "How do you know who to trust?"

"I guess I don't." He hands me his card. He's scribbled his home number and cell phone on it. "Keep in touch."

"How can we stop him?" I ask as I stand.

He presses his lips tightly together and shakes his head. He doesn't have the answer. The despair I feel at that gesture is quickly replaced by steel determination. I will stop Joey Martin, no matter what it takes.

As I walk out of the park, I think about Strohmayer's cute boys and his wife at home. If he's digging around and this is as corrupt as it appears, he's also risking his life. A small flicker of guilt washes over me. Is all this my fault? Is it all because *I'm* digging around?

Getting in my car, I see that I've missed three calls from Donovan. I wonder if it's an emergency and dial his number, but I only get voice mail.

"It's me. I was meeting with Detective Strohmayer. Hope everything's okay. Call me back."

I'm relieved that Strohmayer believes my theory that Khoury was taken out for what she knows, but I'm not sure it will help. What I do know is that Lucy will end up in the arms of a killer if we don't stop him. I have two days to prove Joey Martin was in town when his family was killed.

Chapter 38

Donovan is on his computer and barely looks at me when I come in. Maybe he's angry with me for the other night? I wanted so much to respond to his touch, but lately I'm as cold as stone around him.

"Busy day today?" I ask and lean over to kiss him while trying to get a glimpse at what he's looking at. It looks like he's writing a long e-mail.

"Huh?" He looks up like he just noticed me.

"You never called me back," I say.

"Oh, well I figured you were probably too busy hanging out with Detective Strohmayer."

"I left you a message that I'd finished meeting with him and was available to talk."

He doesn't answer. The muscle in his jaw gives him away. He's irritated.

"Are you jealous?"

He stands and closes the top of his laptop, turning his back to me. "I don't know what you're talking about."

"You're acting like this because I didn't want to be rude and answer my phone in the middle of an important conversation?"

He turns now and stares at me, pouring himself a tumbler of bourbon. "What do you want me to think?"

My eyebrows raise, and my mouth opens. *Are you kidding*?

"I want you to trust me. That's what I want."

He sighs and slumps onto the couch, taking a big sip of his drink before he answers. "I do trust you."

I wait for him to say more, but the silence stretches on for several seconds.

"What's going on?" I stand right before him so he has to look at me. I can't read the look he gives me.

"Let's not talk about this right now," he says, standing and grabbing his gun and wallet. He sticks his wallet in his back pocket and his gun in his side holster. "I've had a long day. I'll be crabby until I eat something."

We walk over to Mr. Sushi across the lake and eat dinner. Or, rather, Donovan eats. I eat a few pieces of a California roll but plead an upset stomach. Donovan downs several cups of sake and eats the entire fried green tea ice cream we usually share.

Back in his apartment, Donovan is slightly drunk, which surprises me. He's usually a man totally in control. He grabs me as I'm getting dressed for bed and kisses me so fiercely that my body responds wildly to him, filling me with relief. At the same time, I can't help but think it's such a waste.

Long afterward, as I lie in the dark next to his sleeping form, I'm empty, hollow. Even though the sex tonight was more like it used to be, there was something there between us, something nearly tangible, that separated us even as our bodies were as close as they could be. I'm not comfortable with the man I'm supposed to marry one day. The reality strikes me so hard that I have to choke back a sob. What has happened to us? I try to reassure myself that it's nothing. I tell myself that if I can only get pregnant, everything will be fine. But doubt swells within me. I push it way back into the furthest recesses of my mind.

Chapter 39

MARSHA BITES HER pencil as she watches me.

My heart speeds up. I know her enough to be able to tell she is about to say something I don't want to hear.

I've spent the past hour confiding in her. About my secret sleuthing to find Frank. About hiding the e-mails from Donovan. About my hunt to prove Joey Martin killed his family and how unless I do something, Lucy's going to be in his custody tomorrow. About my longing to be a mother to Lucy. I've spilled it all, given up the ghost, talked about it all until I feel empty, drained. She's sat and listened thoughtfully without saying much.

She asks how I'm sleeping.

Horrible.

How's my appetite.

Almost nonexistent.

How are my moods?

Shitty.

She leans back and steeples her fingers. Uh-oh.

"I think you are suffering from postpartum depression."

Her words make sense, and at the same time, they seem completely absurd.

"It is also complicated by the fact that you are mourning the death of a loved one."

"My sister?"

"Your baby."

Her words make me clamp my mouth shut.

It doesn't seem real that I'm mourning someone I never met. But she's right.

It explains a lot.

"I'll write you a prescription for Prozac."

I stare at her until she looks up from her scribbling.

"I can't take it."

She raises her eyebrow.

"I'm not going to have any of that in my body in case I get pregnant. I don't want anything to jeopardize another . . . baby."

"Studies show that mothers who take most antidepressants go on to have healthy babies. It doesn't seem to affect the child at all."

"Seem to?" I say. "They didn't think thalidomide affected babies, either, until they linked it to all the babies born without arms and legs. I'm just not comfortable with that."

"I get that," Marsha says. "It actually takes three months to see any benefits from the prescription anyway." She stands and holds out the small slip of paper. "I'd feel more comfortable if you'd just have the prescription filled. You'll have that as an option in case your depression gets worse. We can talk about it more next week, okay?"

I shove the piece of paper in my bag even though I have no intention of ever getting it filled. The best cure for me is to get knocked up ASAP.

Chapter 40

TODAY IS THE day Joey Martin is going to pick up Lucy.

I couldn't stop it. I don't know why I ever thought I could.

I'm a failure. I couldn't save that girl from her father, who, according to his mother-in-law, is, at the least, a jerk and, at the worst, a mass murderer. And now with Khoury's murder, the missing evidence, and a cover-up that extends to the U.S. military, I'm more convinced than ever that Joey Martin had something to do with the massacre.

I'm also a failure in my relationship, which I can sense slipping into an abyss that will be greater than both of us. It seems like Donovan and I have barely spoken in days. We have a date tonight. In the morning, he's leaving for a weeklong conference on policing in Washington, D.C. I already miss him, but I'm too exhausted to care.

A little after noon, Tricia calls. I've been expecting her call all morning.

"He just picked her up." She is whispering. "I'm watching him take her to the car right now.

"What's he like?"

"He's hugging her and stuff, but there was something about his eyes. He looked a little off, you know."

"Tricia, okay, now this part is important. Can you describe his car? Can you write down the license-plate number?"

"I'll try. It's a little hard to see. Oh God, I'm practically leaning out the second story here, Jesus. The things I do for my *famiglia. Ohibò, cosa mi tocca sentire*!"

"Try really hard." I'm squinting my eyes, as if I'm her trying to see the license-plate number.

"It's a dark green four-door sedan. Maybe Nissan or Toyota, I can't tell these things, for Christ's sake. Oh Jesus wept, he's blocking the plate. He's standing right in front of it, putting a bag in the trunk . . . okay, now he's in the car . . ."

"The plate. The plate, Tricia." I practically hiss the words.

"Okay, okay. S . . . M . . . or maybe it's an N. D. It looks like a one, a six. Oh shit, he pulled out. I can't see the last number. Oh crap. He pulled out on the street. I'm sorry. That's all I got."

Not good enough.

I slump back in my chair. I was leaning forward in excitement.

"Sorry. I'll see if I can find out more about him. Maybe where he's staying or something."

I sigh. She didn't have to call me. It's not her fault. "Thanks, Tricia."

"No problem, babe."

I hang up and close my eyes.

He got Lucy. I didn't save her in time.

MY FAILURE FILLS me with a heavy sludge of inertia all day. I don't want to do anything except curl up into a little ball and sleep for three weeks, but I manage to pound out a few stories before deadline. As my car slips into the Caldecott Tunnel into Oakland, a motorcycle with its light on pulls up so close to me I can't see anything in my rearview mirror except his form. We are the only two vehicles in the tunnel, but he keeps revving his engine, as if urging me to speed up.

Every time I try to look behind me, the bright light from his headlamp blinds me. He's dangerously close to my bumper. I gently tap on my brakes, but it only makes the motorcyclist angry, and he weaves back and forth behind me, stepping on the gas and letting off.

I did a big story a few months ago on motorcyclists who did these types of stunts on I-680. Sometimes a dozen of them would line up in a row and zoom down the freeway with their front tires in the air, popping wheelies. Others stand on top of their bikes at speeds of nearly eighty miles per hour. It seems pretty cool until someone dies, which eventually happens to many of them. What triggered this story wasn't the death of one of the bikers. It was the death of an innocent bystander. A teenage girl.

The motorcyclists were doing their stunts down the freeway, and one smashed into a car carrying a fourteen-year-old girl. The impact killed her instantly. As fate often has it in these types of things, the motorcyclist was not killed. He might walk funny for the rest of his life, but he's alive.

I named him in the story and received a flurry of hate mail, saying that I wrongly blamed him for the death and that if the girl had been wearing a seat belt, she'd probably still be alive.

The logic of the hate mail infuriated me. I wonder if this motorcyclist behind me somehow recognized me and is taunting me.

When we emerge from the tunnel, we come up on some slower

traffic. I slam on my brakes to avoid hitting a slow car in front of me, and the motorcyclist zips off to the side of me on the shoulder. For a few seconds, he is right beside me, head turned to look in my window. His helmet's visor is opaque and pulled down past his chin. I dart a glance at him. Then he is gone, zooming down the freeway on the white line, leaving all of us behind.

My heart is racing, and a small part of me wants to keep on driving into San Francisco rather than keep my date with Donovan. I want to go home and lock my door and get in bed. But I drive to his place on autopilot. I need to take advantage of any time I have with him before he leaves for his trip.

He wants to see a movie at the Grand Lake Theatre. Usually, I love watching the elderly woman play the Wurlitzer organ before the show, sitting on a small platform that rises as she plays. She seems to float up from the floor, stopping five feet above the ground and playing the entire time. The haunting organ notes reverberate throughout the older theater, and raucous whistling and applause always follow the performance. After, there is a small light show as layers of curtains part in a swishy flourish.

About once a month, we walk over here from Donovan's place on the lake. Although I like listening to the organist, tonight I'd rather be home in my pajamas snuggling on the couch and watching classics, such as *Houseboat* with Cary Grant and Sophia Loren.

I'm irritated that we are going to waste tonight together sitting side by side in a dark movie theater, where we can't even talk. Even though my body seems numb lately, I do want things back to normal. That's why under my dress, I'm wearing sexy lace stockings and a garter belt that match my red lace bra and panties.

As the previews play, I lace my fingers in Donovan's. In the flickering light from the big screen, I study his face and give his hand a squeeze. He returns the squeeze, but it seems halfhearted. In the light from the big screen, his jaw seems set. Hard. The muscle along his sculpted cheekbone is tight. I take his hand and put it in my lap, moving it down to my thighs to let him touch the lace top of my stockings, but he erupts into a cough and removes his hand from mine to cover his mouth.

I stare at his profile for a few more minutes until the main feature begins. He doesn't look over at me even once. I know things have been tense lately. Losing the baby wasn't easy on him, either. The night I told him is the only time I've ever seen him cry. It didn't last long, and he would be mortified if I ever brought it up, but the fact is, he was as heartbroken as me.

So how come he seems to have gotten over it so much easier than I did?

At first, after I miscarried, I was probably no picnic to be around, obsessed with my cycle. But I'm over that now. Or at least trying to be better.

In the back of my mind, I remember him complaining the other night about me obsessing on the Mission Massacre. He also didn't like that I'd lost weight. Well, I can't help either of those things. As the movie plays, I zone off. No matter how hard I tried, it's too late now. Lucy ended up in her father's care. Every once in a while, I dart a glance at Donovan's profile. At one point, I try to hold his hand again, but he withdraws it almost immediately to dig into the popcorn tub in his lap. That's when I know I'm not imagining it; something is wrong. Hopefully we can get over it when we get back to his place. I didn't wear this lingerie for nothing.

We are nursing drinks at The Black Cat Café down the street from the theater, and a lot more than my garter belt feels uncomfortable right now. Donovan is downing bourbon, and I'm sipping a Pellegrino. Donovan thinks it is because I'm trying to get pregnant, but the truth is I can barely make myself sip even water.

The dark bar is lit from the ceiling with turquoise neon lights, giving everyone an unearthly glow and making all the silver mirrors on the walls glitter. The room is the size of a large hallway. Its few black velvet chairs are taken, so we sit at the bar. I study his reflection in the mirror. He hasn't smiled at me once tonight. I swing my legs around to face him.

"What gives?"

He presses his lips together, and my heart seems to stop for a second.

"I've been thinking a lot about us, our relationship," he finally says, turning to face me on the stool so our knees are touching.

"I know it hasn't been easy—" I start, but the look on his face silences me.

"I know this miscarriage was hard on you. It was hard on me, too." He exhales. "It still is hard on me."

My heart melts at these words, and I reach for his hand. He doesn't return the pressure. My throat seems to swell until I can't swallow the lump that has appeared there.

"What I'm trying to say is, I'm sure losing the baby triggered all of this, but that doesn't make it okay."

All of this?

"Your obsession with Frank? I get that, too," he continues. "These are things I can handle. Because I love you." He pauses and looks me so deeply in the eyes that I feel naked in the dark bar.

A weight lifts from my chest. No matter what he is saying, he loves me, and that means we can handle everything else, right?

He looks away for a second as he presses on.

"But what I'm not sure I can handle is your . . . obsession . . . transferring that fixation to every story you report about. And frankly, I don't think you can handle it, either."

"I can—" I interrupt, but he holds up a hand so he can continue, and he says the words that lodge themselves like a knife in my heart.

"We shouldn't even consider having a baby until you get this . . . handled. You've checked out completely. Our sex life—it's like we're in a laboratory. I don't want to have a baby under these circumstances. I don't think you do, either."

I'm stunned into silence. I blink, and he continues.

"I love you too much to sit back and watch you destroy yourself."

Destroy myself? Because I want to put a killer behind bars? He watches me and waits for my response. I take a long drink of water before I speak.

"You're a cop, Donovan," I say finally. "You of all people should understand."

"It's because I'm a cop that I do understand. I've watched many of my colleagues get too close to a case and let it destroy them. It's always that one case—the one that got away—that leads them to ruin their lives. But what worries me the most about you is that there will always be a new one. At least that's the way it seems to be going."

"What are you trying to say?"

Silence stretches between us.

He sighs and stands. "We need some time to think about all of this and our next step."

I know my mouth is open and my forehead is wrinkled in confusion. What the hell does that mean?

Chapter 41

AT HOME IN North Beach, I peel off my dress in front of the mirror and stare at my image in my wasted red-and-black lace lingerie and stockings.

We walked home from the bar in silence, then I got in my car and peeled out. He must be serious about taking some time, because he didn't even try to stop me. We'll still talk, he says. But he needs to "think" about our relationship, so we're taking a "break." He still loves me. Like that matters. If we're not together, his love is no good to me. I don't need to be loved from afar. What does that even mean?

He didn't even say how long the "break" would be, and damn if I'll ask him and beg for him to be with me. Part of me hopes he will come around and call me tonight. Or maybe in the morning? Because despite it all, I can't help but mentally calculate every missed opportunity to conceive a baby. But things must get better between us if we want to be parents. They have to. Even as I think this, I know this only proves that at least some of what Donovan said is true. But I can't help it.

Staring at the mirror, my image grows slightly blurry. As I give myself one last glance, I try to ignore the fact that my bra, the usual size I've worn all my adult life, is slightly too big and that you can see my rib cage below it.

A few minutes later, I've changed into a cotton nightie that falls to my knees, and I've curled up on my couch with the lights off. When I first got home, my apartment smelled like cat pee, so I threw open the door to my balcony.

Now I close my eyes and listen to the foghorn as the cool breeze licks at my bare legs. Dusty meows at me and leaps on the back of the sofa, pacing. He's hungry. I know I should get off the couch and feed him, but it seems like more effort than I can manage right now. After a few moments, guilt overcomes me, and by the light coming in from the street, I sloppily fill his water and dump three times as much cat food as he usually gets into his bowl, spilling it onto the floor around the bowl before I crawl back onto the couch.

After a few minutes of staring at the curtain to my sliding-glass doors, which is whipping in the wind, I turn and bury my face in the back of the couch, closing my eyes.

A kaleidoscope of images flashes before me: Caterina in her coffin. My mother clawing at the dirt as the coffin is lowered into the ground. The last look Jack Dean Johnson gave me as I plunged the shard of glass into his chest. The way the blood seeped out around my hand so warm. Mark Emerson's lifeless eyes as he stared up at the ceiling, dead from my bullet. The blood in the toilet. So much blood. How could so much blood come out of me and I'm still alive? The bloodbath that awaited me in that Mission apartment, bodies strewn everywhere, blood smeared across the walls, heads tottering on shredded flesh.

For once I let the images wash over me without trying to tamp them down.

This is your life.

I bury my face in the soft dark velvet of my couch. I want to cry, but crying does not come easy for me. And damn if I'm going to cry over a guy. I'll cry over something worthwhile, like the death of my sister, but not over some guy wanting to take a break from me. Not over that.

All this makes me exhausted, spent, empty. My eyelids so heavy. When I close my eyes, anticipating the nightmarish flickering of horrific images from the apartment, there is nothing. Blissfully, there is nothing—just blackness.

The phone ringing wakes me up, but I don't move. Only open my eyes. The apartment is black. After a few minutes, the ringing stops. My answering machine clicks on. I hear a dial tone. If it's Donovan, he'll leave a message. The last thing I want him to think is that I'm waiting by the phone for him to call. In case it was my mother, I call her but get her voice mail. I lie and tell her I'm super busy at work and won't make it to Nana's on Sunday.

The sliding-glass door is still open, and now the air in my studio is icy. I pull the quilt that is wadded up at my feet over me.

The next time I open my eyes, the light around me is gray. A typical foggy San Francisco morning. Dusty is wadded up in a furry semicircle around my head. I move him over and sit up. Unearthed from the blanket, my body instantly prickles with goose bumps. My breath appears in a cartoon bubble in front of my face when I exhale. Wrapping a blanket around me, I pad over to the sliding-glass door, slam it shut, and crawl back onto the couch, where I drift off into a dreamless sleep.

Throughout the day, the phone rings a few times, but I can tune it out now. In the distance, I hear voices leave messages, but I just bury my face deeper. The day is punctuated by Dusty occasionally getting up to poke around the apartment. I hear him drinking out of the toilet and am relieved that he's this self-sufficient and I don't have to get up. If I twist my head, I can see the corner of the kitchen where his food bowl is. Food pellets lay scattered on the floor, so I close my eyes again. Dusty comes back to snuggle with me for most of the day, sometimes at my head, sometimes stretched out against my back, sometimes at my feet in a puffy warm ball.

At one point, I open my eyes, and it is dark again. I could be dead and nobody would even know. Donovan will regret wanting to take a break when he finds out I died and nobody found me for days while he was at his goddamn training, won't he?

My mom will be pissed. My whole family would blame him. I can see them all at my funeral. My brother Dante trying to take swings at him while my oldest brother, Marco, holds him back. My mom and aunts glaring at him. Maybe my mom would even slap his face? My sweet nana cursing him out in Italian. She might even hold up her hand, pointing her pinky and index finger at him, giving him the *malocchio,* cursing him with the evil eye.

I clutch at the small golden horn hanging from a delicate chain at my neck. My father's *cornetto.* It didn't protect him from the *malocchio*; why would I think it would protect me?

I'm doomed to a wretched, cursed life. I lost my sister, my father. And then I killed two men. I'm being punished. Isn't that what Frank was trying to tell me in his e-mails?

Pounding on the door awakens me. Donovan. He came back for me.

I stand on weak legs and run my fingers through my hair,

which is knotted and tangled so much that it feels like I now have dreadlocks. I vaguely wonder if I have time to stick a glob of toothpaste in my mouth to disguise my nasty breath, but the pounding continues, a rapping that makes me realize it's not Donovan. He has his own key. He wouldn't keep knocking—he'd let himself in.

The knocking stops and I hear voices, low, outside the door, then Nicole's no-nonsense voice.

"Gabriella? If you're in there, open up, or else your landlady here, Mrs. Cossetta, is going to unlock the door."

Mrs. Cossetta?

"I'm here. Give me a second." My voice cracks.

I throw a robe around me and open the door. Nicole stands there with a big pink scarf looped around her neck and her nose pink from the cold. Lopez is with her, dressed in camouflauge pants and a big army jacket.

Mrs. Cossetta just rolls her eyes, lets out a big puff of air, mumbles in Italian, and shuffles off in her backless slippers to her apartment down the hall.

"What's up with the old biddy?" Lopez says, jutting his chin at her retreating form.

"She's okay." I defend her even though we avoid each other as much as possible.

Mrs. Cossetta is the sister of my old landlord, who died last year. She only keeps me in my rent-controlled place because before her sister died, she insisted her tenants be allowed to stay.

Nicole is bustling about my apartment, turning on all the lights, folding the quilt on the couch, and feeding Dusty. I slump back on the couch as she starts banging pots and pans around in my kitchen. Lopez is checking out my wall—a gallery of pictures that mean something to me. They are the main items I would grab if my building caught fire.

There are pictures of my family. Me and Caterina as little girls. My mother and father with their arms around each other. My brothers playing bocce in the park. Me eating gelato. Caterina petting Nana's cat.

"Some of these are amazing," he says, squinting. "Who took them?"

"Nana used to dream of being a photographer when she was in Italy," I say. "But her father, my great-grandfather, said women were meant to be wives and mothers."

"What a waste," Lopez says. "She is an artist. This is some motherfucking cool shit."

It makes me sad to think of my grandmother being told to abandon her passion because of her gender. But then again, I've contended with some of my Italian relatives discouraging me from pursuing my career as a reporter, as well.

Lopez pulls out one of my dining room chairs and straddles it backward. Both of them are doing a good job of not talking about why they unexpectedly showed up. I'm not going to be the one to bring it up.

"Set the table." Nicole sets a stack of bowls and spoons in front of Lopez.

He stands and starts whistling as he sets the table, grabbing some of my cloth napkins and making fancy shapes with them. "I used to wait tables on Union Street, man," he says over his shoulder.

I curl up on the couch, watching as Nicole stirs a pot of something on the stove and Lopez puts in my Afro-Cuban All Stars CD, picks up Dusty, and dances around with him, wiggling his slim hips like a belly dancer. Dusty gives me a look but stays as malleable as a rag doll. Nicole's blond head bobs to the music, and she shakes her hips a little as she stirs. I know I should get up and help or at least stop them, but moving my body off this couch seems impossible.

"Dinner is served, my darling," Nicole says, unwrapping my pink polka-dot apron from around her waist. My stomach grumbles as I get a whiff of the garlic bread she slides out of the oven.

I stand on weak legs. When was the last time I ate? Yesterday? No. Two days ago? Maybe.

"It's Monday, right?" I vaguely recall talking to Kellogg this morning, telling him I was staying home sick.

Heading toward the kitchen, I try to finger-comb my hair and straighten my clothes, but it's no use. A glimpse of myself in the mirror across the room confirms what I suspected: I look like an extra in a horror flick. I have zombie hair, and my bony knees are sticking out of the bottom of my stained nightgown.

"Oh, Gabriella," Nicole says softly as she watches me. Her face, her cheery façade, fall away. Lopez hears her voice catch and turns to look at me, as well. "Holy shit you've had us worried. I've been calling for two days."

"I'm sorry," I say and hang my head. Nicole grabs me in a hug. When she releases me, I try my best to cheer up for their sake. I don't want them to worry about me. They are the best friends a girl could have. I break off bits of the garlic bread and chew it as long as I can before I swallow, hoping I can keep it down despite the turmoil in my stomach.

I take small sips of the red wine Nicole brought to wash the bread down.

The chicken noodle soup Nicole heated on the stove goes down a little easier, but I take it slow, too.

Nicole and Lopez make small talk at first, but then Nicole turns to me.

"Kellogg said you could take as much time off as you need, so you don't have to worry about that."

For the first time in my life, being a reporter feels like a waste. It seems like so long ago that I loved it so much I gave up boyfriends for my job. That seems like another lifetime and another person. Like a woman I read about in a book or watched in a movie. Was that really me?

My fiancé, the man I love and want to spend the rest of my life with, doesn't want me the way I am. He wants me to change, and I can't. I just can't. Even if I wanted to. Which I don't. And I don't care anymore. I'm too exhausted to care.

I'm slightly more alive after I eat a bit.

Nicole puts the leftover soup in the fridge and tells me to eat it for lunch tomorrow.

"I brought a baguette for your breakfast. Do I have to drive over here and feed it to you, or can you promise to eat it for breakfast?"

She already is leaving her husband and baby to be with me tonight. The least I can do is agree. I nod.

She lifts an eyebrow.

"I promise."

Lopez is scratching Dusty behind the ears, when he stands to leave. Nicole pulls on her jacket and picks up her bag. "By the way, I almost forgot. I brought a message for you," Nicole says, digging around in her purse. "It's from Lucy's grandmother, so I thought you might want to read it."

She puts a pink slip in front of me before she kisses me on the cheek as she and Lopez leave.

Mrs. Castillo's message says she's going to clean out her daughter's apartment on Tuesday morning and wants me to meet her there to help.

Despite the cloak of apathy that presses down on me, my heart beats a little faster reading this. I grab my phone.

A few minutes later, I hang up. I told her I'd meet her in the morning. Even though the rent is paid to the end of the month, the landlord wants all the family's belongings moved so he can start cleaning and getting the place ready for new tenants. She wants my help with packing and sorting. She said she doesn't know anyone else here and doesn't think she can do it alone.

I look at the clock. I'm not supposed to meet her for fourteen hours. I need to visit the apartment now. Alone. As soon as I saw the message from Mrs. Castillo on that little pink slip, I've imagined being in that apartment again, looking for some type of clue that can prove Joey Martin killed his family.

Maybe if I find something soon, they can stop him and get Lucy back before something bad happens—if it hasn't already. What that something is, I don't know, but as soon as I heard Lucy would be in his care, I've been filled with a sense of dread and foreboding.

I rush to get dressed.

Chapter 42

My knuckles are turning white from clutching the bump key that Lopez gave me as I stand in front of the apartment door. Images of that day rush back. The door that was ajar, the baby staring at me, so still she looked like a doll. The blood. The horrible, nightmarish scene that awaited me. I swallow and stick the key in the lock, pulling it back ever so slightly one notch and giving it a slight bump with the handle of a hairbrush I brought along. Lopez said any hard-backed object would work. Click. The door creaks open under my hand. I glance around me down the hall, but no heads emerge from closed apartment doors.

My heart is pounding in my throat, but there is no way Martin would be back in this apartment, is there? Even so, I reach for the light switch before I step foot into the apartment. After I was attacked, the cops had plugged the light back in. Its beam reassures me that he hasn't been back. I slip inside the apartment and shut the door softly behind me, leaning back against it.

The apartment is empty, but in my mind's eye I can still see the bodies sprawled where there are now only dried puddles of blood on the floor, or dark stains on the couch, or a Rorschach splatter pattern on the walls. The air has a faint metallic smell that must be from the leftover blood.

I blink and shake my head to rid myself of the images.

I've been in this apartment twice already. Maybe three times is the charm. Be methodical, I tell myself and start at the wall closest to me, examining photographs in frames for clues and working my way clockwise around the room, pulling out bureau drawers and sifting through the contents, not bothering to push them back in. After I'm done in the living room, I head toward the bedroom.

Near the bed, on the nightstand, I find the book that Maria Martin was reading—*Healthy Sleep Habits, Happy Child.* For some reason I hadn't read the title before. Underneath, more parenting books are stacked. This woman had intended to give her daughter the best of herself and be the best mother she could be. And for some reason, her husband took this away from her. Why? There has to be some clue. Where are the letters that were under the floorboard? Did Martin get them before I arrived last time? I lift up the mattress to the bed and pull out all the dresser drawers looking for something that will explain this, but there is nothing. I pull the furniture away from the walls and look for anything taped to the backs and bottoms, but there is nothing. I know that most detectives check in all these places as well, but right now I can't trust the police department's job. Not now that I suspect they were never interested in solving this murder.

In the bathroom, I stand in the tub, peering out the window and trying to imagine how Martin escaped after killing everyone in his family. Did he have to go out the window because the UPS guy was knocking at the front door with that package from Babies"R"Us? By sitting on the windowsill in the bathroom, he could have leaned over and grabbed hold of the metal rungs on the telephone pole before climbing down to the alley, like he did after I found him hiding here.

In the kitchen, I get started with what I had planned on helping Mrs. Castillo with in the morning—I fill a big trash bag with all the rotten food that is stinking up the refrigerator. I tie the bag in a big knot and haul it with me into the hallway. I leave the trash bag near the back door before I head upstairs to the in-laws' apartment.

After I look around, I do the same thing there—empty the rotten food out of the refrigerator, even though a bag of mush in the produce bin makes me gag. Holding the garbage bag, I give one last look around the small apartment. Everything is as it was the first time I came in. There is nothing to find. No clue. Disappointed, I lock the door and head downstairs with the trash bag.

I'm halfway down the stairs when I realize there was only one thing not like the other. It was so slight that I nearly missed it. I rush back to the apartment and jimmy the lock with the bump key again.

This time I head straight for the coffee table. I thought it was strange that the cops didn't search and confiscate everything in the in-laws' upstairs apartment, but I guess they gave it short shrift, since it wasn't the crime scene. Now that I'm here again, I think Khoury's men lied to her about even coming into this apartment. I wonder if it had to do with the cover-up, someone not wanting the crime solved at all.

Unlike everything else in this extraordinarily tidy apartment, a stack of magazines on the coffee table was slightly askew, ever so slightly off kilter. As if someone tried to stack them in a hurry. Or as if there is something other than a magazine underneath. I scatter the magazines and unearth it. A small black journal.

The first entry is dated March.

I sink onto the couch and open it, holding my breath. On the first page of the Moleskine, it offers a reward if found. It belongs to Maria Martin.

My heart speeds up, and I flip to the first entry, which is preceded by a quote. *"For to be free is not merely to cast off one's chains but to live in a way that respects and enhances the freedom of others."—Nelson Mandela*

It is followed by a space before her first entry:

"Joey left today. I think my heart will break from missing him, but at the same time I feel so free, as if a great weight has been lifted from me, and this makes me so guilty. Isn't a wife supposed to want to be around her husband? But sometimes his attention is overwhelming. If I go visit his parents in their apartment upstairs, he calls me on my phone and says he misses me and to come back down to our apartment. If I'm in the shower too long, he comes in and sits on the toilet to talk to me. He gets jealous if I talk to the clerk at the grocery store. Isn't that proof of his love?

"I know it stems from his love of me, but it is stifling sometimes. Are all American men like this with their wives? I am looking forward to some time alone. I guess I'm just not used to being married yet. And not used to the American way of life. I love his family, but they are always asking me questions, making me feel inadequate, telling me how I do everything wrong. I can't help it, I want to be as American as them. I really do. Don't they know that I have dreamed of living in America my entire life? That I don't want to do things the way my mother does. America is a dream come true. Land of the free. Where the *Federales* can't come into your house and kill your father and rape your mother."

Mrs. Castillo was raped? I remember the sadness in her eyes, the weariness that I assumed stemmed from the grief of losing her daughter.

I read on.

"My mother told me not to marry Joey. She is old-fashioned. She doesn't understand love. I see how other women look at Joey when we are out. They look at him and look at me and wonder why he is with me. I know I am so lucky to have him. He says he never knew what love was until he met me. My heart is so full of love for him. I will make up for the love his parents never gave him. And even so, after all that, he takes care of them. Even though they never loved him, never wanted him, he pays for their rent so they can live in a safe neighborhood. He is a true man. He knows what honor and love truly are. I am so lucky. My mother doesn't understand because my father was not like this.

"He is so frustrated that we have not been able to have a baby yet. He will lose that anger when I have his baby inside me. It might even be inside me right now. I didn't want to say anything to him before he left because I couldn't bear him thinking I was pregnant if I was only late. I could never do that to him. He has enough evil to deal with without heartbreaking news from me. But I am going to see the doctor next week. They will know for sure. I will call him, and he will be happy, and he can leave his frustration behind."

I read as fast as I can, flipping ahead. Skimming, I stop cold on a name.

"Abequero came over again." I freeze, then read on.

"I know that Joey would be upset if we were alone, so I always invite Mama and Papa Martin to come, too. Otherwise it looks bad. It's not proper for me to be alone with Abe. I don't know why he doesn't bring his wife. Maybe because she doesn't like me. Or at least that is how she acts."

Abequero. Abe. Mrs. Castillo said it sounded like a girl's name. Abe. Pronounced like "Abby." This is the good friend.

I skim ahead, looking to spot Abequero's name again.

"I want to die," the entry begins. "He will not stop. He says it will make our love stronger. It will make our marriage last forever if I just do this. But I would rather die. I can't take it anymore. He talks and writes of nothing else."

What does he want her to do?

"He would have never said any of this before. Oh why, oh why, did he have to go to Iraq? It is not fair. He should never have believed them. It was not his fault. He was following orders. I know he will never forgive himself. I try to tell him this, but he won't talk about it anymore.

"And he has changed. Now, he is different. Now, he is cold. Where is the man I fell in love with?"

I can't figure out what Joey Martin is asking her to do. Something so horrible she would rather die? Flipping back a few pages, I find what she is referring to.

"He called me and told me he knows I want to have sex with him."

Him?

"I told him no, I would never break the sacred vow of marriage. Never. He told me that it is okay. That Abequero is his friend. And that it is okay if we have sex because I was a virgin when we met. He says I will never know how special our love is unless I am with someone else."

The next day:

"He called again today. He says it is the only thing that will make him happy if I make sex with Abe. I wish Abe had gone to Iraq with Joey and none of this would be possible. If only Abe hadn't broken his arm that day, he'd be with Joey and maybe talk some sense into him. Joey sounds crazier every day. Now he says having sex with someone else will show me I did the right thing to marry him."

He wants her to have an affair with his best friend, Abequero. *Mother Mary and Joseph.*

I flip ahead to the next week.

"I want to die. Every letter he writes. Every time he calls. He begs me. He says it is what an angel told him God wants me to do. He said it is in his dreams that I do this. I am losing my mind. Who can I tell this to? That my husband wants me to have sex with another man—his friend—and he says it is what God has told him is right? He is not right in the head after what happened. It has changed him. But he won't admit it. He says he is the same. He is breaking my heart. I want to tell him I have his baby, but the doctor says to wait until I am twelve weeks along and we know for sure it is safe and the baby will live. The doctor says it is too hard to tell a man in war he will be a father, only to tell him later he will not."

Sitting on the couch, reading Maria's journal, my heart goes out to her. Alone in a new country with a husband who's mentally losing it? What happened to him in Iraq? Something horrible that has made him turn on her. No wonder she was so confused about how to handle her husband's crazy request. The next page skips forward a few days.

"I told my mama. I drove to San Juan Bautista and told her I was having a baby and that Joey wants me to have sex with his friend Abe. She cried and told me to leave Joey. To stay with her and we would hide from him. I told her I could handle it my own way. I would handle my own husband. She pulled at me, snagging my sweater as I tried to leave, and we argued. I told her she couldn't control my life anymore. That I was a grown woman. She said something mean then. She told me that Joey didn't really love me or he would've never asked me to do that. How dare she talk about my husband's love for me? Of course he loves me. Why else would he act so crazy? Then I said something I deeply regret.

"I told her I would do whatever it took to keep my husband alive, something she had not been able to do. Now I want to die more than ever. She will never forgive my cruel words. I am a horrible, horrible person."

The next entry is two days later.

"I told Joey it will happen tonight. His parents are visiting some friends in Pinole and will be gone all night. Abe's wife is out of town. In Los Angeles for shopping or something. I told him I will go to Abe's place tonight."

She's going through with it?

The next entry is not dated.

"Everything is worse than ever. I told him I was pregnant and he still won't change his mind about me sleeping with Abe. I dumped a bottle of aspirin into a glass of orange juice, but I couldn't make myself drink it. Not with this baby inside. I felt the baby move. Suicide is a sin, I know, but I don't care. I don't care what happens to me anymore.

"Before I drank the juice, I called my mama and asked her to forgive my cruel, heartless words. She said she forgave me the minute they came out of my mouth. How did I ever get blessed with such a mother? Her words make me remember that if I kill myself, I kill my baby. I cannot do that. I want my baby to live. If I can be half the mother to my baby she is to me, my baby will be blessed."

The sentence "I want my baby to live" grows blurry. When I turn the page, the rest of the journal is blank. It ends on those words, only halfway through. I look at the date. I do the math. She was probably three months pregnant.

Why did she stop journaling? What happened? Did she have sex with Abe?

Maria's mother knows more than she is saying.

Chapter 43

I'M AT THE Mission apartment early Tuesday morning.

Mrs. Castillo is waiting at the end of the hall in front of the door to the apartment. She wears boots and a silver wool cape that matches the streak in her hair. She wilts as I thrust Maria's diary in front of her. The look on her face—resigned, not surprised—tells me she knew about this journal the whole time.

"Did you want me to find it?"

She purses her blood red lips and gestures toward the closed door to Maria's apartment. "I couldn't go in there by myself. I couldn't see where it happened. But I knew Maria had hidden the journal somewhere. I thought it might be hidden with the letters." She looks down as she says it.

"How did you know that the cops didn't have it already?"

"Detective Khoury. She was going to go back to the apartment that day to look for it. I think that is why she was killed. I come from a country where you can't trust the *policia*. The *Federales* are all crooked. America is supposed to be different, but it is not. Who am I to trust?"

"You didn't tell me any of this." I wave the diary around a few inches from her face. I'm angry. "You didn't tell Khoury. Did you know I didn't even find it here? It was upstairs, in her in-laws' apartment."

She shrugs. "Did you read . . . did she write about . . . everything?" Mrs. Castillo closes her eyes, as if she is in pain.

"You mean, how Joey messed with her head and forced her to have sex with Abequero? That's why he killed her, isn't it?"

Mrs. Castillo wearily leans against the hallway wall.

"He wasn't always like that. He wasn't." She closes her eyes, shaking her head. "He even helped me get my green card to come to the U.S. because Maria missed me so much. He was different then. Until he went to war. There something happened. Something awful. Maria wouldn't tell me, but she called me, crying. She said something went horribly wrong in Iraq and that Joey had tried to kill himself. She begged him to come home so she could help. He refused. He didn't call or write for a month. When he did, it was as if something had changed."

"You should've gone to the police with this," I say, angrily waving the journal around. "Why didn't you? Now Detective Khoury is dead and Lucy is in the hands of a murderer and you could've stopped it."

She reels back from my angry words, as if I have slapped her. Seeing her face, I soften for a second. "Is it because you didn't want people to know Maria had an affair with Abequero? It wasn't her fault. Joey drove her to it. That is mental, emotional, and psychological abuse."

Mrs. Castillo doesn't look up, just shakes her head.

I take her arm and lead her out of the building. "I'll come back here and get what you want out of the apartment. But first you and I are having breakfast, and you're going to tell me everything."

I drag her into a Starbucks a few blocks away from the apartment building and settle her in with a hot tea, while I order a cappuccino.

"Tell me what she told you that day on the phone when you said you forgave her as soon as the words came out of her mouth." I take a sip of my coffee and watch her expression.

She looks up in surprise that I know about that conversation.

"That was in there?"

I wave the diary at her. "It's *all* in here. All except parts of what she said when she called you that day. That was the last entry in her diary. What happened next?"

She raises her head slowly and meets my eyes. "You did not know my Maria. She did not sleep with Abequero. She told Joey that she would so he would stop asking her about it. But she will not betray her morals and values because he asked her to. She told him it would happen that night, but it didn't."

"What happened? Why is she dead?"

"I don't know why she is dead. I only know what she told me about that night."

She tells me the story.

Maria was in her pajamas, curled up with a blanket, drinking milk and watching TV, when the phone rang.

It was Joey.

She was caught. She was not at Abe's apartment.

Joey didn't even say hello. "It's a good thing you were home, you slut. I was just testing you. You fucked him before, though, didn't you? That one time I came home and he was there. You fucked him, didn't you? That is how you got pregnant, isn't it? That baby is his. I had a doc do some tests over here. He said the chances of me getting someone pregnant? Yeah, I got a better chance of winning the Nobel Prize."

"No!" she cried. "I swear. I have never been with anyone but you. That doctor is wrong. I swear. We can do tests when you get home. We can show that I am right. You have to believe me."

The line was silent, then his voice came across in a menacing whisper.

"You think you are safe in your cozy little apartment I pay for? I almost got leave last week. I almost got to come home. And I was going to come home and surprise you with Abe. I was going to kill you and kill him and that bastard baby inside you. Just like I kill all these ragheads. It is so easy. Easiest thing I've ever done. And if you think I wouldn't kill you . . . you are wrong."

She pleaded and begged and even said, "Wait. Wait until the baby is born and we will do the DNA tests. Don't kill our baby, Joey. It is our baby, I swear to the Virgin Mary and all the Saints. The baby is yours."

"How can I believe you?"

"We will go to the doctor together," she told him. "We will do the DNA tests. You can pick the doctor. You will see I'm not lying. If we do tests and the baby is not yours, then I will kill myself for you. You will see. I promise."

Tears drip down her face as Mrs. Castillo finishes her story.

"She begged me, asked, 'What do I do, Mama?' Every letter he writes. Every call he makes. He begs her to do it. What else could she do but tell him yes, it will happen. Even if she never was going to go through with it. She finally said she was, so he would stop."

Lucy is ten months old.

I ask Mrs. Castillo if the DNA test was ever done.

"I don't think so. He has only been home once in the past eighteen months, and it was when Lucy was born. He seemed so happy then. I think he wanted to believe she was his. But then that woman—that wife of his friend said Maria and her husband were sleeping together."

"Carol Abequero?"

"Yes, that is the name. And his name was Abe."

"When did this happen?"

"Last month?" Mrs. Castillo says. "But I know Lucy is his. I wish she was his friend's, Abe's baby, but she is not."

So, he came home and killed her for an affair she didn't even have. I wonder if Mrs. Castillo knows Abequero is dead. I decide now is not the time to tell her.

"How do you know for sure the baby is Joey's?"

"I know my Maria. She would not lie to me."

"What did Maria tell you about the DNA test? Did she mention it at all?"

"After she thought she had placated him by offering the DNA test and saying she would kill herself, he made her promise to stop talking to me about it. Every time I brought it up, she shushed me, she acted afraid. She told me she had to do it. She was afraid that if she didn't do everything he said, he would come home and kill her and the baby."

He killed Maria anyway. I don't say it out loud.

How to prove that he came home and killed her when the military says he was in Iraq? They are protecting him for some reason. But why?

"You're right, the police need to know all of this. It's the only way to get Lucy away from him," I say.

Mrs. Castillo closes her eyes for a few seconds. When they pop open, the look in them is one of sheer terror.

"He does not want to care for her. That is why I wanted to get Lucy away from him. At first, I was going to kill him on my own. I came to you so you could find him for me so I could kill him. He's going to kill Lucy. He told Maria that. She sends me this note the day before she dies."

Mrs. Castillo fishes a note out of her low-cut black leotard and reads it. It is from Joey Martin and is short, but not sweet. It was dated a few weeks before the massacre. It says that Maria will die for betraying him, and so will her bastard baby.

"You need to give that to the cops."

"The police? You cannot trust them. I give it to you." She hands me the note.

I hold it in my palm for a minute before I stick it in my bag.

Martin was going to kill the baby, too, but something must have stopped him. Was he interrupted by UPS knocking on the door? Is that why she was spared?

That's why he wants the baby now. To kill her and finish the job. Maybe in some way that appears to be an accident or not, but either way he's going to do it and disappear. If I don't find him, he's going to go underground forever, and that baby is going to die—if she's not dead already.

Chapter 44

THE PALACE OF Fine Arts has always been an ethereal and peaceful spot in the hustle and bustle of San Francisco. It has a calming effect on me and has always been a great place to gather my thoughts. When I arrive this morning, the sun has broken through the morning fog and illuminated the clouds behind the palace in pretty pinks and oranges.

I park out front, sipping the rest of my coffee. I wince, remembering how Donovan and I came here last winter because we were considering holding our wedding reception here.

From this location, I can see both Alcatraz and the Golden Gate Bridge.

As I look at the island prison, it triggers a memory of a dream I had last night:

I was playing a game of chess with Joey Martin. We were sitting in a damp prison cell. We had bet Lucy's fate on the game.

She was sleeping in a bassinet nearby. If I won, I could take her home with me. If he won, he would leave her here to be eaten by rats. As we played, rats kept coming out of holes in the cell and scaling the legs of the bassinet. I was trying to concentrate on playing the game at the same time I was kicking the rats away from the baby.

It was my move. I was close to losing. He was a better chess player than me, and I knew it. At first I panicked, but then I realized I would employ the technique of "craftiness."

According to my chess book, craftiness is described as winning without actually cheating but doing something close to cheating to throw your opponent off his game.

For instance, a chess player can eat three heads of garlic the night before so he reeks terribly and disarms the other player with his pungent smell. Or wear his pajamas to the match instead of a nice shirt. My favorite example was when a player suffered a back injury and took part in a tournament while lying on a couch. It irritated his opponent so much that he took to playing all his matches while lying on a massage table. It's all part of psychological warfare to throw someone off his game.

Now I realize that this is how I will trap Martin in real life.

I come up with an idea, a plan to lure Joey Martin out of hiding. Everyone is chasing him. I will throw him off his game, surprise him with what he least expects, and force him to come to me.

Right now he has no reason to surface. He thinks he's gotten away scot-free and he'll kill Lucy and disappear. If he hasn't already. I need to flush him out of his hiding spot.

I grab my phone and call in to my voice mail at work. Scanning my old messages, I finally hear Dave Schrader's voice again asking me to appear on his *True Crime Tuesdays* show.

I listen to Schrader rattle off his number, and I jot it down in my reporter's notebook.

A few minutes later, I hang up with Schrader. We have a date.

Tonight at eight. I'll show up at his San Francisco studio down by the waterfront under the Bay Bridge. He'll talk about my guest appearance as much as possible beforehand, pulling in some favors from anchors at three Bay Area news stations.

It may not work, but it's worth a try.

THE DAY AT work goes better.

Having a plan to trap Joey Martin makes me feel like my old self again. Then, it gets even better. My jailhouse interview request was approved.

Carol Abequero looks like she's a movie star playing the role of a glamorous prisoner. Her stint in jail has not smudged her looks.

Her complexion actually seems complemented by the orange of her jail jumpsuit. Her hair, tightly pulled back in a chignon, accents her sharp cheekbones. Above them, her makeup-less eyes are striking, slanted and arctic blue, like a Siamese cat's. Her pale pink lips are puffy in a way only an injection from a doctor can achieve.

She arches one impeccably groomed eyebrow when she sees me.

"You look better in person than on TV," she says.

"Same for you." The footage of her being arrested was not pretty. She had on sweatpants, an old T-shirt, and a green beauty mask.

"Of course they had to come on my beauty night," she says and gestures with one French-manicured hand. "I almost wonder if they hadn't planned it that way. Humiliate the murder suspect." She scoffs. "Murder suspect. Have you ever heard anything so ridiculous?"

"So you didn't do it?"

She gives me a look of disbelief. "You're kidding, right? Isn't that why you wanted to talk to me? To put why I'm innocent in the paper?"

"Sort of." I don't want to give her too much too soon. "What is your connection to Maria Martin?"

She purses her plump lips together in a long, drawn-out sigh. "I believe you would call me the aggrieved wife, the cuckold—or is that word only for men?"

"You think your husband cheated on you with Maria Martin?"

"Honey, I know he cheated on me. He spent every damn second he could over at her place. If a man does that, he's obviously getting some. You don't do that out of the goodness of your heart, or whatever crap Richard tried to tell me. Helping her while Joey was gone, my ass. Helping himself to her goodie bag is what he was doing."

"You don't seem very broken up about your husband's death."

"He was in love with her." She says it in a soft voice and examines her cuticles.

"You didn't answer my question."

She rolls her eyes. "So what? I'm not sorry he's dead. He was going to divorce me anyway."

Her attention returns to her nails.

"Am I boring you?"

She sighs exaggeratedly. "Yes. I'm not interested in talking about Maria Martin. As a matter of fact, I'd be perfectly happy to never hear her name again." She widens both eyes and sits up straighter, as if daring me to argue with her.

"Okay," I say. "But that's unlikely, since you're in jail for her murder. So you've made it pretty clear that there was no love lost between you and Maria. Who do you think killed her?"

"Not a clue. Maybe some jealous lover."

Here's my in.

"What about a jealous husband?"

Her tinkly laugh startles me. "Joey? Oh Joey wouldn't hurt her. She was his prize belonging. It's the first time I ever saw Joey in love. Not that she deserved it."

I don't answer. An old journalism trick. Most people can't stand an awkward silence and will rush to fill it. She doesn't disappoint.

"A man will overlook a lot of flaws as long as he's getting laid by a beautiful woman on a regular basis."

"Have you known Joey for a long time? You seem to think highly of him. You said she didn't deserve his love."

"Haven't you met him? He's all man. Virile. Hard-bodied. Doesn't put up with any shit. And yet he has the most gentle, loving side you'll ever see in a man."

The alarms are going off in my head. Not just her words, but her smile as she speaks about Joey Martin.

"You love him."

"Oh, yes," she shrugs. "He'll always take care of me. That's why I'm not worried about being in here. Joey will figure out a way to get me out. You know . . ." She lowers her voice to a whisper. " . . . he's part of a secret military group. The best of the best. Now, how sexy is that?"

"Not too sexy, since he killed his wife and parents."

She recoils, her lips baring her teeth. She shakes her head. "Not possible."

"He killed them and framed you. That is why you're in jail. You'll go away for the rest of your life for a mass murder you didn't commit. Do you have any idea what they'll do with your pretty face in prison?" I eye her body like a hungry man would. "Trust me, honey, you will be extremely popular."

She swallows and looks off to the side—the only indication that I've gotten to her at all. I push on.

"What if I told you he's here? In the Bay Area."

A small twitch of her lips, an attempt to hold back a smile, tells me everything I need to know.

"But you already know that, don't you?" I say. "You've seen him, haven't you?"

She twists her lip a little. That's my answer. She has. For sure. She stands.

"Looks like our little visit is over. Nice chatting with you." She starts to take the phone away from her ear to hang it up, but my words freeze her:

"You're taking the fall for him. I hope it's worth it."

"Joey will take care of me. He'll get me out of here. I'm the only one who was honest with him and told him his dear innocent little wifey was actually a whore sleeping with my husband."

I stare at her for a second, feeling my face turn red with fury. "If what you say is true, then it looks like you are actually the one who should be behind bars for Maria Martin's murder."

I slam the phone down.

For a second, I see what she doesn't want me to—a flicker of fear and doubt running across her face.

Chapter 45

THE FOX TV reporter flutters her eyelashes at Dave Schrader, who is doing a great job of keeping his eyes off her bulging cleavage. His radio show must have some pull. I called him this morning and within a few hours, he's on the five o'clock news.

I'm perched on the edge of my couch with the remote in my hand. I automatically like Schrader, since the overly made up TV reporter is practically falling out of her white silk blouse and he's not even sneaking a glance. The one time I ran into this reporter at a crime scene, she was whining because she'd gotten some mud on her beige Manolo Blahnik heels.

Now she is clearly reading from a cue card, her eyes squinting.

"Dave, you say Gabriella Giovanni will reveal the identity of the killer—or rather who she suspects is the killer—in the Mission Massacre?" she asks.

"That's right. She has proof of who did it. She'll talk about it tonight, on my *True Crime Tuesday* radio show. Even I don't know what evidence or proof she has." He leans back on the couch.

"That's tonight, right, Dave?"

"Yes, today is Tuesday."

"Shouldn't she go to the police with this information?" the reporter asks, simpering.

"From my understanding, this investigation is so sensitive that Ms. Giovanni is not sure exactly who to trust, so she wants to go public with the information first. After, she will turn it over to the San Francisco Police Department."

My phone rings, so I don't hear the rest of the brief interview.

"What the hell are you doing?"

Donovan. He decides to call me now. Too little, too late.

"I've got it under control," I say with gritted teeth, wondering how he heard about all of this in D.C.

He knows he has no say about what I do right now. He wants a "break," he can have one. But I still feel compelled to take away his worry if I can. I'm not a total bitch.

"Donovan, you don't have to worry about me, it's a trap. C-Lo will be watching the whole time. It's a chance to lure the killer out of hiding."

The line is silent.

"What was that line about SFPD?"

"Come on. They lost the evidence, Donovan. Nobody loses evidence unless they want to. Something is going on. Someone powerful is protecting Joey Martin, and I'm going to find out why."

"You'll do whatever the hell you want because you always do. But this time you're messing with the U.S. military. You are way out of your league. I'm tempted to catch the next flight home."

"I don't need you to come in and rescue me. I'm not a damsel in distress. If the military or the cops wanted to get rid of me, don't you think they would've a long time ago? They're not worried about me, and that's where they are making a mistake," I say. "Besides, I'm not going after the U.S. military. I'm going after a man who killed his family and is probably going to kill his daughter if he hasn't already. If there is any chance she's alive, I can't sit back and do nothing. Anyway, you don't have to worry I'm not going into this alone. I have someone from SFPD on board—Detective Strohmayer."

The line is silent. Is he jealous? He doesn't have anything to worry about. The last thing I'm interested in right now is complicating my life with another man—a married man to boot. Besides, like it or not, I'm in love with Donovan.

"I've got to go." I hang up without waiting for his response.

And if things go as planned, I won't be alone for even a second. As soon as we hang up, I dial Strohmayer's cell. I sort of fibbed to Donovan. I planned on bringing Strohmayer into the loop, but I haven't actually reached him yet. I called him three times already today, but I didn't get a response.

This time he answers. I tell him all about my plan for tonight and the note from Maria I have in my bag. Joey Martin is going to kill Lucy if he hasn't already. Why he didn't the first time, I don't know. It doesn't make sense. But his intentions in that note are clear. And if he has killed her, I will not stop until he is punished for it.

At first, Strohmayer isn't happy about my plan, but he warms up to the idea and agrees to help. There are at least three cops he can trust at the department, he says. Then he hangs up to make arrangements.

Less than four hours until go time.

Slipping on my old worn jeans, a stocking cap, and my Oakland Raiders hoodie, I lace up my combat boots and pound down the stairs. I also scrubbed all the makeup off my face. Now that I've been in the paper and on TV, I'm worried my chess buddies will recognize me. Part of what I love about playing chess on Market Street is that it is one place where I'm always anonymous, where I can go to escape and not be baggage-laden Gabriella Giovanni for a few hours. Glancing at my clock, I see I have time for a few quick chess games on Market Street, dinner, and, after, my interview on live radio.

An hour later, Georges looks worried as I try to hail a cab on Market Street. I've lost four games in a row. And I bet big. Twenty-five bucks a game.

"Natasha, today is just not your day," he says, and his big brown eyes under bushy eyebrows seem sad. "You maybe want to go home now and get in bed. Luck and fortune are not shining on you today, my friend."

I think about that for a second. He may be right. Either way, it's too late. Game on.

Chapter 46

GO TIME.

Lopez calls my cell to let me know he's downstairs. I buzz him in, and when I open my door, he gives a low whistle; I threw on a low-cut navy velvet dress, my highest black sandals, and long silver earrings that dangle to my shoulders.

"Man, I don't want to have to be the one to tell you this," Lopez says, "but nobody can see you on the radio."

"Very funny, C-Lo."

Behind him is an older man with a receding hairline and wide smile. He wears jeans and a fleece pullover. I can tell he's packing.

"Detective Werner?" I say, turning toward him. "This is my friend Chris Lopez."

"Met on the way up," he says and extends his hand. "Call me Mac."

"Thanks for coming on short notice, Mac."

"Amanda was my friend."

I meet his eyes and nod.

"I made some *pasta fazool.* It's simmering on the stove, and there's a baguette on the table and beer in the fridge. Oh, and there's the remote control. Please make yourself at home. I think we'll be back around ten or so."

"Oh boy, does that smell good," he says, smiling and rubbing his hands together. "Dinner, too? This is the best security gig I've ever had."

"Well, thanks again. I really appreciate it."

Downstairs, Lopez opens the passenger door to my Toyota Avalon for me. I've asked him to drive. I pull down the visor and attempt to fix my lipstick in the mirror as he swerves through town like he's got a guest spot on *The Streets of San Francisco* TV show.

"This baby handles like a Maserati, man. No shit. Who would've thought," he says, accelerating through the Stockton Street tunnel and downshifting through a curve.

Satisfied with my makeup, I lean back and close my eyes, replaying what I'm going to say. He won't be able to resist. Joey Martin will be listening to the show. He will know what I mean and he will rise to the bait. I'm certain.

"Do me a favor," I say as we near Van Ness Boulevard. "Pull over near that mailbox."

He pulls over, and I lean over and stick a package in the mailbox.

"What was that?"

"The evidence that will convict Joey Martin."

"Cool, man. Who did you mail it to?"

"The district attorney's office."

"You think you can trust them?"

"Nicole told me which D.A. was for sure on the up-and-up. A young one. Kimberly Fowler. You heard of her?"

"Hell, yes. All the Bay Area photogs call her 'the Babe D.A.' "

Fowler may look like she stepped off the cover of *Vogue* magazine, but according to Nicole, she's a shark.

When we pull up, the streets are filled with TV vans, their satellites stretching up into the sky.

"What the fuck are they doing here? Since when do TV stations show up to cover a radio show?" He looks over and squints at me. "That's why you dressed up. You knew this, man, didn't you?"

I give him a smile and raised eyebrow. He fiddles with his radio, plugging in a Beastie Boys CD while we wait until the car clock clicks to 8:45 p.m. Out of the corner of my eye, I see the TV reporters prepping to go live for the nine o'clock broadcast.

"Showtime," I say, opening the door and swinging my legs to the ground.

"Ms. Giovanni, are you going to reveal who the Mission Massacre killer is on tonight's radio show?"

"Why are you talking to Darkness Radio instead of the cops? Do you think you're above the law?"

"What do you hope to accomplish with this interview tonight?"

I smile and pause, like I'm on the freaking Hollywood Red Carpet. My acting better be up to that standard if what I have planned is going to work.

"I'm sorry, there must have been some confusion about my interview here tonight," I say. "I'll talk about what I saw that night in the apartment, but I'll let the police reveal who the killer is. There is just one more puzzle piece that needs to be played before that can happen."

The last sentence is the only true thing I say. A few reporters turn away in disappointment, so I talk fast.

"I have something that specifically names the Mission Massacre killer."

I pause dramatically and look right into the camera of Channel 5, which is the most- watched station in the Bay Area.

"What is it?" a reporter finally asks.

"One of the victims, Maria Martin, kept a detailed journal. In that journal, she names her killer. She describes him in detail."

"Who is it then?" a reporter asks impatiently.

"Well, here is where it gets really interesting," I say. "And, also, tragic."

The silence is only broken up by the sound of a car a street over zooming past.

I wait until they are leaning toward me, then I give them my rehearsed spiel: "The lead detective on the case, Amanda Khoury, was so dedicated to solving this case that she found what all the evidence techs had missed—Maria's journal.

"As soon as Khoury saw the journal and read it, she knew she had solved the case. Because she lives near Maria Martin, she stopped to walk her dog before she headed into the police station to turn in the journal as evidence. She knew she'd probably be pulling an all-nighter in preparing arrest warrants for the killer, so she wanted to make sure her dog, Shelby, was fed and walked, because she wasn't sure when she'd be back home again.

"Tragically, when she was walking her dog, she was murdered.

"Here is what the police aren't telling you," I continue, raising my voice. "Detective Amanda Khoury was murdered because she found the journal. She was not the victim of a random robbery gone bad. She was killed because she had figured out who the killer was."

There is silence as they wait for me to go on.

"But the killer never found Maria's journal. The good news is that journal is now in my possession—well, not actually in my possession. I'm not stupid. I have it in a safe, secure place, and I'll turn it over to the police first thing in the morning. I hope you will all be there. Nine a.m. Front steps of the San Francisco Police Department. Now, if you'll excuse me, I have a radio interview to do."

I turn and go through the big glass doors without looking back. I can hear the reporters scrambling to pack up their equipment. Chattering excitedly, they're calling their producers.

And just in case Martin missed the TV news, I go in and meet with Dave Schrader and tell him the exact same thing.

But this time I also talk more about what I saw and how disturbing it was. I owe Dave that for cooperating with me and for pulling out all the stops to make sure all his TV news pals covered my arrival.

It is crucial that Joey Martin come out of hiding to try to get the journal before I turn it over to the police in the morning.

I'll make it easy for him to get it, but it will be a fake journal. I spent some time earlier carefully copying a few passages from Maria's journal into a new black Moleskine. It won't matter if Martin gets the fake, since I've already mailed the original to the Babe D.A.

Strohmayer and another one of his buddies should be somewhere nearby the radio station, waiting to tail Lopez and me back to my apartment. After Lopez drops me off, Mac will move outside the building, and at least two cops will stay on stakeout near my place overnight, waiting in case Martin shows up.

When I leave in the morning, they'll follow me—or Martin, if he shows. I'll pretend to retrieve the journal from a storage locker at the BART station and put it in my bag. Then, amid the rush-hour crowd, I'll set my bag down on a table at a sidewalk coffee shop while I go to the counter to get some cream and sugar. If Martin's followed me, he'll grab the journal and run. The cops who've followed us from my place will tail him so they can find where he's keeping Lucy. And then arrest him. Strohmayer said that once Martin is in custody, he's going to bring in the big guns, some buddy in the CIA to help him investigate Khoury's death and figure out what the military is up to.

The detectives will also do their best to find out why the military is giving Martin an alibi. That will be their job. My job is to get Lucy safely away from him. I know the clock is ticking. Martin has had Lucy for five days now. That's a lot of time for a sociopath to have a baby in his care. The darkest side of me wants to scream that it's too late—that she's dead—but I can't go there.

I only hope that wherever he is hiding, Joey Martin is someplace where he tuned into the radio or TV and saw me. Otherwise, this whole exercise is a waste of time.

Tricia called me this morning to tell me that Martin said he was leaving the country. When Lucy's caseworker asked him where she could forward some immunization information she'd gotten from the pediatrician, he told her he'd have to get back to her with a forwarding address. When she pressed him on it, he got angry and rude, saying he was going to be out of the country soon and could give a shit about their stupid paperwork. The woman was shocked enough to blab about it in the break room yesterday. If my plan doesn't work, he may disappear with Lucy forever. If she's still alive.

Chapter 47

WHEN WE PULL back into my neighborhood, I glance into every parked car. I wonder if Joey is already out there somewhere. I don't see signs of Strohmayer or his cop friends anywhere. That's good, though. It wouldn't do to have them be obvious.

Lopez drops me off out front and waits for me to enter the building before leaving to hunt down a parking spot on my crowded street. The plan is for me to get a good night's sleep while Lopez and Strohmayer and his buddies keep an eye on my place from below.

Trudging up my stairs, I can't wait to change into a pair of sweatpants and a T-shirt. My feet hurt from my heels, and my dress is itchy.

I'll thank Mac and get in my pajamas. Thinking this, I step inside my apartment. I automatically close the door behind me, ready to greet the detective. The words are frozen on my lips as fear shoots through me. In the millisecond it takes before cold steel presses against my neck, I take in the scene before me—my apartment is in shambles, and there are two jean-clad legs sticking out of my bathroom. Mac.

"Scream and I'll slice your head right off your neck. You've seen what I can do. Understand?" I start to nod, but as soon as I do, I feel the prick of the blade.

"Where are they?" The voice is warm on my neck, and I feel a beefy chest pressed against my back. Joey Martin. He smells like cologne and toothpaste. Like he groomed himself carefully before this attack.

"On the table," I say, gesturing to the journal I bought today. Why did he say, "Where are *they*?" as if there were more than one?

"Don't fuck with me." He growls the words in my ear. "That's fake. It's not Maria's handwriting. What do you think, I'm stupid?"

He puts his arm around my waist and lifts me, pulling me back from the door. "Where are they? Give them to me and you won't die."

Again it is plural. *They. Them.*

I flash back to earlier—sliding the package in the mailbox on Van Ness Boulevard. I can't give the real journal to him anymore. And he's serious about killing me. In my mind, I can clearly see his father with his throat cut. He'll do it. If he can do that to the people he loved, he won't hesitate to kill me.

"It's not here." My voice is shaky. "It's in a storage locker at the Embarcadero BART station. I was going to get it in the morning. I'm not stupid, either. I'm not keeping something like that at my place." The pressure on the blade seems to ease slightly. "What you saw was what I copied out of the journal for the story I'm writing for my newspaper. If you tell me where Lucy is I'll tell you exactly where to find it."

He presses the blade into my neck. "You'll tell me anyway.

Where's the key to the storage locker?" I still haven't seen his face. He's staying behind me, holding the blade to my neck. "Empty your bag."

He prods at my bag on the floor with his foot, and I lean down and empty it onto the floor. Of course, there is no locker key.

"Where is it?" he growls as I stand and he puts the blade on my neck again.

Flashing to all possible spots in my apartment where I can say the key is, I pick one that means he'll have to let me go to reach it. "On top of the kitchen cabinet. Against the wall. If you tell me where Lucy is, I'll tell all the cops to go away. I'll give it all to you myself. Tonight. Just tell me where she is."

The pressure of the blade is removed, and he shoves me against the wall. I hit it hard and slump down. "You don't seem to understand who is in charge here," he says and then moves so fast I only feel him pass before the light in my kitchen flicks on. Joey Martin's dark hair is buzzed in a crew cut. His full lips and bushy eyebrows might be attractive on someone whose face isn't ravaged by fury. His body is pure muscle, his chest as wide as a doorway, his neck as thick as a telephone pole. He's probably only a few inches taller than me, but twice as bulky. He wears tan canvas pants and a matching shirt with lots of pockets—some sort of desert military fatigues. A samurai sword dangles in one arm by his side.

His eyes wander down my body in a way that makes my skin crawl. I eye Mac's legs sticking out of the bathroom, but it's not clear if he's dead or injured.

I try to distract Martin. "Why did you do it? Why did you kill your whole family?" I don't disguise the disgust in my voice.

His dark eyes meet mine without flinching. "Unless you've been over there—to Iraq—and seen what I've seen, you can't understand. In Iraq, I saw more people I know die than you've met in your entire life. Dead bodies are nothing. Killing someone is the easiest thing to do in the world."

He taps the sword on my wooden floor, watching me, waiting for me to react to his words.

"Killing is easy? Even your parents? The people who raised you?" I'm hoping to jar him, give myself time to figure out a way to escape. I stand, keeping my back against the wall.

"Anyone can raise a kid," he says, his eyes growing even darker. "Your family isn't the two people who fucked and brought you into this world. I didn't choose them, and they didn't choose me. I was a mistake. My mother would have told you that. She never wanted me. They mean nothing to me. I'm a trained and paid killer. The government pays me to kill. I kill to keep people like you safe."

His smirk at these words makes me angry, so I decide not to hold back.

"Don't act so honorable. You didn't kill them defending America. You killed your entire family because you were jealous. It's that simple."

His eyes narrow and his lip curls up. "I am not jealous."

"Then you're insecure. You thought Maria cheated on you. But guess what, you were wrong. She never cheated on you. Never. It says so in the journal. Carol Abequero lied to you because she's in love with you."

He stomps closer to me, eyes blazing in anger. "You think you know so much? Pure little Maria fucked everyone. Abe. My nephew. Even my goddamn sensei. My family covered it up. They all betrayed me. Traitors deserve to die."

"What happened in Iraq?"

He whips his head to look at me, eyes wide and then narrow.

"I know something bad happened. What was it?"

"It was nothing." His face grows bland again, expressionless. He flicks the pillows off my couch with his sword as he talks. Caught up in the conversation, it seems like he's momentarily forgotten about the key in the kitchen.

"If it was nothing, why did you try to kill yourself?"

In less than a second, he is before me, and his meaty hands are wrapped around my neck.

"Who told you that?"

"I don't know what happened over there," I say. "But I know that it was fucked up enough for you to want to die." I stare into his eyes, looking for any warmth. There is none. His fingernails dig into the flesh on my throat. I can't breathe for a second, and then he eases up. The light in his eyes fades. He lets go, and his eyes grow flat again, dead.

"You don't know. You are fishing. You are a good actress. But I am trained to read people. You are lying."

He's only a few inches from me. I can smell his dinner. Something garlicky.

"Why did you kill Javier?"

He doesn't act surprised that I know this.

"Javier was okay. His only problem was being in the wrong place at the wrong time. He saw me come in with blood all over. I couldn't trust him to keep his mouth shut. Sort of like you." He smiles at his cleverness, then his eyes grow hard and his lips press tightly together, as if he remembers why he is here. "Enough bullshit talk. Give me the goddamn key before I slice your fucking head off your neck." He breathes the words in a hiss. Instead of his fingernails, the cold steel is pressed up against my throat again. Another prick, like a needle, and he draws the blade away from my neck. He holds it up a few inches from my eyes. A drop of my blood slides down it.

"Up there," I say and point to the kitchen cabinets. Without turning completely away from me, he eyes the cabinets. "I'll get it if you tell me where Lucy is."

"You'll get it anyway." He shoves me toward the kitchen. I need him to make me get up on the counter, if he does and finds there is no key up there, I'm dead.

I hold my breath, waiting for him to make the decision.

"Get up there and get it," he says. I try to hide my relief. This is my only chance. As I walk, my heel catches in my dress and rips it. I can feel his breathe on the back of my neck as he follows me.

Out of the corner of my eye, I spot Dusty's tail sticking out from behind the couch. It is waving angrily. *Stay put, Dusty.* I don't doubt that Joey Martin will kill a helpless animal.

Grabbing a chair, I put it in front of the sink, giving him as wide a berth as I can in my tiny apartment. He rotates his body so his eyes never leave me. I climb onto the chair and turn my back on him. His hands are on me, moving up my legs to my lower back. "Nice." The word sends a ripple of terror down my body, and my mouth goes dry.

"One last question," I say, turning toward him and effectively eluding his grasp. "Do you really think you can get away without anyone knowing you killed your family?" I know if I keep him talking there is a chance Lopez or Strohmayer below might figure out something up here is awry since Mac hasn't come downstairs yet.

"Much bigger issues are at stake than that. They'll leave me alone if I keep quiet."

"Who are *they*? Keep quiet about what?"

His eyes grow wide. "Son of a bitch. You don't have the right journal. You don't have the original letters, do you? You don't even fucking have anything, do you? I've come here, risking everything, and you don't even have them." He spits on my wood floor, and my eyes narrow.

"I didn't read the whole thing. Or all the letters," I add at the last second. He said the "original" letters. He doesn't have the letters under the floorboard? Then who does?

But he's not done talking. "I told them if they leave me the fuck alone, their secret is safe with me. But that means staying low, off the radar. Anyone gets a hold of the originals to those letters, it's all over. You put it in the paper that I killed Maria, they will have to come after me so they can get me before the cops do. They don't trust me not to crack under pressure to the cops. If the cops find me, *they* will find me, and I'm a dead man."

"Who are *they*? The military? Does this have to do with why they lied about where you were?"

"I was totally going to play it cool and keep their goddamn secret, but they wouldn't give me leave to come see Maria, so I had to take off on my own."

It's a gamble, but I'll take it. "Why did you tell Maria everything in the letters? And what did you do with the copies you found under the floorboard?"

It pays off.

"It was a mistake." He spits the words out. I was right—he got the letters under the floorboard. But they were copies. Where are the originals? He goes on. "I told her before I knew she was a cheating whore. I wanted her to know to never trust the American government. They don't care about anyone. Not Flight 93. Not you. Not me. Nobody. That's why I'm going underground and they'll never see me again."

"What?" Flight 93 was the plane that crashed in the field on 9/11. When it happened last year, I interviewed the family of one of the victims, because he was from our newspaper coverage area.

"You think the government cares about its people?" he says. "It doesn't. Flight 93 is proof of that. The government only cares about itself and its upper echelon. They didn't know I knew everything until I went AWOL. When they threatened to court-martial me for desertion, I told them what I heard. What I knew. The deal is they will leave me alone if I keep quiet. If the letters get out, I'm a dead man. There will be no place to hide."

"What do you mean? What about Flight 93?" I shoot a sideways glance at Mac's legs sticking out my bathroom door. Did they twitch, or am I imagining things?

"We shot it down. Our country. We did it."

"What?" The blood drains from my face. What's he talking about?

"I heard everything in that Blackhawk. They didn't know. I heard it all."

"I don't understand."

"That morning on 9/11, they ordered me to get the general to the White House safe and sound," Martin says, tapping the sword on the counter, the vein in his temple throbbing as he grows angrier telling his story. "They forgot to turn off the headphones. I heard the whole thing. Heard the general give the order to shoot down Flight 93 before it got to the White House. Only ones who heard it was me, the general, and whoever shot the flight down."

I'm trying to digest what he has said, the revelation he has made. Can it be true? Is he that deranged, or is this why the military lied about his whereabouts? Because despite what he thinks, they don't want him arrested. They want him dead.

The United States government shot down a plane carrying forty Americans. Martin might be one of the few people in the world who knows about it, and he thinks they will let him live with this knowledge?

He's a dead man walking.

"What's done is done," he says when he sees the look of horror on my face. "Now quit stalling. Get up there and get me the key. I got some business in Oakland before I split town. Hurry."

"Is that where Lucy is? In Oakland? Is she alive?"

"Get up there."

I step from the chair onto the counter. Leaning forward, I swipe my hand across the top of the cabinet until I find what I'm looking for. Out of the corner of my eye, I see him watching.

He sweeps his sword up and down with a swishing sound. "Is it up there or not? If you're fucking with me . . ." He stands on the chair and rubs the smooth edge of the sword against my bare thigh. Across the room, a loud crash signals that Dusty has tried to escape his hideout behind the couch but has taken down some lamp cords and lamps with him. "What the fuck?" Martin swivels his head toward the living room for a second without taking the sword off my leg.

Taking advantage of the distraction, I twist at the waist and bring my hand down from the cabinet right when Joey Martin turns back and finds the tear-gas canister at eye level. I push down with my finger, and pepper spray squirts in his eyes.

He howls and jerks, and an intense pain sears my leg. I collapse onto the small counter before tumbling, taking Joey Martin off the chair with me. We land in a thud, and I hear Martin smack his head on something. Fortunately, his chest cushions my landing. Rolling off him, I hope he's dead or knocked out, but he's only stunned. The sword is still in his hand. I jerk in time to hear the zing of the metal hitting something hard beside me. "Motherfucker." He grunts.

The samurai sword's blade is embedded in the wooden kitchen floor a few inches away from my head. He tugs at it, but it doesn't budge. It's stuck in the crack of a floorboard. Thank God for these old floors. The veins on his arm bulge near my head and neck as he pulls even harder, his face growing red. I try to roll away, but he notices and kicks at me, striking my left thigh with his boot heel. I scream in pain. The floor is slippery underneath me as I try to crawl backward away from him.

"Where is she?" The words are thick in my mouth. "Where is Lucy?"

He keeps tugging on the sword. I wonder how long before it will spring free. I eye the front door. I'm only a few feet away now.

"Is she dead?"

He shrugs. "She isn't mine. Don't you understand a thing I said? Maria was whoring around. God knows whose baby that is. Probably that traitor Abe."

She's alive. That is why he shrugged. He wouldn't hesitate to tell me she was dead.

"She's yours. The DNA test proved it." It's a lie, but it stops him in his tracks. He looks down, hand frozen on the scabbard. For a second, he closes his eyes. His fingers go for the cell phone clipped to his belt. They linger there for a second before returning back to his side. He was going to call someone. To stop her from being killed. I know it.

"Who were you calling? Who has her? Tell me!"

"There was no DNA test. You're lying to me. I can see it."

It's true. He spots my lies instantly.

"Where is Lucy? Is she dead?"

He avoids my eyes.

"She's not dead, is she? You couldn't do it."

He doesn't deny it. I know I'm right. She's still alive. For whatever reason, he hasn't killed her yet. Relief floods me mingling with a burst of hope and adrenaline. There is still a chance to save her.

"None of that matters." He stands. The sword is in his hand, free of the wood. He starts walking toward me. "This sword has taken many lives. It will now take two more. I have no reason to keep that baby alive. Too bad you don't understand what the sensei does—death by sword is an honorable way to die."

A loud knock on my door echoes throughout the apartment, and he freezes.

"Giovanni? Mac?" It's Lopez.

"C-Lo!" My voice tells him everything he needs to know, and within seconds I hear a click and a bump, and the door handle turns.

Martin gives one look at the door and sprints to the sliding-glass doors leading to my balcony. "He's here!" I shout it as loud as I can, but my words are stuck. I scramble toward the door as it swings open. "He hurt Mac!"

Lopez rushes in with gun drawn.

"The balcony," I say. I try to stand, but there is something wrong with my leg.

The curtains to my sliding-glass doors blow from a slight breeze. I can't see anything beyond them.

He's trapped. I live on the fourth floor. There is a reason I live this high up. I don't want anyone able to get in my windows or onto my balcony.

Lopez rushes toward the balcony and rips open the curtain. Even from where I slump, I can see the balcony is empty. Lopez goes to the edge and leans over. He fires one shot, which echoes loudly.

"Damn. Missed." He rushes back over to me and slips in the blood on the floor, sliding into me. I wince in pain.

"How did he get down?" I ask.

"Dude is like fucking Spiderman or something, jumped from balcony to balcony. Come on." He reaches and pulls me up. When he sees my leg his brow furrows. "What the fuck?"

"Just a little samurai sword slice."

He races to the open door of my closet and rips a shirt off a hanger. I see it is my Calvin Klein blouse. He starts to rip it in strips. "No, not that one," I start to protest but instead grimace in pain.

He wraps it tightly around my thigh and says, "You're goddamn lucky. He missed slicing your femoral artery to shreds. You should've lost a shitload more blood than you did. You're still gonna need stitches, though. An assload of them maybe. I can only delay the inevitable here."

He pauses for a minute and draws back, looking at me with an odd expression. "Maybe your guardian angel is watching over you tonight, Giovanni."

"Maybe," I say solemnly, thinking of Caterina, but I grow frantic, remembering. "Mac! He's in the bathroom."

Lopez rushes over. He's on his knees, checking for a pulse on the detective. I'm clutching my phone, waiting for Lopez to speak. "He's alive."

I hear a small groan.

"Thank God." I breathe a sigh of relief and dial Strohmayer. "Call nine-one-one. Joey Martin was here. He hurt Mac. He's going to kill Lucy. We have to get to her first. He said he had business in Oakland. He's either heading for the dojo or to this club Fellatio in Oakland."

Strohmayer swears softly before he talks into his radio, his voice strained. "Officer down." He gives my address and says to me, "We're on it."

"We're coming out and heading to Oakland. Meet you there," I say and hang up.

Lopez comes out and gestures to Mac behind him, who is sitting up. "He'll live."

I grab my bag and open the door. "Lucy. We have to get her first."

"Where is she?" Lopez asks.

"I don't know for sure." I hate that these words are true. "He said he had two more lives to take and that he needed to get to Oakland. There are only two places I know about in Oakland where he might be. He said Javier saw him come in with blood all over him. It has to be the dojo or the sex club."

"Think. Which one do you think it is?" Lopez asks, holding my arms. "Think, Giovanni. Trust your gut on this one."

I squint my eyes closed, and the answer leaps to my mind. The kid on the street, Tre, said he thought there were rooms that people stayed in at Fellatio. That would be the perfect place for Martin to hide out and keep a baby. After the massacre, he was more likely to go to a room at the sex club to change than the dojo. It has to be Fellatio.

"The sex club," I say, opening my eyes and scrambling to my

feet as the sounds of sirens fill the streets below. Mrs. Cossetta peeks out of her apartment.

"Mrs. Cossetta! There's a police officer injured in my bathroom. Will you please sit with him until the paramedics get upstairs?"

Her mouth is wide open, and I cast one last glance back at Mac's legs before I follow Lopez, leaving my front door wide open.

We are heading for the sex club first. I hope I'm right because if I'm wrong, Lucy is dead.

Chapter 48

I'M FREEZING ON the back of Lopez's motorcycle in my ripped, bloody, velvet dress, which is flapping in the wind like a tattered flag. When I asked to go with Lopez, I didn't realize he had his motorcycle outside. But it is infinitely faster than taking a car. At this rate, we might even beat Martin to Oakland. We ride the white line all the way across the Bay Bridge.

My hair is whipping in the wind, so I bury my face in the back of C-Lo's leather jacket, clutching him around the waist and hoping we don't crash and die before I can get to Lucy.

Finally, we exit the bridge. Lopez parks half a block away from the sex club.

"Stick here until I figure out what's up," he whispers.

"Forget that," I say and leap off the bike onto my good leg. Even so, a sharp lightning bolt of pain shoots up my other leg.

"Was worried you might say that." He hands me a gun from his ankle strap. "Try not to shoot me."

"Thanks for your vote of confidence." I stick the gun in my purse.

"No problem, man."

We hug the walls of the buildings across the street from the club, looking up at the dark windows. Every time a car pulls up, we duck into a doorway, but no vehicles stop.

"Let's get the kid and let's scram and let the cops deal with that crazy fuck Martin," Lopez says over his shoulder to me.

I don't see Strohmayer anywhere. Maybe he's already inside? I dial Strohmayer's number but get his voice mail. "Where are you? We're already at Fellatio on Fifth Street in Oakland. We're going to go in."

Lopez grabs his pick lock kit and a bump key out of his back pocket, and we slink over to the door of the sex club, looking over our shoulders every few seconds. A shadowy figure turns onto the street and we freeze, but it turns down an alley.

Lopez ignores the doorbell. With the bump key, it only takes him a second to unlock the door. We slip inside, closing the door behind us in the pitch black. Lopez snaps on a small flashlight attached to his keychain.

"You're a regular MacGyver," I say with admiration.

"Damn straight, man," he whispers back. "Once a Green Beret, always a Green Beret. *MacGyver*'s a really good show, by the way."

Following him up the steep staircase, I can feel the pounding of music somewhere close, vibrating through my bones.

At the top is another door, locked. Even in the blackness, Lopez opens it within seconds. The door noisily creaks open, and we freeze again. We are in a small foyer. It is lined with coats hanging on coatracks. A man sitting in an easy chair jumps to his feet, pointing a gun at us.

Before I can react, Lopez has the man's arm behind his back, and the gun clatters to the ground.

"Easy now, we didn't mean to scare you. The door was unlocked. We're just here to have some fun." Lopez lets go of the man's arm and backs off, holding one arm up and putting the other one around my neck, drawing me close. The other man, who has a tightly shaved head, keeps his eye on us as he reaches down for his gun. Lopez lifts his shirt a few inches to reveal the gun tucked into his waistband and waits until the man puts his own gun away before lowering his shirt. Lopez reaches for his wallet. He tucks a hundred-dollar bill into the man's palm.

The man looks at the money in his hand and smiles. He holds out his palm again.

Lopez extracts two more one-hundred-dollar bills and sticks them in the man's jacket pocket. The man bows and presses a small button near the table lamp. A solid steel door to our right clicks open.

"One more thing," Lopez says, turning, as if it's an afterthought. "If we get too tired to drive home, can we get a room?"

The man doesn't answer for a second. "Find Claudio. He's got a green hat on."

As soon as the steel door swings open, we are greeted by low, throbbing music. The room is lit with lights that run along the floor, like in a movie theater. Long, flowing fabric hangs from the ceiling in oranges and reds and blues and pinks. A small, elevated dance floor contains stripper poles wound with tiny white lights. Nobody looks up when we come in. All the attention is focused on the elevated dance floor. On it, it looks like four bodies are pressed close to, around, and between a naked woman's legs.

We scan the crowd. They are dressed in a variety of gear, from three-piece suits to lingerie with garter belts, to nothing at all. But nobody is wearing a green hat.

With a hand to my back, Lopez guides me toward another doorway. My leg is smarting from the cut. It feels sticky and wet, but I don't have time to worry if the makeshift bandage is leaking.

The next room is a soft, hazy, red color, and the music is different, more pounding and rhythmic. In that room, a few couples are having sex on an assortment of plush velvet furniture flanked by Tiffany-style lamps with red lightbulbs. One woman wears a period costume from the Victorian era, complete with hoops, and the dress is thrown up over her head as her partner thrusts against her. Another couch is home to two men and a woman wrapped around one another. In a shadowy corner, a woman in a garter belt and corset has her legs wrapped around a man who is pressed tightly into the corner clutching her ass, his head over her shoulder, biting his lip and moaning. The combined moaning in the room is nearly louder than the music. No green hats.

We push on. This room has two doorways. Lopez motions for me to wait as he sticks his head into a particularly dark room illuminated by a large TV screen showing naked entangled bodies. Dark silhouettes cover a bevy of couches and are contorted in ways I can't quite figure out. I'm so intent on watching Lopez wend his way through the clusters of bodies that I don't realize someone has crept up until I feel hands cover my breasts and a body presses tightly against me from behind. I buck away right when Lopez arrives. His eyes grow wide, and I grab his arm before he swings a punch. I lean into his ear. "*Look.*" He follows my gaze.

The man who fondled me wears a mask that makes his face look like a pointy-beaked bird. On top of his head is a giant green top hat.

"Sorry to startle you," he says in a thick British accent. "I'm

Claudio." He takes a deep bow. "Gigi," I say, nodding back. "This is Chris."

Lopez is gritting his jaw tightly but manages to nod.

"You are new." He says it as a statement. He wears tight jeans and an equally tight black T-shirt that shows every ripple on his abdomen.

"Yes." I try to see his eyes past the mask, but it is too dark. "I thought maybe this would be good for our relationship, but maybe we need some time alone first. To warm up, you know. I heard you had rooms to rent?"

"Yes. Follow me." He puts his hand on my back so low I cringe and scoot away, making my leg erupt in pain from the sudden jerking movement. I clutch Lopez's arm and give him a look. He picks up on it and places himself between the birdman and me. The man leads us through another room.

This room is dark except for one giant spotlight shining down on a man getting oral sex from another man. Claudio takes a key and opens a door to a small passageway. Once the door behind us closes, he uses a different key and opens the door to a bright hallway with about a dozen doors. He opens the closest door to our left and hands us the key. He catches me eyeing a doorway at the end of the hall.

"There is a doorway to the street for our regular guests to use. But I suggest you come back through the club. That way you can pay me for the room. Come find me."

"You trust us?" I can't help but ask.

He leans back and lets out a laugh. "No. But I'll take a gamble. I'm going to take a chance that you will come back and find me, and that way I can think of a creative way for you to pay for your room. Money means nothing to me. I have more than I will ever need. It is so boring. I weary thinking about it. You, however, I'm fairly certain I would never tire of." He runs a finger down my cheek and across my lips. I am frozen by his touch. I stare at the black orbs of his eyes beneath the mask until Lopez pulls me into the room and closes the door.

"Jesus H. Christ, I thought you were leaving with him. What's the creepy Pied Piper done to you?"

"Nothing," I say and can't bite back the anger I put into the word. I'm not mad at him. I'm mad at my traitorous body, which was responding to that man's touch.

Lopez has his ear pressed to the door. Within seconds, he turns the knob. "He's gone. Let's go."

We start down the hall, pressing our ears to each door before moving on. At one door, I hear a few moans, but most are quiet.

Then, in the stillness, I hear a sound. It's a baby making a loud cry that is abruptly silenced.

Chapter 49

"OVER THERE," I whisper, pointing to a door halfway down the hall.

When I get to the door, I press my ear against it. Yes. A baby is whimpering.

Lopez tries the door first. Unlocked. He raises his eyebrows, steps to the side, and pushes the door open, his gun held in front of him. The door creaks open. We step inside, leaving the door behind us wide open. Inside, a small table lamp illuminates the scene. A woman with teased hair and a slinky nightgown is sitting on a desk chair. She holds Lucy. The baby gurgles in her arms, clutching a bottle. The woman's eyes are wide with fright.

"He made me. He called me and told me to give her this bottle." The woman says it in a daze. Her eyes are bloodshot, and her arms are scarred with needle marks. "I'm babysitting. He said he'd give me money and more smack if I did what he said."

It takes a second for her words to sink in. Did he poison her? I race over and grab the baby out of her arms. "Someone call nine-one-one. We need poison control."

"Nobody is calling anyone." Joey Martin's voice sends a chill down my body. I turn. He is standing in the hallway just beyond the open door, a small gun aimed in my direction. Behind the door, Lopez lifts his gun. Before I can react, the room erupts in a chaotic cacophony of gunfire and screaming and shouting. The last thing I see before I dive for the floor is the door exploding in shattered pieces of wood. Dragging Lucy with me, I roll under the bed. When I turn my head, I'm face-to-face with the woman in the negligee. A black bullet hole gapes between her eyes. After a few seconds, the sounds of scuffling recede and are taken over by feet pounding down the stairs.

The room is dead quiet. Lucy is cooing above my head. She doesn't appear to be hurt from the fall, and she seems happy to see me. Was there poison in that bottle? Is that why he ordered that woman to give Lucy the bottle? I have no idea how much Lucy ingested. We need to get her to the hospital to have her stomach pumped.

I push and slide us out from under the bed, forced to shove the half-naked woman's body out of my way. I try to avoid looking at her face again. Once I'm standing on wobbly legs with Lucy in my arms, I scan the room. Lucy and I are the only ones here—except the dead woman.

My eyes widen as I take in the room for the first time. In one corner is a small bassinet. It contains a pink puppy stuffed animal, and a tiny musical mobile dangles over it. Some milk crates are stacked into a makeshift dresser. The top one holds a neat stack of diapers. The second one has more than a dozen folded baby outfits. The bottom one has baby shampoo, lotion, and diaper cream.

I smell Lucy's hair. Freshly washed. I check her diaper. Dry as a bone.

It is now so clear. I search the floor until I find the bottle I tore from Lucy's grasp. Leaning over, I pick it up, unscrew the nipple, and take a tiny sip. It tastes like regular milk. I thought that woman was implying the bottle contained poison and maybe in her drug-addled brain she thought it did, but it tastes normal.

Joey Martin wanted to kill Lucy. In fact, he might even have tried to kill her. But in the end, he couldn't. All this flashes through my mind in a few seconds.

I spot a thick manila envelope on a bureau. With the hand not holding Lucy, I dump the contents on the bed. Photocopies of letters. Maria's letters.

Shouting and gunfire erupting from down on the street send me heading toward the window. At the same time, the bone-shuddering thump of a helicopter arriving sends a chill down my spine. The entire building is vibrating from the reverberation.

The dead woman is in my way, but instead of going over her to the window, I take the long away and go around her. I'm limping, clutching Lucy to my chest, and trying to ignore the pain in my leg. I push aside heavy blackout curtains, and my breath fogs a small circle on the window as I peer out.

Kicking up dirt and trash, a small, dark helicopter lands in the middle of the street below. Within seconds, five men in full body armor spring out a door and grab a figure dressed in black. Joey Martin. They have his arms and legs and basically throw him in the helicopter in one fluid movement before the buglike aircraft shoots straight up and disappears into the night.

The whole operation—landing, scooping up Martin, and taking off—takes less than thirty seconds.

Blinking, I take in the scene on the street below. A group of people huddles around a figure prone on the ground. An icy chill runs down my spine until I see it's not Lopez. He's nearby, hunched over the body lying in the street. I squint and realize who the man on the ground is—Strohmayer. People dressed in rubber and leather and lacy lingerie are pouring out the front door of the club.

The noise of sirens grows closer, and the room lights up with red and blue strobe lights as emergency vehicles arrive on the street below. More than ten squad cars, a fire truck, and an ambulance.

Holding Lucy's head against my chest, I hobble down the back stairs with one hand grasping the rail. My leg is screaming in pain now. Outside, I push through the crowd in the street, but by the time I get there, they've loaded Strohmayer on a gurney and are pushing it toward the ambulance. His eyes are closed, and his face is ashen.

"Oh Mother Mary, please let him be okay." An image of his wife and kids flashes into my mind. "His family needs him."

I head toward an ambulance that pulls up.

"The baby. Can you check her? There's a slight chance she's been poisoned." Two EMTs take Lucy from me and bring her in the back of the ambulance. I want her checked out. Just in case. Even though I don't think there was anything but milk in that bottle.

"What did she ingest?"

"Maybe nothing, but can you check? Here is her bottle." I thrust the bottle at them. One EMT rips the nipple off, smells, and crinkles his nose.

Inside the ambulance, they have Lucy strapped down. They're checking her pulse and heart rate, looking at her eyes, inside her mouth. They feed her something. Lopez is at my side.

Without warning, my legs give out, and I slump to the ground. A wave of vertigo washes over me. Maybe the bottle did have poison. The next thing I know, I'm guided to the back of an ambulance. I look down, and the blood has soaked through Lopez's makeshift bandage. The sight makes me even dizzier. At the same time, I struggle to get up and go back to Lucy.

Lopez's face peers down at me from the back of the ambulance. "Hey, man, don't worry. I'm riding in the ambulance with the baby girl. She's doing okay. She's in good hands."

I lay back in relief as the ambulance doors slam shut. He'll take care of her.

"Let's get you to the hospital and patched up. Looks like you've lost a lot of blood," one of the EMTs says.

I want to fight, but I don't have it in me.

In the emergency room, I call Lopez on my cell after the doctor has stitched up my leg.

"Where is she?"

"Right here. Grandma's got her. They don't think she ingested any poison. In fact, they don't think the bottle had anything poisonous in it at all. But they are keeping her overnight for observation."

Thank God. Then I remember. "Mac?"

"Concussion. He's having an overnighter, too."

I chew on my lip for a second, the events of the evening replaying themselves in my mind. Lopez was right about the black helicopters all along.

"Who was in the helicopter?" I ask. "Who took Martin?"

"You don't ever have to worry about that punk ever again," Lopez says. "Wherever they took him, he's not coming back."

"Will they kill him?"

"Probably already have."

"Guess that's justice of some sort."

"Yeah. We almost had him. He pulled this fucking knife out of his ass or something and poked Strohmayer in the back. I probably could've got him, Giovanni, but your cop buddy was bleeding so bad, the helicopter landed, and bam. He was gone." He clears his throat for a minute. "How is Stroh, anyway?"

I scramble to find my clothes so I can get dressed. "I don't know. You saw him up close. How bad was it?"

"Hard to say. Could've been a lot worse, though. He could've bled out. Hell, you could've bled out, too."

"Well, it sounds like you saved him and me. Thanks."

"Ain't no big thing, *chica*." He waits for a second, and I know something is wrong.

"What is it, C-Lo?"

"The sensei. He was already dead by the time the fuzz got there."

"Thanks for letting me know." I hang up, remembering the bundle of pussy willow branches the sensei gave me for good luck, now sitting in a vase in my kitchen. All he wanted to do was protect his niece.

A doctor and nurse come in with release papers, and although I'm limping, I move as fast as I can down the hall toward the lobby. The nurse told me someone is waiting for me. The way she smiled, I know it is Donovan, so I hurry, filled with both excitement and nervousness. He must have taken the next plane after we spoke earlier. I round a corner, and a petite woman with short red hair and a pink scarf grabs me in a giant hug. I recognize her from the picture. Strohmayer's wife.

"He'll be fine," she says. "It was only a scratch. A deep one, took a few stitches, but no permanent damage."

"Oh, thank God," I say with a big exhalation. I stick out my hand. "I'm Gabriella."

"I'm Mary. We have a lot to talk about. Scott told me you might be interested in going skydiving with me. I need more friends like you. As soon as the hubby gets on his feet again, we'd love for you to come over and have dinner with us. That is, if you don't mind two crazy energetic twins talking a hundred miles a minute as part of the dinner package."

I can't stop the smile from spreading across my face. "That sounds perfect."

Chapter 50

DONOVAN WRAPS ME in a hug as we walk out of the hospital. He hasn't stopped touching me since I practically threw myself in his arms in the ER lobby. He put his mouth against my hair as he breathed into it. "Thank God you're okay."

I reach up and whisper in his ear. "I love you, but let's get the hell out of here."

He supports me as I walk. I have twenty stitches in my leg. The E.R. doctor said I was pretty damn lucky and the only reason it didn't hurt so bad earlier is that the adrenaline kept me going. But now that everything is over, the pain is intense. I downed a few painkillers and hope they kick in soon.

We are both pretty quiet on the drive back to my apartment. I sink back into the leather seat of his Saab, feeling warm and sleepy. "I think the drugs are kicking in," I say.

"Good. I'm taking you home and putting you to bed."

"Sounds good," I say with a sleepy smile. It's becoming hard to keep my eyes open.

He reaches over and squeezes my hand every once in a while.

Upstairs at my place, I get a second wind.

"I'm starving. Can I eat first?"

He flashes me an appreciative look, and I realize it's been a while since he's heard me say those words. He takes out a loaf of sourdough, some olives, and some cheese, and pours a couple of glasses of red wine.

"Sit." He points to the table.

I sink into the chair, glad to be off my leg, which still smarts a little.

He drains his wine in one gulp and runs his hand through his hair. Uh-oh.

"I've been doing a lot of thinking," he says.

The bread in my mouth seems to expand into a mushy pile of newspaper.

"I'm not going to lie to you," he says. "I want a family almost more than I want anything else in the world."

My heart sinks.

"But I want one thing more than that." He reaches over and grabs my hand. "I want you. I want you with or without a baby. I want you. That's why I need you to let all of this go. Let go of wanting to get pregnant. It's destroying you. If it happens, it happens, but it won't be worth losing you. Nothing is worth losing you."

He takes a breath. "But I need to know. Can you let go? Can you let go of having a baby, even though we both want one? Can you let go? For me. For us?"

It takes me a while to answer. I take my own huge gulp of wine before clearing my throat. I can't lie to him. He deserves the truth.

"I can't let go, Donovan. I'm so sorry. This is who I am. This is what I am. I can't change, Donovan. I can't give up wanting a baby. I don't have it in me."

He stares at me for a second. I hold my breath, waiting to see how he will react. He heads to the counter and opens another bottle of wine before he turns back.

"I've thought about what would happen if you said that. I thought about it on the plane, imagining my life without you."

I watch his mouth as he says these words, and I wait.

"I've decided that I'll do whatever it takes to help you," he says finally. "I want you to let all this go. But if you can't, I'll be here for you."

Hot tears form in the corners of my eyes. He takes my hand. "I promise you I will put you first. If it means blowing off Finn, I will do that. I can always make up for it later. Hell, he can handle the slack. I will put you first no matter what. I promise."

Even though it is what I've dreamed of hearing him say, it doesn't stop the despair from rising up into my chest. I bury my face in Donovan's shirt.

As if he senses the dark pit I've fallen into right on my own couch, Donovan takes my chin in his hand and starts to kiss me with a fury I have never felt before, his mouth traveling across my skin with an urgency and intensity that make my body respond wildly. I'm moaning, and clawing at him, tearing his clothes off him and myself until I'm naked, straddling him on the couch.

Nothing exists except our bodies.

In our wild desire, I distantly register objects flying off my coffee table, glass breaking, pillows flung to the floor, sudden darkness as a table lamp is knocked over. We don't stop or care—all over the apartment, on top of the kitchen table, under it, I lose track of time and can't distinguish between his body and my own. There's definitely something to be said about a lover who knows how every inch of your body responds to his touch after years of practice.

When we finally collapse on the bed, the only thought in my head is wondering when we can do it again.

It's not the first time I've turned to sex to squash pain and doubt and feelings of helplessness. But I don't care. It is what we both need so badly. After last month's sterile, obligatory, hoping-to-get-knocked-up, clinical sex, tonight's session is one for the record books.

Because this time, everything is different. This time, maybe for the first time ever, I'm not afraid to lose myself completely in someone else. And not just anyone—it's the man I'm hoping will be the father of my children.

Chapter 51

FINALLY, AFTER WRITING for ten hours, I hit send and slump back into my chair at my desk.

Kellogg, who has been hovering over my shoulder for the past twenty minutes, sprints back to his desk like a wide-end receiver.

The newspaper attorney reads over Kellogg's shoulder and after a few minutes, gives the thumbs-up. Kellogg stands up, knocking his chair onto the ground and throws his fists up in the air.

The entire newsroom erupts in cheers. A few bottles of champagne are uncorked, and waiters start carrying in plates of food and setting up on a conference-room table.

I close my eyes and smile. My story is flying through the ether. Kellogg is sending it to the Associated Press and then it will appear in newspapers around the world.

I try to keep my eyes open as my colleagues pat me on the back and toast me with bottles of beer and plastic cups of champagne. I've barely slept for the past two days nailing this story down. It *is* the biggest story of my life, just like Maria Martin said it would be.

It turns out General Hightower is in deep shit.

And my story is telling the world all about it. We found proof of what Martin told me, in letters he sent to his wife. We have the photocopies, and the cops have the originals. Maria sent them to her mother's post-office box in San Juan Bautista the day she called me at the newspaper. In her note, she wrote that she was giving me copies to write a story, but she wanted her mother to have the originals for safekeeping.

Mrs. Castillo doesn't check the box often. But she did yesterday.

The letters from Martin outlined what he told me about Flight 93. In the package to her mother, Maria Martin said she was going to go to the press with the information. *The press.* She trusted me with all that information. But Martin killed her in a fit of jealous rage first.

But now the story she trusted me to tell is going to be told.

GENERAL ORDERED FLIGHT 93 SHOT DOWN

When General Craig Hightower learned during the early morning hours of 9/11 fthat Flight 93 was on a direct crash course to the White House, he made the hardest decision of his life: To shoot the plane down.

The revelation comes less than 24 hours after Hightower announced his plans to run for president.

In a conversation secretly recorded by military investigators in his office, Hightower explained that he had no choice but to order the plane shot down.

"Is it a bad thing? Yes. Do I regret it? Yes. Would I do it again? Yes. Of course I didn't want to do it, but would I do it again? In a second."

The president has denied any knowledge of

Hightower's actions, saying the military leader acted independently and under no direct orders from the White House. A congressional investigation has convened.

It's also been revealed that to keep its secret about Flight 93, the general was involved in a massive cover-up involving a U.S. soldier suspected of killing his family.

Joey Martin, a member of an elite, secret unit of the U.S. Army, accidentally heard the general's orders to shoot down the plane while he was in a Blackhawk helicopter escorting the general to the White House in the wake of the first two planes hitting the Twin Towers.

Senator Kate Corvin has confirmed that based on information provided to her office by the Bay Herald, an investigation into both the president's and General Hightower's actions is underway.

Sgt. Martin's account of what he heard was laid out in a long letter he wrote to his wife, who he is now suspected of killing, along with other members of his family.

At the time of the flight to the White House on the morning of 9/11, Martin's headset was accidentally tuned into the same frequency as the general's when the order was given. Officials realized later that someone else had been listening into the conversation, but they did not know it was Martin until he came forward recently with what he knew.

Martin revealed what he had heard after his commanding officers refused to grant Martin leave to come visit his family in San Francisco. When he went

> *AWOL and was threatened with desertion, he contacted the general, saying that if anyone came after him, he would reveal the conversation he had overheard in the Blackhawk.*
>
> *Police say Martin came home and killed his wife, parents, and nephew. The motive for those slayings is still under investigation.*
>
> *As police searched for Martin, the general lied about his whereabouts in an elaborate cover-up, telling his staff, including Lt. General David Cooper, that Martin was still in Iraq.*

I left a lot out of this story. I know why Martin killed his wife and family. He told me himself that he killed her because he thought she was unfaithful, but by even saying this, I'm opening up scrutiny of Maria she doesn't deserve.

And this story would never have come together without the help of Moretti's friend, Lt. General Cooper, who has been on our side ever since we told him what was going on. He arranged the secret recording of Hightower spilling the beans and has taken care of every small detail to make sure nobody will get away with it.

And surprisingly, the recruiter came forward with a statement against the general, saying the general had lied to him, as well. Guess it goes to show that being a jerk doesn't mean you automatically break the law or do something nefarious. Some people are jerks for no good reason.

The letters also revealed what happened to Joey Martin in Iraq. I think that is why he spared Lucy.

Joey and three other men in his unit had been ordered on a covert night mission to destroy a building believed to be a military stronghold and hideout for Osama bin Laden.

Using a Stinger shoulder-fired missile, they firebombed the building. Then, to make sure the job was done, they stormed the rubble of the building to finish Bin Laden off in case he had survived the fire and bombing.

But when they approached the partially collapsed building, they were met with the sounds of women screaming and babies crying. The building was a military hospital with a special newborn unit. Wounded Iraqi nurses wielding machine guns took out two of Joey's fellow soldiers as they approached. Joey and one other U.S. solider took out the five remaining nurses before they left, convinced that Osama had not been there.

Twenty-four babies died that day. Most were the children of military soldiers. The intent had been to send a strong message to Iraqi forces.

The other surviving soldier was shot dead when he opened fire on his commander on the base. Joey believed it was a suicide mission, because he had contemplated suicide, as well.

Maria somehow talked him out of it. But afterward, although he didn't kill himself, he grew cold, vicious, and jealous. She told her mother he had changed.

This must be why Joey Martin couldn't kill Lucy. His taste for blood didn't extend to babies after what he did in Iraq. It explains why he set up a makeshift nursery for Lucy in his room at Fellatio. I think he was going to take her with him and care for her as his own, whether she truly was his or not. Maybe it was his own form of penance. Or maybe he wasn't fully the monster we all believed. We'll never know.

All the charges against Carol Abequero were dropped. She was released from jail the same day that Martin disappeared and she has gone underground.

None of this makes it in my story. That is a story to tell another day. Along with my story about how what soldiers do and see in Iraq can destroy lives if they are not given proper support and help from our government.

My story about Joey Martin goes on to explain how the general's influence extended to Khoury's lieutenant, who had already been arrested on suspicion of killing her after SFPD internal affairs investigators say ballistics analysis matched the bullet to his gun. Apparently, he was so sure he would get away with it that he used his service weapon. The general had promised the lieutenant a position in his cabinet if he was elected president in two years.

The only loose end was Martin. On my drive home to Donovan's, Kellogg calls.

"The general just offered his resignation on CNN. Took the fall for the president. Said he acted alone. One out of two isn't bad. Nice work, Giovanni."

Chapter 52

FATHER LIAM FINISHES sprinkling holy water over Lucy in the baptismal font and hands her to Donovan as the congregation erupts in cheers.

"Up high. Over your head. Like she's the Lion King," he says in Donovan's ear loud enough for me to overhear. He winks at me as he says it.

Donovan holds her high in the air as we process down the aisle at the church, passing faces wide with smiles. We make our way back to a small room, where Lucy will be dried and changed back into a flowing white baptismal gown.

Later, Mrs. Castillo hands her to me as we sit at a picnic in the park. The congregation put together a small feast to celebrate Lucy's baptism. Several colored tablecloths and blankets are spread on the grass. One portable table holds the food—a roast pig, bowls of fruit and vegetables, rolls, and an assortment of salads, wine, lemonade, and cake.

I fold Lucy into my arms and breathe in her hair, trying not to cry. I've been a weepy mess ever since Lucy was found safe.

Luckily, Donovan and Mrs. Castillo are distracted as they talk about something near the fountains, so they don't notice. Lucy coos at me, patting my cheek and wrapping her little fingers through my hair. All my melancholy fades away as I laugh at this delightful little creature in my arms.

We sit down on a soft blanket near the food and play patty-cake, and I watch her as she squeals with delight when a trio of geese comes by looking for scraps of food.

Later, when Mrs. Castillo buckles Lucy into the car seat in the back of her Lincoln, a wave of sadness returns, swooping over me. I open the door one last time and kiss the baby on her forehead. It's the third time I've done so.

"I'm sorry. I'm being silly," I say with an embarrassed smile. "I just wish you didn't live so far away."

"You can come visit Lucy anytime you want. She will need her godmother around to help guide her spiritual growth."

I smile as they drive away, watching the car until it disappears around a corner.

LATER, DONOVAN AND I are having a nightcap with Father Liam in his study. The fireplace is lit, and the hearth is covered with candles, the flames flickering, illuminating all our faces in an orange glow. Soft music is playing in the background. I'm mellow and sleepy and relax into the love seat, smiling at Donovan and Father Liam as they argue about who is a better filmmaker—Francis Ford Coppola or Steven Spielberg. A half-played chess game is on a small table near Father Liam's armchair. I can't help but glance at it every once in a while, figuring out the next few moves for both black and white. Donovan is refilling our drinks at the bar against the wall when Father Liam spots me eyeing the board.

"Donovan has me in a pickle there, you see. I'm black." His blue eyes sparkle, and he presses his lips tightly together in a mischievous smile.

My eyes grow round. Donovan? I glance at his back and see his head drop. He turns with a sheepish smile.

"Ah jeez, it was supposed to be a surprise," he says. "I asked Father Liam to teach me to play. I was going to surprise you when I got a little better."

He walks over and hands us our drinks. For some reason, my face feels hot, and I grab my vodka and gulp. I haven't been drinking lately, so the alcohol hits me with a rush, and I'm sure my face turns even redder.

Donovan is watching me, and I can't stop smiling. He leans over, and his lips brush my forehead. "You did good, Ella," he says in a low voice that sends a ripple of desire coursing through me. "That baby girl is right where she belongs."

I sigh and close my eyes for a second. He's right. She's safe. But there are still too many loose ends.

"What if he's not dead?" I say, voicing a worry that keeps creeping into my mind. "What if Joey Martin is still out there and kills again?"

Donovan's forehead scrunches. "He thought his wife was cheating and about to go to the press with all his secrets. He thought his parents and nephew were in on it. He killed Abequero because he thought he was betrayed by him. Yes, he was delusional, but he had specific targets."

We found out the connection with the sex club when the cops questioned the owner, the man in the green hat. A few years ago, before Joey Martin was deployed, he and Carol Abequero used to rent a room at the sex club to consummate their affair. While they were there, they met and became friends with Javier. Joey Martin introduced Javier to the dojo.

It appears that after he killed his family, Joey ran into Javier at the sex club when he went to change his clothes and hide. The sensei must have known this, and that's why he is now dead, too.

Joey Martin killed everyone who got in his way. Everyone but Lucy.

Despite what everyone says, I'm not convinced Joey Martin is dead.

Lopez said that the Army "Combined Applications Group" soldiers were the best of the best. That even Navy SEALs and Green Berets wanted to be like them. They were sort of like the James Bonds of the world, but even more ruthless and dangerous.

Hell, this guy was the only other person in a helicopter taking a five-star General of the Army to the White House in the early hours of 9/11. From what Lopez explained to me, the only one higher than Hightower at that time was the president. The designation of five-star General of the Army is only given during wartime, he said. What if Joey Martin is alive and not done seeking revenge?

I'm staring at the fire in Father Liam's rectory, thinking of all this, when a hand is placed on my shoulder.

"The more important question, I fear, is this Frank Anderson." Father Liam's words hang in the silence.

Donovan sits up straight. "As usual, you are right," he says. "I've—"

His cell phone ringing interrupts him. Once glance at the screen tells me what I already suspected. It's his partner, Finn.

Of course.

Donovan gives me an apologetic look and leaves to take the call in another room.

Father Liam gets up to refill my drink.

"Let's talk about you," he says with a wink as he settles back into his winged armchair.

"I'm fine."

"Really?" He raises one eyebrow, and I know I can't lie to him.

"No, I'm not actually fine at all." I scoot toward the edge of the couch. "I'm relieved that Lucy is safe." I take a sip of my drink, but I'm not done yet. "Even though it's been more than twenty years, the man who killed my sister Caterina is still out there, possibly, God forbid, preying on others. And I don't think I will ever have a child of my own." I look up at Father Liam, fiercely blinking back tears. "I don't even deserve to be a mother."

"My dear Gabriella," he says, getting up and settling beside me on the love seat. He pats my knee. "How can you hold onto all of this? Why do you feel like you need to take on the weight of the world? You can't stop or control all the evil in this world. I know. God knows I've tried. I can only do my small part in spreading goodness. I can't stop all the bad things from happening. Do you know how many nights I've sat here in this room weeping for the parishioners who have confided in me about their tragedy and heartache, and me knowing I can't stop their child who has cancer from dying? Or that I can't make the wounds from being sexually abused as a child disappear from the elderly man who is still haunted by it to this day? Or my friend, Gabriella, who will not forgive herself even though God has already forgiven her."

I close my eyes. I will not cry. I breathe slowly in and out. In the other room, I can hear the low rumble of Donovan's voice as he speaks on the phone. Opening my eyes, I reach for Father Liam's hand. "Tell me what to do. Tell me how to do it. I'm so tired of feeling this way. I'm exhausted by it all. I want to sleep for a year. I don't want to feel this way anymore."

A beatific smile spreads across Father Liam's face. "It's simple, my dear. It only takes two words for me to give you the key, the secret to finding your way out of the hellhole you've crawled into."

I wait, feeling hopeful.

"Let go." He squeezes my hand.

I mull the words over. I think about what those words mean in my life. Let go of my obsessive desire to get pregnant. Let go of trying to find Frank Anderson so I can wreak my revenge. Let go of worrying about what Joey Martin will do let loose in the world.

"The question is, my dear, can you do that?"

I stare into the flames of the fire across the room. I'm not sure, but I'm also not sure I can go on the way I am anymore.

A FEW MINUTES later, Donovan comes in and looks right at me. "Can I talk to you a sec?"

I already know what he's going to say. I'm ovulating. Tonight was supposed to be the night we tried to get pregnant. His face is creased with concern as I follow him into a spare bedroom and he closes the door. He runs his fingers through his hair.

"Geez, I'm not sure what to do. I told Finn I'd call him back. It's another prostitute. With the same john as the one strangled last week. The pimp is trying to send a message. She's the one who came to us about her friend's death. I can't let this one go, but I promised you. I promised I'd put you first no matter what. Maybe we could run home for a bit and I'll catch up with Finn later?"

He is so torn and earnest. With sudden clarity, I know what I want him to do.

"Go."

Donovan lifts an eyebrow, as if it is a trick.

"No, really. You need to do this. Go. We always have next month. That woman came to you for help. She did what she thought was right, and now she's dead. You need to seek justice for her. I get it. Go. I love you. But you need to go."

He grabs me and kisses me so fiercely I can't breathe.

When he pulls back, I gasp for air.

"There's more where that comes from," he says. He turns to leave but stops.

"By the way, what I was about to say when Finn called is that the FBI is taking over Caterina's case."

My mouth is open in surprise. I quickly close it.

"FBI?" I ask.

"That's fantastic news," Father Liam says, clapping his hands together.

"Yep," Donovan smiles. "An FBI buddy of mine is looking at a case in Nevada that is similar to Caterina's, and that makes it cross state lines. FBI jurisdiction." He turns to me. "I was going to give you the good news when we got home. I have a bottle of bubbly chilling. Getting the feds involved is just what we need to find that asshole. No offense, Father."

Father Liam's eyes sparkle. "Sounds like a good description of that man, from all the accounts I've heard."

My heart pounds, and adrenaline spikes through my body. This is like Christmas come early. I'm a little light-headed at this news. I close my eyes for a second and blink back the roller coaster of emotions swarming over me. Finally, after so long, there might be justice for Caterina.

DRIVING ACROSS THE Bay Bridge, I find comfort in the city skyline, as I have so many other nights in my life. The sight of the soaring buildings against the midnight blue sky always makes my heart leap with joy. This city is my home. Even if I do end up getting a place with Donovan in Oakland, I will never be far from San Francisco. It will always be the place where I'm most alive and most in touch with myself.

Tomorrow I'm visiting a dojo in San Francisco's Chinatown. I'll ask them if they'll teach me to use my kubaton and which martial arts I should study for self-defense.

Thinking about my conversation with Father Liam, I soak in the night before me—the dotted lights that make up the skyline of San Francisco, my soul city, welcoming me home. Right when I'm halfway across the Bay Bridge, high above the water, I realize I'm at the point where my two lives—the one with Donovan in Oakland and the one so rooted in my past in San Francisco—intersect. It is right there that I roll down my window. Feeling the cold, crisp air against my face, whipping my hair, I imagine tossing all my fears and worries and anxieties out the window into the cool, dark waters of the Bay below. In my mind, I can see them float down into the darkness and sink into the bottom of the Bay. Good riddance. Hitting the exit to Market Street, I crank up my radio, singing along to U2's "Elevation" at the top of my lungs with a smile plastered across my face. I wonder if it actually worked, because strangely, I now feel lighter. I feel free. I feel a surge of hope and joy. Maybe, just maybe, if I try hard enough, I'll be able to let go.

Acknowledgments

Biggest thanks to you, my reader, who made writing this book possible and who motivated and inspired me with your enthusiasm and encouragement. I'm so grateful. I'm incredibly lucky to work with such a stellar team at HarperCollins: My biggest thanks to my super smart and talented editor, Emily Krump; Danielle Bartlett, publicist extraordinaire; and online guru Dana Trombley.

As always, thanks to my powerhouse agent, Stacey Glick!

My heartfelt thanks to Jana Hiller, Sam Bohrman, and my mother, who rushed to read this so I could make my deadline.

Thanks to Sergeant Paul Paulos for answering a tricky crime-scene question. Shout- out to Troy Denning for his encouragement before my first book ever came out and for letting me use his Facebook page to garner Star Wars quotes from his fans. Thanks to my parents and my brother, Bill, who gave me some great plot ideas for this book.

And of course, thank you to my husband and children, who are my everything.

About the Author

KRISTI BELCAMINO is a writer, photographer, and artist. In her former life as a newspaper crime reporter in California, she flew over Big Sur in an F/A-18 jet with the Blue Angels, raced a Dodge Viper at Laguna Seca, watched autopsies, and interviewed serial killers. She is now a journalist based in Minneapolis, and the Gabriella Giovanni mysteries are her first books. Friend Kristi at *www.facebook.com/kristibelcaminowriter* or follow her on Twitter @KristiBelcamino.